COPPERS END

STEF LYONS

STEF LYONS WRITER

❀ Created with Vellum

This book couldn't have happened without the massive support of my partner, Graham. You have been my biggest cheerleader and so, so patient with me. Even when I wanted to give up, you wouldn't let me.

My two children. You are amazing. All my books will be dedicated to you and your life-affirming cuddles.

To Jill Dawson, my mentor. Back in 2017 you took me under your wing and gave me the confidence to be a real, actual, bone fide writer. I will always be grateful for the magic you have put into my work.

CHAPTER 1

Coppers End was dark when Deborah arrived. It was bigger than she had been expecting. And gloomier. Shadows inside the windows moved as street lamps came on automatically above her head. Deborah took hold of the brass door knob, shivering as cold ran up her arm. For the third time today she wished Peter was with her here instead of back in London

The front hall of her new home, a big stone floored area with wood panelled walls, wasn't much warmer than outside. Deborah moved her feet through a thin layer of fog that was circling the ground. Leaves, old letters, and the odd piece of gravel had scattered themselves on the stone flagging. With only the feeble light from the street lamp outside it was hard to see what lay ahead. The wind blew more detritus inside and bitter cold turned Deborah's arms to goosebumps. She ran her hands along the wall. The light switch must be here somewhere. At a click, a single bare bulb flickered on. The weak glow only served to illuminate the darkness further inside the cavernous house. Another gust blew and every hair on the back of her neck stood on end. Pulling her coat closer round her body, Deborah pushed against the railing wind and closed the door. The movers would be here in less than an hour and she needed to get a lay of the land.

"Hmm" Deborah said aloud. Taking a large torch from her handbag, she switched it on as she made her way around. To her right was a large room. *A dining room perhaps?* She moved through a connecting door to one side that led to what must have formerly been a kitchen. *Bloody hell.* There was at least working electricity here, but that was all. Out a different door, a downstairs cloakroom. To the right a utility space with a sink and a tap that produced mainly sludge until something resembling water flowed out.

Then the main living room. The darkest part of the house by far. As Deborah went in her torch flickered, before going off entirely. Hitting it till it worked, Deborah swore an oath which echoed off the bare walls. A small amount of illumination once more, and Deborah could finally take in the room. A huge old fireplace. All bricks. Coal scattered in front of it. No warmth in here though. No light. The cold stone gave off only a chill. The dark pressed against Deborah and for a moment she felt like she might choke. She stood up and moved away. The torch went out once more. Forcing herself to think practically, she backed out of the room. *It needs light and warmth, and lots of paint. That's all.*

Upstairs there were five bedrooms. Two very large, three smaller. *They would do as studies or if Lissa and the family come to stay.* Going around looking for and turning on more lights showed that about half the house had working electricity. Some of the switches were broken. Everywhere else was too old and had never been updated. There were a few radiators but they only screamed as Deborah attempted to turn them on. Upon inspection in the twilit garden, the oil tank outside was empty too. *No heat tonight then,* Deborah sighed.

Standing back in the wreck of what should have been the kitchen - no fridge, an old broken-looking oven, filthy cupboards with hanging doors - the movers arrived. They had been such a pain when packing up the London flat. Right now Deborah felt very grateful for every moment they were here. Working till late, they made sure beds, tables and large furniture were in all the right places. Deborah nearly kissed the gruff man who installed her old refrigerator. By nine they were done. Deborah paid them and once more stood alone in her new abode. Tears welled up in her eyes. Her lip trembled. What had she done? *No,* she decided. *No.* With a long day looming ahead of her tomorrow, Deborah went upstairs to the master bedroom. Putting as many layers of clothing and blankets on, she lay in her old bed and forced herself to sleep.

Even in her dreams this house, Coppers End, was not far away from her thoughts. Deborah writhed as she slept, picturing boxes having their contents spilled, lists that didn't end and movers that refused to move anything. Her mind switched from room to room and then quite suddenly she was outside and everything was dark. The heavy front door was closed, just as it had been this afternoon when she had first arrived. Only this time the door wouldn't open, no matter how hard she pushed.

"This is MY house," she had started shouting at the door. "Mine! Let. Me. In!"

She kicked and forced it but it wouldn't open. Finally it started to yield to her, but not without the hinges, or something, screaming as she did so. And what a terrible scream it had been. Guttural and from some depth inside the house that Deborah could not see. It pierced her skull as she tried to get into her house and then it rang through her ears. At once the screaming stopped and the door stopped resisting. She was in her hall. The lone bulb flickering. And each time it came on a shadow appeared. And then moved.

First it had been on the stairs. Then halfway, then at the bottom. Each time the light flashed it got a little closer and each time that happened the shadow seemed clearer, less vague. It was a man. His face got closer to hers. She could see the whites of his eyes now and the dark clothing he wore. He was in uniform. Perhaps. And something was in his hand. As his body neared hers she could just make out what it was. A snake? No. Old rope. Thick rope. Fraying and hanging heavy in his arms. He was almost right in front of her now. Deborah felt like the air was being squeezed out her lungs. Her throat was closing. She wanted to call for help but no noise came from her mouth. And who would hear her? Her heart hurt, like it was breaking into pieces. A few tears streaked her face as she desperately attempted to breathe in.

But then there was a light. Bright light. She closed her eyes and put her hand up to shield them and in doing so realised this was the real sun. It was really there.

Opening her eyes, she saw the sun shine in through paper thin curtains. She grimaced, remembering only fragments of what she had been dreaming, only moments ago. Most of it had dissipated like birds startled from a tree. All that was left was her unease. The feeling didn't fade as she remembered she was here, in this old house, alone. She sighed and told herself not to indulge in any wallowing. *Self pity wins no wars*, she reminded herself.

Groaning, she stretched out. Once her arms and toes left the warm cocoon of her swaddling blankets, the chill outside caught her. Avoiding the sharp teeth of the frosty air, she retreated back into her cave. *It's nice in here*, Deborah pulled the blankets tighter.

"Peter would have been up and out, frostbite be damned," Deborah said to the pillow next to her. *Damn him*, she added just to herself. Three deep breaths later, Deborah had thrown off the covers and ran to the sink in the nearest bathroom. The pipes sputtered and choked, and a rust coloured liquid squirted out. Grabbing some with her bare hands, Deborah washed her face and managed to splash a little under her armpits and between her legs.

"That'll be just fine!" she paced back to her room, searching for a clean pair of knickers but throwing on yesterday's dirty clothes.

The morning was spent looking for a way to turn the few radiators on, eating some bread, and working out how many windows weren't cracked or broken. She inspected the garden and looked out over the local terrain. As much as she could. Fog was gathering in the nearby hills and beginning to roll towards the house. She turned around to go back inside, but took a long look at the back of the house. Once more, the hairs on her neck stood up but on this occasion her mouth curled up at each corner. Her heart was beating fast but her shoulders relaxed for the first time since she had got in her car in Hampstead, waving goodbye to Peter for the next twenty-four hours. *It's not so bad, I suppose... A cup of tea now, I think.* Deborah walked back indoors, still smiling. It only faded when she realised she had no kettle.

After boiling water on a camping stove, Deborah made herself some tea with a little of the milk she'd brought from London the day before. A table had been placed in the ruinous kitchen so she could sit and let the heat of her drink warm her up in the glacial space inside her house. Once she had feeling in her fingers again, she took a sheet of paper and a pen from her handbag and began to write.

Coppers End,
The Querneys
Bourtonshire.

12th January 1973

Dearest Lissa,

We're finally in. However, not only is it a complete mess, it's bloody freezing too. I'm cursing Peter for this. I suppose it cannot be helped. His mother has been finding it so difficult to get around. So she says. One only gets the one mother; seeing as ours is long dead I'm sure it's the right thing to do to let Peter be near his. Even so, he's going to be spending lots of time in London at the Chambers' flat. I don't blame him. This place is uninhabitable at the moment. Nothing has changed since the late 1940s. Hardly any working electricity. No working central heating. The oven is one of those old coal things mother used to have and there are holes where lots of the windows are supposed to be. Peter has said I might grow fond of the project.

Can I confide in you? The thing is, I've found myself feeling rather sick. The excitement I had about this back in London is long gone. Now I'm here I don't know why I did it. Every part of me that I love is back home. In this little village I am alone and surrounded by the unknown.

There are two things that are stopping me from falling fully into despair. First is that Peter is so enthusiastic and happy about this move. I hardly knew how much he had missed country living. It is quite a surprise to me and I can't bring myself to rain on his parade. Secondly, and you will probably laugh at me for what I am about to tell you, but it is this house. Yes, it is a pile of rubble, surrounded by fields and sheep and not much more, but there is something else. Something I can't put my finger on. A crackle in the air when I walk about the place. I felt it in the garden earlier and maybe this morning. Makes the hair on my neck stand on end. Call me mad, but there it is. Hopefully that feeling will turn out to be happiness once we are unpacked and living our ordinary lives.

Apologies. I'm rambling on when this was really only meant to be a quick note to tell you we are in. I miss London terribly and our lovely flat. I miss you most of all, but there's nothing new there. Love to Jonathan and the children. Looking forward to seeing you out here when you are next able to get away.

All my love,

Deborah xxx

SHE FOLDED THE LETTER. After a difficult rifle through her brown leather satchel she located a stamp and placed it on the envelope, before walking to the post box a few yards from her front gate. The air was now thick with fog and mist was settling at knee height. The green hills that she knew surrounded her house must be behind it all somewhere. Shivering, Deborah rushed back inside and pushed the large door shut, grabbing an extra cardigan from a pile near an open suitcase. Boxes filled every nook of the stone-floored hall, and each of the downstairs rooms. Several large mirrors and boxed-up paintings leaned against walls. Deborah groaned. The work that she now had to undertake was gargantuan.

"Where to begin?" she said aloud.

Let's start with the easy bit. Within moments suitcases were placed in bedrooms. Checking into the tops of a few boxes, Deborah found the thing she wanted most. Placing the turntable gently on the floor, Deborah took a record out of its sleeve. The needle touched down and *Lyric Pieces, Book V, Opus 54: Nocturne* by Grieg began to play. Deborah sighed loudly and smiled. *That's better. Now for the rest of the unpacking.* When it was time to break for lunch, Deborah stopped for some bread and cheese. Later on, she cut up pieces of cardboard: some to fill in the cracks in the windows and some as kindling. It was mid afternoon and it was already getting dark. The agent had provided lamps and a few candles for the parts of the house without electricity. Deborah set to lighting them once she had made a fire, before sitting down at a makeshift table for a little more bread, cheese and pickles, and opening a bottle of beaujolais.

The fire created a paltry heat that didn't fill the vast living room with its dark wood walls and matching floor. Pulling her leather armchair as close as she dared and staring into the flames, Deborah listened to the sound of the wind rattling and moaning its way through the house. *Coppers End...* she wondered at the meaning of the name of this place. Deborah was jolted out of her thoughts as an outside light came on, glaring through the curtainless windows. She grabbed another shawl from the back of her chair and went to the front door, undoing the locks from the inside.

"Come in, come in. Quick, quick," she said. A strong gust blew dead leaves into the house with her husband as Deborah fought to close the door. "You're back earlier than I expected," she added, smiling.

"Friday. Not much to do. Excused myself and got an earlier train,' Peter Gordon QC said, kissing his wife on the cheek.

"I'm afraid there's not much in for supper. I've had some cheese and bread and a few bits. Though what I've lacked in sustenance I've made up for by opening a lovely bottle. Would you like some?"

"Gosh. Yes. Lovely. I'll just go and wash my hands."

"Good luck. The water was running brown earlier."

'Probably just needs a run through. Old pipes. I'll get onto it in the morning."

Peter made his way gingerly up the stairs, over cases of books, and boxes of ornaments that had been placed there in anticipation of being moved upwards.

After dining on a small but tasty supper, Peter and Deborah went back to unpacking. Peter moved cupboards and sideboards, Deborah found homes for clothes and made a list of all the renovations they would need to get on with.

"It's a lot to do you know," she said as they finally sat down in their bed, heads resting on the rattan board, the room lit only by two candles. "We're going to need to get the place rewired. A new kitchen. I can't possibly live with that oven for long. A fitted one would work well. There's only a small larder here. And yes, we've got our fridge in now but it doesn't exactly fit. It's almost in the middle of the room... Perhaps there's a Home Stores in town."

"I'm sure you will make this place wonderful very soon. You picked everything at the old flat and it was all lovely."

"Yes, but I didn't have to start that almost entirely from scratch, did I? I've no idea how to do a full renovation. And I haven't even *begun* thinking about the garden. It's a huge load of mud. And fences. Why so many fences?" she stared into the distance. "I still can't believe you managed to get me to leave Hampstead for this pile of old rubbish. I must be mad," she smiled weakly.

"I'll make it up to you. I promise," he took her hand. "It'll be good to be closer to mother. And country life isn't all that bad. The fresh air, nature abounds, open spaces, friendly people. A number from chambers commute from this part of the world."

"Hmmm. Staying over in London all the time too, I'll bet."

"That's the only downside really. A pretty minor one all things considered. Once the house is sorted I'll be here during the week more often. It's far too disorganised and a terrible mess here. There's no study for me to work from yet. Plus I haven't got anywhere to keep my clothes smart at the moment. I can't very well turn up in front of a judge all wrinkly and covered in plaster and wood shavings."

"If you don't want to turn up all wrinkly when I suppose we will need to find a way to iron out those," Deborah giggled as she pointed at Peter's forehead and eyes.

"Now, now, when you're as old and wise as I am, you will have them too," Peter kissed her tenderly on her forehead.

"I'll just have to work hard and fast to make sure I get to see you more than just on the odd weekend."

Deborah turned to her husband. His eyes were closed as he sat, listening to the continuing sound of wind hissing through window cracks, and swirling round the outside of their house. A heavy feeling came over her. A sickness in her belly. *What are we doing here?* She bit her lip, looking at Peter, wondering if she could ever tell him about her doubts. And about the way she got goosebumps in certain rooms in the house, even wearing several jumpers, or sitting by the fire. *He'd only laugh,* she looked away.

The cardboard she had put up over the biggest window breakages were rattling noisily now, making a whistling noise when there was a particularly strong draft against the side of the house. She got up and grabbed another blanket from a box near the bed.

"Here," she said, placing the blanket over them both, "it's freezing. I have no idea where the hot water bottles are. So we shall have to make do with layers until the oil tank can be filled and the heating is working."

"Thanks," Peter replied, pulling the covers over himself. "We'll get to work on the place. I promise. I'll wake up early in the morning and empty more boxes. Perhaps I shall walk into the village shops to stock up and enquire about where we can find what we need. Introduce myself to the neighbours while I'm at it."

"Yes, good idea. Night."

"Night."

Deborah rolled over. She ached from the day and it wasn't long before she was sleeping deeply, soothed by the sound of the storm outside her window.

Deborah woke with a start. It was still night. One of the cardboard patches on the windows had blown in and was making a loud buzzing sound and it was raining inside. Running quickly, she shoved boxes up against it to keep it in place and then back to bed to warm herself up. The seconds she had been away from the cover of her duvet had caused her skin to freeze over. Peter was snoring. It wasn't long before Deborah nodded off again, waking only when sunlight was once more streaming in through the curtains.

Peter's side of the bed was empty. Deborah smiled to herself. Putting on her dressing gown and placing a shawl over her shoulders, she went downstairs, avoiding tripping on the many items still there.

"Peter?" she called.

"In the kitchen!" he yelled back. "I've been out already. Much nicer day today. Went and got the paper from the newsagents. Met the proprietor. Lovely chap and his wife. Perkins, he's called. Placed a weekly order for The Times for me and The Guardian for you."

"Oh great, thanks," Deborah smiled as she turned on a camping stove and searched for a kettle. "Tea? It'll take a short while. I'm not entirely sure where the kettle is... ah. Here." She let the water run for a few moments. Once it was clear of rust, Deborah filled the stainless steel kettle and placed it on the stove to heat up. "I might even be able to fry up a couple of eggs or something on this. It's like camping isn't it? Except we're inside. Although the outside does seem to want to come in. We really are going to have to fix these windows as soon as possible."

"Don't look so concerned, I've already started working on that."

"You have?"

"Oh yes. I asked Mr Perkins about it all. There are quite a few shops and tradesmen operating from the main village. East Querney."

"East Querney?"

"Yes, just up the road from here. Perkins told me all about it. The Querneys is actually Four Querneys. North, South, East and West. We're right in the middle. And!" Peter exclaimed, causing his newly forming jowls to move slightly, "what I had no idea about was this house. The name. Coppers End. We said it was strange when we first got the place." Peter picked up his paper and began to read the front page.

"Yes, odd name..."

"Well it's an old police house. Not been one since the early nineteen-twenties or something. But it was a real police house. It had a couple of cells and everything. I can't imagine what criminal behaviour would ever take place in a small village like this. But there was always an officer living here. Sometimes with his wife. Sometimes with a more junior officer too. Fascinating."

"Very," Deborah shuddered. "Well isn't this bizarre? I'm sure I dreamed of a policeman. Maybe last night. Or the night before. I can't remember now."

"Oh really?" Peter dipped the corner of his newspaper and looked at Deborah, one eyebrow crooked.

"Oh not like that, you silly boob," Deborah shook her head. "I really did. He wasn't doing much. Walking down the stairs, I think. Maybe. It's hard to remember. Don't you think that's strange?"

"Oh, you probably figured it out from the name. It's not that hard to infer. Coppers and coppers and all that."

"I suppose," Deborah looked out the window as she continued to wait for the water to heat.

"Well, Perkins and his wife told me that the house was cleared after one of the senior officers died, or maybe they didn't, but something happened and the police decided to modernise and moved the jurisdiction to the main town up in Bourton. No need for such a small force out here all the time. The house was sold privately. The previous owner did very little work to it and died about twenty years ago and the house has been empty ever since. Absolutely fascinating."

"Gosh, yes," Deborah was pouring tea. "What a lot of history," she rubbed her arms. "It's a shame no one did much to the house... Now. There is bread and there are eggs," Deborah said, looking through their larder. "I am sure I can do something. But we must pop into this East Querney to get more food and talk to the right people about sorting the place out."

"Of course."

After breakfast, Deborah and Peter Gordon donned their coats and woolly hats and made the short walk to the area known as East Querney. It was a bigger village than Deborah was expecting with a pub and many small shops and larger premises. There was a butcher and a baker, an antiques shop, a grocer, an ironmonger as well as a hardware store. There were two tea rooms and Perkins' newsagents. All of it was quintessentially quaint, old stones and dry stone walling and little cottages with trellises and chimneys. *I bet in spring and summer this is a beautiful village to live in,* Deborah conceded.

Everyone already seemed to know who they were. People would grin or wave at them as they walked past. A couple of old ladies asked if they were the ones who had moved into the old police house and Deborah and Peter nodded and smiled, explaining about Peter's mother living in Bourton etc. etc.

"That's nice, isn't it, eh? You don't see much of people lookin' after their ol' mums these days," one of the old ladies said. "It's nice to have a younger face in the village though," she added, looking at Deborah, who blushed.

"I'm hardly young anymore. But it's kind of you to say." Deborah pulled Peter's arm and they continued their walk. Lowering her voice to a low whisper she asked, "Does everyone stop and tell you their business round here?" Deborah laughed.

"Maybe." Peter sighed and laughed along with his wife.

They made their way to the small grocery, parting at the door as Peter went to ask in the hardware store. Alone, Deborah perused the aisles of the little shop. Its limited space was packed with produce. *Mainly potatoes and cabbages. Oh, and carrots too.* Inside a small fridge Deborah found milk and one glass bottle of orange juice. A different section sold packaged bread loaves and there was sugar and tea, and chicory coffee that looked like it had been left over from the war. Once she was done, Deborah unfolded her hessian bags ready as she approached the till.

"'S all from local farms, miss," the old man behind the counter told Deborah as she paid.

"Pardon?" she asked, looking up from her purse.

"All this. Locally produced, it is."

"Yes, I can see. That's nice."

"I know the cows that made this milk," he added, putting a bottle of it in her bag.

"Good, good. Are you on a first name basis with them all?" she tittered.

"No," the man replied, his brow creased. "Not with a cow."

"Of course not," she shook her head.

"Is it pasteurised?"

"Eh?"

"Pasteurised? The milk."

"Oh yeah. Got to be 'ent it. It's the law now."

"Yes, yes I know. I've been reading a lot about the health benefits of unpasteurised milk. It's quite interesting, don't you think?"

"I don't know. Mebbe. Say, are you the new owner of ol' Coppers End?"

"I am, yes. With my husband, Peter. I'm Deborah, Deborah Gordon."

"Tom Fortner. Pleased to make your acquaintance. 'S nice to have new people in tha' place. Brighten it up a bit. It's got quite a lot of history up there."

"So I've heard," Deborah took the bags from Mr Fortner. "Thanks," she added, making for the door.

"Yeah, that old place," he continued. Deborah paused with her heavy bags and sighed. "It's a funny old story, you know, it's just town gossip but -"

The bell over the shop door rang and in walked Peter.

"Ready to go?" Peter asked, jovially.

"Yes, just finished. Peter, this is Tom Fortner, Mr Fortner, this is my husband, Peter Gordon."

"Oh, call me Tom," he said, holding his hand out to Peter. "Nice to meet you."

"Likewise," he said, smiling and shaking the man's hand. "Good news," Peter turned to Deborah, "I've managed to get someone to come over to the house in the next hour to help us with a few things and give us details of where to start. Very helpful hardware store here, Tom, isn't there?" he said, looking up at the grocer.

"Oh yes, the very best."

"We'd best be going, then," Deborah smiled weakly.

"See you," Tom smiled back and waved them out the door.

Deborah's breath formed icicles as she and Peter walked home.

"Well it's a nice walk into the village, anyway," stated Peter as they ambled along the road. "Not far at all. It'll be easy for you to come and get things when you need."

"Yes..." Deborah strolled silently, wondering where she would get half the stuff she could normally get from the High Street in Hampstead. "I'll need to find some other places to go though, perhaps Bourton town itself," she said after a pause. "You know, to get lentils and things like that. I didn't see any in the grocer's. Also, I wonder if it's at all possible to apply for an allotment. I saw signs for them."

"Oh absolutely. Though I think there's room in the garden for all that. Have you not seen the raised beds?"

"What? No. Must have missed them. I spent most of yesterday and the day before unpacking and trying to fill gaps in windows. This is the last time we buy a complete wreck."

"Ha, one would hope so. I know I went ahead and did it, and I've apologised already. But I really think it will be rather good out here. We aren't that far from London after all. And you've got space to write and work on your doctorate and we can have more of the life that we've always talked about."

"I suppose. Yes, I suppose you're right," she said, turning up the front drive and closing the gate. "Let's work on making this place a nice home," Deborah looked at the dilapidated affront to her senses and dreaded the thought of trying to cook much on the old stove, and trying to heat the house without working central heating.

"Of course we will, darling," Peter put his arm around Deborah. "It'll be a wonderful house. Full of history. You'll get it right in no time."

Peter closed and locked the door behind them both. A chilly draft swept over Deborah and she shivered once more.

CHAPTER 2

The sausages were sizzling and popping in the hot pan. Constable Smith had already cut large slices of bread for them both, and the kettle was whistling at them to make tea.

"Take that off the heat will you, Jacob?" Sergeant Cooke nodded.

Constable Jacob Smith stood at his command and poured hot water into their brown teapot. He stirred the pot, and disguised a yawn.

"I hate havin' Peter Richardson in with us overnight. It's exhaustin'. All he does is talk an' yell. The other sots usually sleep it off an' head out after they've had a cuppa an' a chat."

"Mr Richardson likes the sound of his own voice," Sergeant Cooke replied. "He's not like the others who are mainly here only for a warm place to sleep and a bit of food. He's here because, well, from time to time his wife needs a break from the sound of his pontificating."

"His what?"

"Pontificating, Jacob. Take note and look it up later," Cooke beckoned to his subordinate. "Come on, let's have this before it gets cold."

The kitchen at Coppers End housed a simple wooden table with space for two, perhaps three, to sit at. Here was always the warmest part of the house, perfect for breaking fast on this cold February morning. The two officers sat down with their bread, sausages and dark tea. They ate in comfortable silence. Once they were finished, Sergeant Frederick Cooke wiped his face on his handkerchief and stood up, taking his and his constable's plate with him.

"It's okay, sir. Leave tha' wi' me," the constable protested.

"No, no, Jacob. You've been awake all night thanks to Mr Richardson. You need to get a bit of kip."

"But sir -"

"No, Constable. That's an order. I can't have you getting ill or falling asleep on the job. You look grey. I was hoping the sausages and strong tea would help fix that, but they seem not to have done so quite yet." Jacob nodded and gulped. "You can have a couple of hours, that's all, mind. Then you can get on with your duties and update the logbooks and pop on your rounds." Cooke looked at his pocket watch. "It's six thirty now. I expect you up, showered and dressed and in clean uniform ready to start by nine. Can you manage that?"

"Yes, sir. Thank you, sir. The breakfast did help. Thank you, sir."

"I'd hate to think how terrible you'd have looked without it. Go on. Off to bed. See you at nine sharp."

Cooke knew his protégé would likely fall asleep without removing his uniform. He himself had been that tired many times in his career back in the city. *Up all night with a drunk or on a case,* he recalled. *The next day your tum aches, your head pounds and all you can think about is when you'll next be able to lie down on something soft and close your eyes.* Pouring himself more tea from the pot, Cooke walked towards his study. It was a room near the kitchen, by the front of the house. Practically the whole village had to pass by here to get to wherever else they were going and he could see it all going on from his desk. Cooke sighed to himself with a satisfied smile on his face. Life here was simple. He'd said that to Smith when he first started the job.

"The Querneys is a busy place of course," Cooke had added at the time. "There is trade and farming land. There's the old Querney Mill where lots of people have worked for centuries. There's also the newer, big houses built in West Querney for all those doctors from the local hospital, as well as attorneys with jobs in Bourton or even as far as London."

"Sounds like a bustlin' place, sir," Smith had answered. "I grew up north of here. There was only the farm and two other houses."

"Yes, yes, there's things to be getting on with all of the time. You'll be busy," Cooke had explained two years ago.

Now Sergeant Cooke shook his head as he thought about that meeting. *Smith and I are living on borrowed time.* His work here was small and mainly done at the pleasure of the family at Querney Manor. Taking a well-read letter from his desk with a Bourtonshire Constabulary crest at the top, Cooke unfolded it and read it again. His fingers traced the words as his brow furrowed. Just as it had when he first saw it ten days gone. When he'd told Smith the boy was inconsolable, worried he wasn't being thought of as a good copper.

"Of course not, boy," Cooke had reassured him. "No. Most villages like ours no longer have a dedicated police house. It looks good for them to have one, The Binghams and The Forresters up at the Manor have paid special interest to us and given us more and more over the years for our upkeep. They were the ones who paid to put that new phone in my office. For emergencies and important matters."

"There has been talk of putting one in the centre of The Querneys so anyone can call us for help," Smith had added, excited at the thought.

"Yes, well. Hopefully they will realise in time that Coppers End is also in the centre of The Querneys and so in running for that phone, you'd be outside our front door anyway," he had said, chuckling.

Ah well, he thought now, sipping at another cup of tea and opening the drawer in his dark wooden desk, *such is progress*. Eventually, he knew he and Smith would be amalgamated with the larger force in Bourton who took care of a much wider area and had more advanced procedures. In the meantime, Cooke had resolved to enjoy the peace of his country existence, his private office with a view of the main lanes, and the simple but pleasurable company of Constable Smith.

This morning, there were a number of letters to deal with, and things to sign off. At nine o'clock sharp, Constable Smith reappeared with a cup of tea for himself and Sergeant Cooke.

"Oh, thank you, constable. Get any kip?"

"A little, sergeant. It was nice to lie down and not have Mr Richardson yellin' for me every few minutes."

"You look more fresh-faced. When you've finished that," Cooke nodded at the cup of tea Smith was gulping from, "go on your rounds. Usual route. Pop by Mrs Richardson and check in on her now the husband is home. I've had a letter from Bourton about thefts in the county so see how the shopkeepers are doing, and then go by the Horse and Cart. No stopping for a quick one, no matter what Mr Donaldson insists upon. You're on duty. Mrs Donaldson will want to feed you up with one of her pies, you know what she's like. But no pints."

"Okay, Sergeant. Of course." Constable Smith finished his tea and went out to the cold stone hallway to get his coat. Cooke could see him from his study as he donned his hat and scarf, ready to brave the winter mists. *Poor young'un. We've all been there,* Cooke thought, smiling at the constable as he left.

The day passed as most normally do in The Querneys. Mrs Jennings came by to clean the place at her usual time and made Cooke and Smith a cheese sandwich each for their lunch, followed by strong, sweet tea. She left some ham in the meat safe and a fruit cake in the larder. Cooke worked - filing, taking the odd telephone call from Bourton Constabulary about the thefts. He'd have to do some rounds of his own to let more people in the village know and tell them to keep a lookout. The old ladies would need reassurance over cups of sweet tea and perhaps, if he was lucky, a slice of cake.

Cooke had expected Smith to join him for lunch but he hadn't come. By one thirty, he gave up on the idea and covered the cheese sandwich Mrs Jennings had left for the constable and put it in the larder. *He can have it for his dinner.* Cooke smiled and wondered if Smith had enjoyed his pie at The Horse and Cart. At quarter-past two, the phone rang again.

"Coppers End, Sergeant speaking," Cooke rattled out.

"Sergeant, it's me, Constable Smith."

"Smith? Where are you calling from?"

"The Big House, sir. Querney Manor. I got here abou' ten minutes ago."

"What's happened?"

"It's one o' the maids, sir. She's been found dead. Looks mos' like natural causes, but I think you should come down here anyway."

"Of course, thank you, Smith. Tell Carter I will be along shortly. I will call Bourton before I leave so they can be on alert and also send a medical examiner round."

"Of course, Sergeant."

Cooke replaced the receiver and sighed. After speaking with Bourton, Cooke was careful to make sure his collar was straight and his uniform ship-shape and Bristol fashion. He retrieved his hat, coat and scarf from the stand and locked the door, placing a sign on it saying he would be back later.

The walk to the house was short enough. He strode past others in the village. Some of them smiled weakly and others looked concerned. *News travels fast.* Cooke turned off the main road, up the narrow lane past the church and through the gates which lead through the gardens onto the drive. Cooke knew that somewhere past the fog there were lawns, topiaries and a wood. This deep into winter all of it would be bare and empty. Everything still. Everything waiting for spring.

He rang the bell at the servants' entrance. A footman answered and let him through to the servants' hall. Inside a couple of maids were milling around the heavy wooden table, wringing their hands. Another pair of them were tearful. A scullery maid was passing out cups of sweet tea as hall boys stared through the doors, looking too scared to come in but too fascinated to go away.

"Ah, Sergeant Cooke. Thank you for coming so quickly," The butler, Carter, turned from Constable Smith to greet him. Smith was writing something in his pocket book and scribbling other things out. His top lip was sweaty and he hopped from one foot to the other as he mouthed his own notes back to himself.

"Well, this is serious, and very sad," Cooke directed himself to the maids, "you have my condolences."

"Shall we go to my room to talk before going upstairs to see the, uhhh, the body," Carter looked around at the ladies in the room as his voice trailed off.

"Of course," Cooke nodded his head to the people in the hall and walked towards Carter's study with Constable Smith behind him.

"Would you like some tea, Sergeant? Constable?" Carter asked as they got in and offered them a seat.

"No thank you, Mr Carter. In such cases as these I think it best we get straight to the matter of it."

"Indeed. I suppose you want to know what happened?"

"Yes, please. Tell me what you know. Constable, take notes, please." Smith got his notebook ready.

"Well," started Carter, "the maid in question is called Sarah, Sarah Miller."

"How old?"

"Nineteen."

"Gosh, and you said probably natural causes, Constable?" Cooke turned to the boy. "At nineteen? Was she generally in bad health?"

"Well, sir," Smith gulped, "I wasn't sure, but there's still some of tha' awful flu going round an' Mr Carter an' the other maid, the one who found her, said she hadn't been feelin' well this mornin'."

"Have you seen the body?"

"Only very briefly, sir," Smith said. "Doesn't look to have been a struggle or anythin'. She looked peaceful, like."

"Okay, okay, Smith. Thank you. Carter, what else can you tell me? What happened? Has there been sickness among the staff here?"

"Some, yes. But a number of months ago. The flu was bad here, you'll remember, around the spring of last year."

"Of course, yes. It was awful. Such a terrible tragedy for many families. Especially after the war."

"Precisely. Even so, according to Mrs James the housekeeper, Sarah was up and ready for her duties as normal. Late morning she said she wasn't well with a headache and that she felt sick and faint. Mrs James sent her to bed. After the family was given lunch, the servants sat down as usual for their own, at around one-thirty. At that time Mrs James sent up another maid, Elspeth, to take her some food and to check on her. She couldn't open the door. Once they got in, Sarah was lying there. She had passed away." Carter looked into the distance. "It's an awful thing. Awful. So young. I didn't know her that well but she seemed a nice girl. According to Mrs James she was a hard worker. Never any trouble."

"Very tragic. Very," Cooke shook his head. "I will need to speak with Elspeth and any other staff who had spoken to Miss Miller today. If the door was locked and she was ill, it's most likely natural causes, but it would be good to paint a picture of what happened. Is there family nearby?"

"Not that I know of. I think she has a mother somewhere in North Somerset. I will tell Mrs James to write to her."

"Good, good. I must go up and see the body. I have already alerted Bourton Police who have called the medical examiner. It's something I must do in all cases of a sudden death. Does the family here know what has happened?"

"They do, yes. They are shocked. All of them. Mrs Forrester is very saddened by the passing of a member of the staff. Her husband is in London at the moment. Mr Bingham is here at the house. He is, ahem, attempting to help with the estate and his sister's needs. Shall we make our way to the servants' bedrooms?"

The three men called in on Mrs James for the keys to the women's side of the servants' sleeping quarters. Together, all four climbed several staircases until they were walking along a plain wooden floor in a poorly lit hallway. When they entered Sarah Miller's room the girl was lying on her bed. *Smith was right, she's peaceful.* She was still in her uniform but her hair had been taken out of its cap, and it had mussed up a little where she had lain on it. Her cheeks were red, like they had been gently pinched, and there was a smile on her face, where the corners of her mouth had turned up.

"She's smiling, sir," Constable Smith said.

"Could be, could be. Most likely not. I've seen it before. It's a thing that can happen in some dead bodies, Smith. The medical people can tell you why. I saw it on many occasions during the war. They weren't smiling when they died, I can assure you."

"Yes, sir."

"There doesn't seem to be a sign of struggle," Cooke continued. "There are no drinks on her bed or on the little table next to it. I can't see any sign that she took any powders to help her headache. There's nothing dropped or spilled."

"She would have had to get anything medical from me," Mrs James, the small, thin, Irish housekeeper said, "it's all kept in the kitchen and everyone has to tell me if they need something. She didn't."

"Thank you for clarifying, Mrs James," Cooke smiled at her. She frowned back. "The medical examiner should be here any moment. Before he gets here I would like to speak to the other maids who may have worked with her. And to Elspeth, who found her."

"Of course," Mrs James replied. "I will have them waiting for you in the servants' hall. You can interview them in my sitting room."

"Thank you."

The maids had very little to add to what Carter had told him, including Elspeth. The medical examiner, on first sight, had found nothing interesting. No marks, no signs of anything except slightly blue lips which indicated a possible problem with the heart.

"That, combined with the physical symptoms she had told other people she had earlier. She may have had a mild case of flu, I suspect," the examiner, Dr Simpson said to Cook, Carter, Smith and Mrs James who were all gathered in Mrs James's sitting room a few hours later, "And together it killed her. Most likely a failure of the heart."

"At nineteen?" Mrs James sat down, in shock.

"It can happen," Simpson replied. "We all know how many youngsters were taken off by the flu these last two years." They all bowed their heads for a moment. "And if it is the heart," Simpson started again, "most often it's in the family. She climbs lots of stairs everyday, which probably made things worse. Plus these young girls, sometimes they use medication in a recreational way. It's quite common, sadly."

"But Sarah never -" Mrs James shook her head.

"That you know of. It's this new lifestyle. They all want to be part of it, these young girls," Simpson was adamant.

"I just can't believe it," Mrs James sipped her tea which Carter had topped up for her and added more sugar.

"Will you be needing to do an autopsy?" Cooke asked.

"In a case like this? If I had more suspicions, yes. I shouldn't worry about that sort of thing. It's a sad tragedy, but that's all. Nothing suspicious here. Just a serving girl passing away before her time. No need to waste my time disturbing the body."

"Indeed. Will you have that all in writing to me?"

"Naturally. I shall have it written up for you in the next week. I can see no rush when we both have other things to be getting on with, I am sure. The body can be released to whomever wants responsibility for it," Simpson added, standing up and putting his hat on. Mrs James frowned again and made a low noise.

"Of course," said Carter, leading him out and closing the door behind them both.

"I just can't believe it," Mrs James said, shaking her head. "She was so very young."

"Mr Simpson, though a little blunt, was right, Mrs James," Cooke said in his most soothing voice. "There seems to be no other sign than her heart giving out. Let's not put her body through the indignity of an autopsy, eh?"

"No. But I won't have it said that she was up to no good on her time off. My girls are good girls and I run a tight ship here. We don't have any truck with what other people might get up to."

"No, no, Mrs James," Cooke added. "I'm sure Simpson was just thinking out loud. He works in a large area and sees a lot of the worst things, I am sure."

"Hm."

"Right, Constable. We should head back. We've been away hours now. We must get all this logged properly. Tomorrow I shall call Bourton Constabulary up to inform them of the investigation and conclusion."

"Yes, sergeant."

Both men rose to leave and said their goodbyes to Mrs James and Carter. It was dark as they walked the lanes back to Coppers End.

"Do you think she's righ', sir?"

"Who?"

"Mrs James, the housekeeper. What if we are wrong? Miss Miller was young. And Mrs James said she wasn't into any of tha' nonsense tha' might have made her heart, you know, go funny."

"It's the conclusion of the medical examiner, Constable. He knows rather a lot about medical stuff. More than you or I."

"I know, sir. It's just that you've always said that people in places such as this, well, they know each other. If you watch people enough you get to know them. I know people from my beat, and from calling in and spending time with them. Mrs James will have known Sarah Miller. There would have been a sign her heart wasn't well, wouldn't there? Before now? Or that she was into... those other things?"

"You could have a point, constable. Perhaps. I don't know about you, but my head's a-jumble. When did you last eat? Mrs Jennings left ham. Let's have a cup of tea and some food and I'll have a think about what you're saying."

"Yes, sergeant."

Cooke and Smith made the rest of their way to the police house without speaking. Smith's stomach rumbled loudly occasionally. *He didn't stop for lunch, silly boy,* Cooke thought.

"Get the kettle on, constable," Cooke said as he hung up his coat, hat and scarf in the hall. "I'll get you your sandwich."

Cooke looked out the door before he shut it. *I'll wait for Simpson's report. Then I'll see how I feel,* he thought, hoping to himself that they had all come to the proper conclusion about the unexpected death of Sarah Miller at Querney Manor House.

CHAPTER 3

Coppers End,
The Querneys
Bourtonshire.

15th March 1973

Dearest Lissa,

Sorry I haven't written in a few weeks. Things have been so busy here. Busy but also, strangely, rather dull. I didn't know it was possible for those things to coincide, but it is. With the house, I have taken a path of starting at the bottom and working my way up. The windows are all fixed, the kitchen is almost totally in and I've even managed to restore some of the original pieces in the rest of the house back to some of their former glory. At some point, I realise I will have to tackle the attic. I took a peep in there when we first arrived and it is all cobwebs, furniture and junk. I've asked Peter to help when the time comes to deal with it. I just hope he is around and not on some case that keeps him up in town.

I've used doing up the house as an excuse to pop back to London a few times with Peter on his commute. I have confined my trips to Oxford Street and the aisles of John Lewis etc. At some point I know I will have to brave Hampstead. Old friends have called and written and want to see us for dinner parties. I can't put it off forever. I am hoping that once I feel more settled it will be easier.

It doesn't help that the weather has been bloody awful since we got here. The constant damp is starting to lodge itself permanently in my bones. In my more dramatic moments I wonder if I will ever be truly warm again. This may be nothing to you being so far north. The oil heating breaks regularly, but we have a local man coming next week to fix it once and for all by putting in a whole new thing. Don't ask me what. I am up to my eyeballs in the rest of the house, plus trying to keep up with my writing and research. I have left the heating to Peter.

We see his mother every Sunday and I am obliged to visit once or twice in the week. Should I be irked we moved so Peter could be closer to Elspeth? Yet it is me who brings over groceries and stays while the nurses rub ointments into her ulcerated legs and it most definitely not Peter who throws her old bandages away after. He just goes to Church with her and then for Sunday lunch and a chat about the old days.

I wonder if you felt similar when you upped sticks at all? Or is it just me who feels this way after leaving the hustle and bustle of London? It's different for you perhaps, you did move to another city after all. Once spring is here I am sure it will be better. Prettier at least. I must be positive or this will never work. One potentially exciting thing is that we have been invited up to The Big House - as the locals call it, Querney Manor is its proper name - for dinner at the end of the month. We met the family while out for a walk and got chatting. When they found out Peter is a QC in town they immediately invited us up. They seem nice. Even so, our mother and father would be snorting at me for all this. Upper class twits and all that.

I must dash, my books are calling me to them and this PhD isn't going to write itself. If I have enough done by the summer we should think about a visit. I know Peter would love to go on a walking holiday in the Highlands. Perhaps I can persuade him to make it The Pentlands instead and visit you in Auld Reekie. Fingers crossed.

Love to you and all the family.

Deborah xxx

DEBORAH PUT on her big coat, hat and scarf and set out to post her letter. She smiled at the people going by and offered them the time of day. It was the done thing. She stood by the post box and wondered if there was anything else she needed in East Querney while she was out, not that it was far from the house. Looking around and studying the shops as her breath misted up in front of her, she shrugged and started home. There were puddles on the ground and, though it was March, there were no signs of spring yet. Not even a snowdrop. Not a single sign that the earth was warming up and coming to life once more. The sky was grey, as it had been since she and Peter moved here, and the air felt thick with moisture. Droplets settled on her camel coat sleeves. Deborah shuddered, opened her front gate and went back inside Coppers End.

Peter had left early this morning and his breakfast things were still by the sink.

"I'll get to them when I stop for lunch, I suppose," she sighed to no one. For now, Deborah settled herself into making a boiled egg, toast and coffee. Peter had treated her to a new coffee machine, the french drip type, to go in her new kitchen. Deborah smiled as she looked around the newly decorated room. She had picked out the design herself, knowing Peter would like the wooden units and tasteful little decorations here and there. She had bought new crockery and all new gadgets as well. Lovely Hornsea Saffron serving dishes, gorgeous glassware and a hand-thrown butter dish too. It was everything she had hoped a brand new kitchen could be.

The old one in Hampstead had been a lot smaller and rather old fashioned. Even so, as Deborah remembered it, she felt a wave of warmth. That London kitchen had also been her mother's and it was the room from which she had ruled the house. There had always been some reason or other for Deborah's mother, Evelyn, to be at her stove, one that she had reluctantly converted from coal fired in 1957 a year before she died. By then Lissa was already married with a baby on the way and was living in a flat in St John's Wood. Deborah had stayed living with Evelyn as she studied for her masters degree at Regent's Park. After her mother died Deborah's main comfort was leafing through Evelyn's old, greasy cookbooks, laughing at them with Lissa and reminiscing at how brilliantly their mother had managed for so many years as a widow with two daughters, in London, while working, with rationing, and also managing to be such a force of joyful nature. She made food for everyone and fed every stranger that knocked on the door. No one left their place hungry and all people were welcome. Even now Deborah was in awe of Evelyn's ability to put people at ease and find out their life story after only moments of acquaintance.

Deborah wondered what her mother would think of her now. A secular Jewish girl from an academic, big city family, now living a quintessentially British, Church of England, beef on Sundays, walks in the country, real ale at the pub, Jam and Jerusalem life. *I know exactly what you'd say, mother,* and she laughed to think of it. *You would have liked Peter,* she smiled, imagining the two of them meeting. *Not his mother though. But you'd have enjoyed not liking her all the same.*

After clearing away the breakfast things, Deborah had to make a decision: sort out the house a little, or do some work. She had a deadline coming, somewhere in the future. An academic essay to finish. It was due next month and she was behind with everything else going on. Her new study was still full of boxes so a number of her papers and books were stacked messily on the dining table: a large dark wood thing competing for space with a number of cases from Peter's work, papers wrapped in ribbon and gathering dust. This table was a new purchase as well, to replace the old, battered thing they had brought from Hampstead. Another loss Deborah had felt.

"Don't be silly, darling," Peter had said when he had surprised her with it. "It's just a table."

"It was my mother's," she had replied, feeling tears well up. "I'm not being silly."

"But you were always complaining about it. Saying it had old marks and cuts in it. From where she hadn't used a breadboard."

"But I loved that about her," Deborah reached for her handkerchief.

"But... you didn't say. You always said how thankful you were for table cloths when we had guests!"

"I know! I know! It's just... The memories. It was a part of our old life as well. Dinner parties. Laughter over wine and fondue. Friends. Discussion. Don't you remember any of that?"

"Of course I do. But we can have that here, once we get to know people more." Deborah scoffed loudly in response. "I'm sure of it," he added. "And we can do it on this beautiful antique dining table that I thought you'd love."

"I do. In a way. It *is* beautiful. It's just not my mother's."

"I know. I'm sorry."

"Where did you put the old one? Is it still around? Perhaps I can use it somewhere else."

Peter cleared his throat, "Ahem, I'm afraid to say I sold it for scrap. I got a good price for it, though."

"Scrap?! My mother's old table is scrap? How could you, Peter?"

"I'm so sorry," he had said and repeated that many times that evening. And then a number of times when Deborah had raised it again in arguments days later.

I really must work, Deborah told herself now. Her eyes scanned pages but nothing went in. *Perhaps if I go for a walk. Might clear my head.* After putting on walking boots and her coat, Deborah stared out of the window. The clouds were darkening and rolling wildly. The wind was blowing through bare trees, stripping away what few leaves had tried hanging on over winter. Shaking her head, Deborah took off her coat, walked back to the kitchen and filled the kettle with water. *Tea can fix this,* she nodded her head. Once it was ready, Deborah resumed her seat in front of her books and looked through the few notes she had made last week, sipping her drink and listening to the loud tick tock from the grandfather clock in the hall. Rain started to beat heavily against the windows and there was a howling around the house. Deborah held her cup close, taking comfort from the small amount of warmth it gave her to hands and from the steam in her face. A huge gust blew and the wind wailed. A huge clattering sound came from above. Deborah stood, leaving her tea behind.

"Oh blast. What now?" she grumbled as she manoeuvred towards the stairs.

Deborah opened every door. Every room, checked. Still a noise continued, like marbles rolling and twigs and sticks scratching and breaking. It was coming from above. *The attic,* she sighed. Grabbing the step ladder from a spare room, Deborah pulled it noisily towards the hatch. On the bottom step she managed to loosen the catch and let the attic door fall noisily down, letting dust float around as she guarded her eyes. Once it was clear enough to see again, she took a further few steps up the rungs until her head was through the ceiling. The first thing she felt was an ice cold draft across her face. Light was pouring in on one side, through a hole about twelve inches wide where a few tiles had fallen through. The air coming through them was freezing and bright and flashed across cobwebs and dancing clouds of disturbed dust.

Deborah pulled herself up gingerly, testing the ground with her hands and feet. The attic was the oldest part of the house and had never had a single bit of work done to it. She was in God's hands as she took gentle steps towards the hole in her roof. The place was full even though Peter had only popped a couple of small things of their own up here when they had first moved in. *It's a mystery as to what else could be up here,* Deborah thought as she took a proper look around. There was an old rocking chair with a broken back. Heavy crates that looked mouldy and had merged into each other after decades of being atop one another. There was an old wooden filing cabinet. *Two. No, three cabinets actually.* A large wooden box took up a lot of room. Two walls had bookshelves propped up against them. The wood on them looked quite good. *I wonder if I can get Peter to bring them down? They'd be great in the hall. Or my study once it's sorted.* More boxes hid behind other boxes. There was what looked like a Victorian room divider, or a screen. It had been decorative at one time. The picture painted on it may have been birds, peacocks perhaps, but it had long since faded.

"Right," Deborah said aloud. "Lots to sort in here."

She turned back to the hole in the roof to inspect the damage. As she got closer she could see that years of bad weather and neglect had pushed and pulled at the old slate tiles and they had finally given way, ripping a piece of plasterboard with them from the wall where they had fallen into the attic. *These are still in fine fettle,* she decided, holding the cold, damp pieces of roof in her hands. *They've not smashed too badly on falling, thankfully.* They were so cold and so wet in her hands. *So old,* she thought, realising they must have been placed on the roof when the house was first built. Roofing wasn't something she knew much about, but if it was possible not to go to the expense of replacing the whole thing, she'd try anything. Holding them back in their original place, it was easy to see where they went. *Maybe they can just be placed back on? Hmmmm. The fit isn't quite right.* The damage to the wall where they had come off was preventing them from sitting correctly. On closer inspection Deborah noticed the plaster was peeling, and there was something dog-eared about it too. It was irresistible not to touch. Deborah tried not to pull as she flicked the edge of destruction.

That's weird. There's writing on it. There was writing on the wall. Or was there? This time she gave in, took a deep breath and pulled. Part of the plasterboard came off to reveal some papers that had been stuffed in the wall cavity. The paper was yellow, and delicate, and, in places, threatened to shatter if she held it too hard. The writing itself was in a beautiful cursive script. Even after flattening it, the words were hard to make out in the dark so Deborah leaned in to where the light was pouring in from the hole still in her roof. It looked to be a list of names. Next to the names were other words. Deborah unfolded another page to see what else she could find. Some of the words on those pages were more legible. More names, mainly men's. And dates. A list of what looked like food. There were gaps where words had disappeared over time but a lot of it was clear.

Barthol...ew Smith. 19th Nov. 1912. Evening... Lew... Bread and che..se

Thomas J.... 4th Decem... 1.12. Overni... Bread, chee...e. Po...dge.

A SHOPPING LIST? *No. Why would there be names on it?* Deborah looked for a title page but there were so many loose papers and shuffling them caused fresh dust to go into her face, making her sneeze, which in turn forced more dust into the air. Holding this set of papers in her hand as carefully as she could, she bent down to see if there was more in the wall. There was. Quite a bit.

"What on earth?" Deborah said to herself as she pulled out as much as she dared and walked towards the ladder once more. Stepping down onto safer ground, she put the ladder to one side and went downstairs.

Pushing some of Peter's boxes out of the way, Deborah placed the papers on the dining table. She scanned and searched for more clues as to what she was reading. The writing was clear on a number of pages. In addition, there was a signature that she saw several times: "Serg. John Cooke". Sometimes there was mention of a "Const. J Smith". There were more names, sometimes repeated. More information. Deborah's brow furrowed as something else caught her eye. It looked like the title page of a notebook; it was thicker, dark embossed leather. There was binding hanging off and one side, and it was clear that the pages Deborah was looking at had been ripped from this book. *And stuffed into a wall?* Looking back over the leather cover, another set of words jumped right out from the page: 'Coppers End Log Book'.

"A police log book? That's it..." Deborah whispered. *Dates. Names. What they had been arrested for. What they ate. When they left. Living history.*

Deborah read through what she had found. She could see certain people were brought into this place a number of times to sober up. Others beat their wives. There were thefts, an instance of 'licentious swearing', and most amusingly, 'lewd behaviour from a woman'. Part of her longed to know more than just this basic information. *After they had sobered up, had a bowl of porridge and gone home to their families, what did they do?*

The grandfather clock sounded. It must have done that many times while she sat there, but for the first time Deborah heard it. The click-clack-tick-tock had been the only symphony to accompany her as she read, mesmerised by the people on the pages in front of her. Now the chimes were telling her that the time was rushing past three o'clock. Two hours had gone past unnoticed.

"Oh bugger," she said, looking out of the window. Peter would be back in a couple of hours. She had meant to get something from the butcher for dinner. Putting on her boots and coat again, Deborah stepped out into the darkening light of the March afternoon. The sun hadn't come out at all that day and the charcoal clouds overhead made it seem as though evening was arriving hours earlier than it should. Small droplets of rain fell and Deborah turned to look at the house, wondering whether it was worth running back to get her umbrella. She shook her head, looking at her watch. The butcher would be closing soon. There was no time.

A few people were out in the village. Most of them walking briskly back to their houses. Some of them waved to Deborah, others smiled. Shops were closing. The hardware store was bringing things in from outside, as was the grocer and newsagents. For the first time since moving to The Querneys, Deborah looked closer at the people she saw. In her mind's eye she could imagine those who would have been doing this forty-odd, or fifty years ago. She could see the Constable J Smith (whoever he was) walking up and down, saying hello to people. As a historian, Deborah had always been fascinated by these sorts of things, but her work had never made her think so much about real people, real lives and the ordinary things they did. The houses here had a story and so did the people who lived in them.

She arrived at the butchers and the bell over the door tinkled as she walked in.

"I'm not too late am I?" Deborah asked, a pleading smile on her face.

"Depends what you want, ma'am," the butcher's boys said back. "We got some beef, and sausages. A little chicken if you'd like."

"What type of chicken?"

"Breasts. And a couple o' whole birds."

"Okay, I'll get four breasts please."

The boy behind the counter was probably not really much of a boy, Deborah thought as she looked at him more closely than she had before. His face was familiar.

"Are you... is it your father who owns this place?" she asked, never having had a conversation this long with him before. He went very red and stuttered.

"Uh - uh... y-y-yes. My father. He- he owns it. I'm Lucas. His eldest."

"I'm Deborah. How do you do?" The boy nodded, a puzzled look on his face. "You look like him. I've been here a few times, and I've not seen you in here much before."

"Yeah, I-I'm usually in the back. Dad's just sortin' some stuff out and asked me to finish up in the main shop. I was getting ready to close up, see."

"Yes, sorry, I'm not normally this late. The time just whizzed past today," Deborah laughed awkwardly. Lucas, the not-quite-a-boy gave a quick smile and went back to putting the chicken in a paper bag.

"Lovely, thank you, Lucas," Deborah said, looking at him quizzically once more. "Has your family lived here long? Have you always been the butchers?"

"I guess so, miss. My da' and his da' before him. I don't know much further back than that about what we did, like. But I know we've been here a long time. You'd 'ave to ask my father." The two of them stood staring at one another.

"Okay, well," started Deborah, "thank you for serving even though you were closing up. This will make a lovely coq au vin, I'm sure."

Lucas The Boy smiled clumsily and Deborah stepped out into heavy rain. She half-ran back and opened her gate. This time she stared at her house. Coppers End. Large drops of water tumbled across her face as the rain lashed down and the wind blew it sideways. *That old door. How many people have stepped over its threshold?* Deborah went to do what hundreds of people must have done before; ghosts in her imagination now. Before she turned the handle, something moved in the corner of her eye. A shadow in the window. *No, a trick of the light,* she decided. Deborah pushed hard and went inside, leaving the closing darkness behind her.

CHAPTER 4

Cooke rang the bell by the servants' entrance. In the moments that passed, the sergeant looked at his surroundings. Fog still covered everything. On his sleeves settled droplets of water which he brushed off, only to be replaced by more. He looked up as the door swung open and the face of a boy peered out at him through the thickening gloom.

"Good morning, sir. Can I help you?" asked the boy.

"You're new, aren't you, boy?"

"I am, sir. My name is Charlie, Charlie Bird sir. But seein' as there's already a Charlie here, people call me Bird, sir."

"How do you do, uh, Bird," Cooke stared at the young, skinny lad. "I'm Sergeant Cooke. I've come from Coppers End, the police house in the village. Is Mr Carter in? I need to speak with him urgently. I have news for Mrs Forrester."

"Of course, sir. If you will jus' wait inside in the servant's hall."

"Thank you, Bird."

The young man led Cooke down the cheerless corridor. In rooms either side of him, Cooke could see a busy hive of work and he could smell baking and cooking from the kitchens. *Glorious,* Cooke smiled to himself, sniffing the air. He was shown to the servants' hall where a maid was sewing something at the table. She looked up and nodded her head, getting back to her work. Charlie Bird left him to find Mr Carter.

"Will you take tea, sergeant?" a young girl whom Cooke hadn't noticed asked.

"No. Thank you," he smiled at the timid girl. She curtseyed and hastened away. After another minute, Bird returned. He stood at the doorway and coughed nervously.

"Sergeant, sir," his voice broke and he coughed again. "Mr Carter says I am to show you to his study. He's waitin' for you there."

As Cooke entered the little room at the end of the corridor, Mr Carter was sitting at his desk reading through a ledger of some sort. The butler finished what he was reading, made a mark in the paper, and shut the book, placing a ribbon down the page he was on. He looked at his watch.

"Good morning, sergeant. Just." The man's face was placid. *Ever the professional, he won't let me read his expression one bit.*

"Good morning, Mr Carter. I hope you will excuse my intrusion. I need to speak urgently with Mrs Forrester. I was hoping she might be at home."

"She is," he folded his hands in front of himself. Not a single flinch on his face or registering of wonder at what Cooke might want. "However, she is with her steward, Mr Barnatt. They have been together since breakfast this morning. I believe they will break for lunch soon. Can it wait until then? She does not wish to be disturbed."

"I'm afraid it cannot," Cooke replied. "In fact, it is better that Mr Barnatt is here too. He will need to hear what I have to say as well, I am sure."

Carter glanced at Cooke briefly, his expression implacable, "Of course. I will go up and announce you. If you would wait in the servants' hall, I shall bring you up when they are ready."

Cooke didn't have long to wait in the hall. After a few short minutes, Carter had returned and began leading him up the backstairs. Soon they were in the main house, a beautiful old place filled with antiques and curios from travels to India and Africa. Outside a dark wooden door, Carter stood still, cleared his throat and entered a plush, elegant library.

Eleanor Forrester was sitting in a comfortable chaise. Barnatt, a man in his early thirties, was opposite her on a sofa. On a desk nearby there were important papers and maps of the grounds.

"Ah, Sergeant. Please do take a seat," Mrs Forrester indicated the sofa or any of the other chairs arranged by the glowing fire. Carter stood by the door. "Carter, would you get some tea for us?"

"Of course, Mrs Forrester," the man left, closing the door gently behind him.

"Thank you, Mrs Forrester. Mr Barnatt," Cooke said, nodding his head towards the man.

"To what do we owe the pleasure of your company, sergeant? I hope it is nothing too serious. Two visits to us in, what, a month? Is it more about that sad case of my maid?"

"No, no. Nothing about that. I shan't take up much of your time, if at all possible but I'm afraid I have some troubling news. There have been some thefts."

"Thefts? Good lord." Barnatt asked, shaking his head.

"Yes, I'm grieved to tell you, but one of your farmers, a Mr Porter," Cooke said, checking his notes, "reported it to us this morning. It's your pigs. I've phoned the constabulary up in Bourton to see if there have been other cases brought to their attention in the area, but so far there haven't. I've also spoken to the farmer and his wife, and their farm hands. They say the pig pens were all locked and the pigs were left as usual. They heard nothing."

"Nothing at all?" Barnatt asked.

"Sadly, no."

"How many were taken?"

"All of them, the farmer said," Sergeant Cooke checked his notepad. "He told me that two of them were prize winners. Is that correct?"

"It is," Mrs Forrester's face was stone.

"Damn. And blast," Barnatt hit his fist onto the mahogany table "Forgive my bad language, Mrs Forrester. I simply cannot believe this. How is it possible? Prize winners. All the stock. How did this happen? Why are we only hearing about it now? It's past eleven o'clock."

Sergeant Cooke looked at Eleanor Forrester and Barnatt, "Of course, I know. The farmer, Mr Porter, didn't want to raise the alarm with you until I had spoken with him and confirmed what had happened. Naturally I had to get down there, and see the place myself, take statements, assess the evidence. I got back to the station and spoke to Constable Smith about it and we made calls to Bourton like I told you. Then I came up here. It all takes time, I'm sorry."

"Of course, Sergeant Cooke," Mrs Forrester looked at him kindly.

"From first look it seems, dare I say, like they got in and out quickly. Barely made a mess. It's rather queer. Most common thieves don't care about that sort of thing. They'll happily leave a trail of destruction. This lot were in and out. Gates intact. Fences. They knew exactly what they were doing and exactly where they were going."

"What does that mean?" Mrs Forrester asked, shifting in her seat.

"Could mean many things. Most likely, I think, is that they knew you had a good batch of pigs. Cased the place. Watched for a few days, got to know movements of the farm and farmhouse, and knew how to get into the styes in and out without sounding any alarm."

"Those barns were newly built. Barely up a few months. I was told they offered great protection to the pigs," Eleonor shook her head as tea was brought in by Carter and Bird. "What now?" she asked, looking at Sergeant Cooke and Barnatt for answers.

"We will have to look at the implications of this as a matter of urgency," her steward said.

"I was afraid you were going to say that," she smiled weakly, sipping her tea.

"I'll keep in touch with Bourton," the sergeant said, "they have more officers there. They will hear any local reports of anything similar. And I will keep on the lookout for any mention of any prize pigs for sale or anything like that. I'm sorry this has happened the way it has. The thieves were very professional about it."

"How comforting to know that even in these tragic days that there are still people going about their work with professionalism and care," Mrs Forrester pursed her lips.

"I wish my visits were for better reasons, Mrs Forrester," Cooke sipped his tea. "It's the nature of the job. Only being around for the bad news in life."

"Nonsense," Mrs Forrester replied, smiling at him. "You are a very important fixture at the summer garden party. I want you judging the flowers and vegetables this year, you know."

"That is very kind of you, ma'am. Though I am not sure I am the best man for the job. I know very little about gardening. Just what few vegetables we manage at Coppers End."

"Well, I don't know how to bake a cake, but I judge those every year, don't I?"

Barnatt laughed, "Can I get in on that please? I'd make an excellent judge of cake."

"No, you cannot," Mrs Forrester jibed. "I absolutely adore tasting all those cakes. Anyway, you've got enough to be getting on with. Especially now these pigs have gone."

"Indeed," the steward nodded his head. He turned to Mrs Forrester and muttered, "This couldn't have come at a worse time."

"No," Eleanor Forrester glanced up at Sergeant Cooke and cleared her throat. "But we shall figure it out, Barnatt. We simply must."

"Well, ma'am," Cooke said, placing his empty tea cup on the table in front of him. “I must needs leave you. We both have work to be getting on with.”

“Yes, it’s always the way,” Mrs Forrester stood up. Under her cardigans and a scarf there was a very round belly protruding. *Her confinement must be soon, I’m sure.* Cooke looked away, hoping Mrs Forrester had not seen him stare at her pregnancy.

“I will work on this as best I can, Mrs Forrester,” he said, looking over the room one last time.

“I’m sure you will sergeant,” Mrs Forrester rang the bell and impossibly immediately Carter was in the room, ready to take Cooke back downstairs.

“I’m sure you heard about the theft of the pigs, Carter,” Cooke said as they made their way down the backstairs.

“I could not help it, sir,” the man bristled.

“No. Of course not. I shall be in touch as soon as there is more news on this, Mr Carter,” he said, turning back and putting on his hat to keep the cold off his head.

“Thank you, Sergeant. We have not had a good start to the year here, have we? First the maid and now this.”

“No, sir. I would agree with you there. Crime and tragedy don’t stop, I’m afraid. Sometimes I wish for that, but then I suppose I would be out of a job.”

“Indeed,” Carter nodded as Cooke tipped his hat and walked off into the thickening fog once more.

CHAPTER 5

Coppers End,
The Querneys,
Bourtonshire.
March 31st 1973

Dear Lissa,

Sorry I didn't catch you on the phone the other day. I know you were worried about me being a recluse and not getting out much. Well, worry no more. First of all, the first signs of spring are finally upon us. I even saw the sun shine for a brief moment the other day, which was a welcome respite from the level of rain we've had. The River Wash has run fast and overflown its banks in a number of places. It's been rather dreadful for a lot of the people who live near it. We are lucky that we don't and that we are on higher ground. I attended a community gathering to help those who are flooded and, yes, I talked to some of the villagers. Properly. Not just the time of day as you kept saying. I don't know why I've been so afraid to be friendly. They are perfectly nice people, I suppose I just haven't felt in the mood. I so miss my London friends. I suppose if I actually got to know anyone here it would mean the end of my life back there.

Anyway, the 'second-of-all' part of this brief letter is to let you know that I have not one but two social engagements today. One is with a nice woman I met at the church hall at that community event I told you about. A Mrs Slate. She was very nice and not as old as the other people here and enjoys talking about more than just the time of day and the state of her lawn. I am off to hers for a spot of lunch in a moment. And then, later on of course, is our very exciting evening at The Manor House. Peter is really rather excited. I don't know if I am. It'll be lovely to be at a dinner party for the first time in an absolute age. Though I have a dreadful feeling that they won't be our sort of people. (And by 'our' I mean you and me - Peter is getting more pompous by the day. I do love the silly old so-and-so, but now that he is in line for Head of Chambers and has this house in the right part of the home counties and all that he's gone a bit traditional on me, if you know what I mean. Ho hum. I'm sure it's just a phase.)

So there. I am no longer a shut in. I have even managed to do some of my own work. Well, a little. And I've even got a little personal project of my own on the go: the history of this house. I haven't told you what I found in the attic yet, have I? Don't worry, it's not a mad old woman. It's something much better. Anyway, must dash. Let's speak on the telephone soon, now that you've finally gone and got one. I can't wait to hear news of the children and you and Jonathan. Love to you all.

Deborah xx

DEBORAH HASTILY PLACED her note in the envelope, grabbed a stamp and ran out the door, posting her letter in the box as she walked quickly to her luncheon date. It was definitely warmer than it had been and soon Deborah found herself beginning to perspire under her coat. There were a number of flowers threatening to bloom in this slight elevation of temperature. *They've been desperate to come out,* Deborah thought as she trundled along. The house she was looking for was in South Querney, a part of the little quartet of Querneys that Deborah hadn't been to before. The main village was in the east section. The west was occupied by farmland, the huge mill that had, until fairly recently (it was said), given a lot of the villagers work for many centuries, and there were large Victorian mansions too. The northern quadrant was occupied by Querney Manor House and the huge estate there. The River Wash ran through the village from north to south, and Deborah found her way blocked where some of the flood water hadn't drained away fully yet. *Thank god for wellies,* she intoned, *an item of clothing I never needed before in my life and I am so bloody grateful for -*

"Oh, bugger it!" Deborah's foot had come out of a large puddle of mud, leaving her boot behind. She managed to regain her balance and carefully place her foot back in the shoe. With a great sucking thwunk, Deborah pulled herself free and continued down the increasingly boggy track. She turned off, up a footpath flanked by little cottages. As the road became steeper it became drier and much easier to traverse. It wasn't long before Deborah was outside a charming little country cottage with a rickety green wooden gate and a front yard that she knew would look wonderful when spring was in full flow. There were several cottages along this footpath. Some terraced, some detached. All very quaint.

Deborah walked up the tiled path through the lawn and rang the bell. The woman who opened it was exactly the woman Deborah remembered from a week back at the church hall.

"Mrs Slate, thank you for having me," Deborah smiled at her host.

"Oh, please, call me Theresa. And come in come in. You can leave your muddy wellies in the little porch here."

"Of course, of course. It's finally drying out, thank goodness."

"Yes, a few days without rain has done the trick. Let's just hope it stays that way, eh?"

Deborah took off her coat and hung it on the hooks by the door. There were a number of mismatched wellies and coats there too. Small and large ones. Theresa Slate had two children, Deborah remembered.

"Are your little ones at school?" she asked.

"Yes, yes. And Dennis is at work up in Bourton. He's a carpenter."

"Oh is he? What a skill to have."

"Oh yes, he's very good. Even if I say so myself. Come through!"

Deborah followed her into Theresa's delightful kitchen. Bright colours welcomed her. The smell of homely dinners and stews pervaded, and Deborah imagined love and hugs with sweaty, happy children, and that she was somewhere a pie or a slice of cake was never something longed for for very long. Deborah grinned, enjoying the warmth she felt in this room.

"The kettle has boiled and I've made us tea. I've got us pork pie and some sandwiches. It's not fancy fayre but I made the pie myself and the ham in them sandwiches is from pigs just down the road. I know the farmer. He always gets me a good deal. I also have a fruit cake I made for afters."

"Wow. This is wonderful. You are quite the cook!"

"I like to do it, my mum taught me. My grandma taught her too. And she was a cook at the Big House a long time ago. Well, a cook's assistant, anyway."

"What a wonderful thing to pass down in the family." Deborah took a bite from her sandwich and sipped her tea. "Your husband is a lucky man," she smiled.

Theresa sat opposite her, smiling back and helping herself to pork pie. She was a woman of ample size, round in the tummy and bosom. Deborah noticed Theresa's old fashioned clothes in mismatched colours, but saw that the woman looked very comfortable and content. Theresa's hair was thick auburn curls and Deborah could see she had a very pretty face and strong arms. *Probably from kneading bread and lifting pies in and out of the oven all the time.*

"Do you know much about the family and the manor house now?" Deborah asked, gulping down some hot tea. "I ask because we're going up there tonight for dinner -"

"Oh are you now? How fancy!"

"- yes, and I don't know much about them or the place itself. Do you have family still working there?"

"Oh no, not any more. They've not had lots of staff up there for a long time. It's a funny ol' place. They owned the mill. That's where the town gets its name, did you know that?"

"Querney?"

"Yes, yes, a quern is a type of mill. This village was named after it probably because it practically brought the whole place together. The manor house, the estate and the mill provided all the jobs for most people for a long ol' time. The people at Quernery Manor owned the whole place. They don't own much of The Querneys anymore, mind. Lost lots of their money a few years back."

"Gosh."

"Yes, well, lots of those big families did after The Great War. Couldn't afford all the staff and the land anymore. My grandmother met my grandfather working there. He was a footman."

"Oh yes?"

"Yes, yes. He wasn't there long. Joined just a year or so after the war and then all the sad business happened and most of the people were let go after. The house was never the same after everything that went on there."

"After what?"

"Don't you know?"

"I suppose I don't," Deborah looked puzzled.

"I'm surprised. It's about the only interesting thing to ever happen in The Querneys in all of history. And when I say interesting I know I shouldn't say that, not after what happened. But I guess it is interesting, really. Considering how quiet things normally are in this place. Even so, I'm surprised you don't know much about it. Your house was part of it all too: the police house."

"Sorry, I'm not following."

"Oh, lord, I'm not explaining very well am I? Here," Theresa held out a plate, "take another sandwich. I'll pour more tea as well. And please have some pie! Can't have any going to waste!"

Deborah smiled nervously as she watched her new friend pour tea and put several sugars in her own cup. Theresa took a bite from her sandwich and chewed, clearly longing to finish so she could tell Deborah her gossip. They smiled at each other as the woman opposite Deborah at the yellow formica table swallowed the last of her lunch.

"Now," started Theresa, swallowing and looking eager. "Where to begin. I suppose I would need to go back to early 1920. The misfortunes probably began when that maid died. I don't remember her name. My grandpa said she was just found dead in her room one day. So young, but they thought she must have had a poorly heart or caught the last of the Spanish Flu that had been around. She was buried and that was that but it's such a shame though, to go so very young. They'd already lost so many boys in the war and the all the young people with the flu -"

"Oh yes, that's awful isn't it?"

"Absolutely. Well, that death had nothing to do with it really, but it started some bad times. I think. Well they'd had some more really. My grandmother never knew much as she was in the kitchen most of the time but grandpa, he would open the door at the backstairs, and show the police in. He said he was terrified the first time he saw the officer in his uniform. That's where your house comes in I suppose -"

"Quite, he must have lived there. Was the officer named Cooke, by any chance? Or Smith?"

"Oh I'm sure I don' know. Sorry. I haven't heard the tale told much recently. Both my grandparents died a while back. What makes you ask?"

"Oh nothing, just some names I've read in places. I'm sorry to hear about your grandparents."

"Ahh, 's alright. They lived to a good age. An' they left me this house. This was theirs once. A lot of the cottages round this part of The Querneys housed the staff who wanted to live out. They're small but they are home."

"I can see that. It's lovely here. Your home is so warm and welcoming."

"Oh, well, thank you. I do try," she smiled before remembering herself. "Anyway, as I was saying, the house had a few things go wrong. I'm sure grandpa said somethin' about stolen pigs. I can't remember," she shook her head. "Maybe it was sheep. And that was after the maid dying,

I'm sure. But most tragic of all was the murder of the lady of the house. Mrs Forrester. She'd only recently had a baby an' all. So sad."

"Oh my. Murder? And with a little baby? How horrid," Deborah felt her face flush.

"It really was. Everything changed after that. Mrs Forrester, Eleanor, after she died, her brother inherited and was so torn up about it that he got rid of a lot of the staff and that's when things went down hill and the mill closed, oh, umm a few years later. Maybe ten, but still. It was the beginning of the end. In the second war there was more work because the old mill became a weapons factory. And there is always interest in the place. No one has managed to keep business going there for that long though. So most people who live here don't work here, see. Just those with shops and the like. The rest go into Bourton, or London. Like your husband I think you said?"

"Yes, he works in London. He's a barrister. Criminal Law."

"Well, that's funny isn't it. A criminal barrister living in an old police house," Theresa chuckled to herself.

"I never thought of that," Deborah smiled. "He spends a lot of time in town though. Especially when there are big cases on. The chambers has a couple of flats."

"So are you just rumblin' round that big place by yourself a lot?"

"Quite a bit. So far I've spent most of my time gutting out old rotten things, and decorating, and sorting out putting in a kitchen and glass in the windows, that sort of thing."

"Glass in the windows? Hark at you, next you'll be wanting water in the taps." Both women laughed and drank from their tea. Deborah felt warm and happy and fascinated by what she'd just heard. *I'd forgotten how much I need company from time to time,* she reminded herself.

"Hang on, did you say the name 'Forrester'?" Deborah asked. "I thought the family name was Bingham up at The Big House?"

"Yes, it is. Eleanor Bingham, the one who was killed, married a rich American called Forrester. That's all I know. When she died, it all went to her brother, Rupert Bingham. She didn't update her will to include her daughter so the poor little thing got nothing."

"Wouldn't she have got it automatically?"

"Oh, I don't know. Not sure how these things work."

"Me neither," Deborah furrowed her brow. "What happened to the daughter?"

"I think the child lived at the house for a time but I don't know about it or where she ended up."

"Well, I never. Did they catch who did it?"

"Yes. Well. No. On account that the fella died soon after. It was a vagrant. A tramp. A robbery gone wrong is what my grandpa told me. Fat lot of good it did the guy, he robbed and killed a young woman in her prime and then was found dead in the cold a while later. And then something about the officer in charge. I can't remember what. I think he left soon after. It's been a long time since I last thought about it, so I can't quite remember. And I'm sure my grandparents spared me some of the details because I was too young to hear 'em, you know? They didn't want to upset me. And people here talk about it a little, in hushed voices, but not all that much. Pretty soon it will be long gone from people's memories, I'm sure."

"That whole story is just so... so sad."

"Yes, yes. I know. I bet you didn't realise you were moving to such a fascinating village, eh? Boring old chocolate box, tiny English place somewhere on a map. Well, nothing else has happened in our history except that. And it's a great tragedy."

"It is. And I'm going up there tonight. I suppose it's something I shouldn't mention?"

"Oh I'm not sure. I don't have much to do with them."

"I've met Bernard Bingham and his wife, Diana. That's who invited us."

"Yes, yes, that's Rupert Bingham's eldest son. They run the place now. Rupert is still around but getting on in years and hasn't been too well of late." Deborah nodded her head.

"Bernard and Diana have children, do they?"

"Yes, yes. Two. A daughter and a son. They are pretty much grown up now themselves. Time just keeps on marching doesn't it. Now. Come on. Have a slice of fruit cake. It's been maturing nicely for a few weeks. Should be just right."

"Oh, yes please," Deborah giggled.

It was another hour before Deborah left the cottage, full of food and happy feelings. It was impossible to imagine how she was going to eat a big dinner after such a delicious and filling lunch. *For the first time I might even be enjoying living in this bloody village,* she smiled to herself as she squelched her way through the mud back home.

Once she was back in the relative warmth of Coppers End, Deborah took off her coat and went to the kitchen for another cup of tea. As the kettle boiled, she flipped the radio on, switching it from Radio 4 to Radio 1. *It's nice to have a change sometimes,* she considered. A song was playing and it seemed to be quite nice. When it was over the DJ said it had been by Mott The Hoople. Then he announced a song by Elton John next.

"Ooh, this is a good one," Deborah said, turning up the volume. Singing along, "Rocket maaaan, duuh-duh, duh-duh, duh-duh, bam, bam, baam..." Deborah also swayed, letting her hair move around as her head went back and forth. When it was over, she turned off the radio, looked around and placed her cup of tea on a coaster on the dining room table where her work was. An hour ticked by. The clock in the hall struck half past and Deborah checked her watch. It was four-thirty. *Gosh, I haven't done much.* It wasn't that she was unmotivated.

Why am I so distracted," Deborah asked aloud to the empty space. She knew she didn't really need an answer to the question. She looked at her watch again and thought, *not long till this dinner.* She shuddered. *The story of those people in that house was awful.* And she was going there this very evening.

Peter had promised he would be back on time and ready to go out just before seven. He was true to his word and was back at the house at ten to six.

"I'm home!" he called as he closed the door behind himself.

"Evening!" Deborah called from upstairs. She was finishing spraying her hair and pinning it back. Standing up, Deborah looked in the mirror, satisfied with her new earthy green, floral maxi dress from Laura Ashley. She walked down the stairs and found Peter in the living room at the drinks cart, making himself a whiskey and soda.

"You're starting early, aren't you? On the strong stuff?"

"Well, it's been a bit of a day," he replied, replacing the bottle of single malt. He turned and looked at his wife, "Well, don't you look lovely," he smiled at her, "a sight for sore eyes."

"Well, thank you. You'll need to go and get showered and changed yourself. We need to leave in about an hour. I'm not sure what to wear on my feet. It's so muddy. I'd wear my lovely new boots, but wellies seem better. But that doesn't seem, well, glamorous enough to head up to a manor house in."

"Nonsense, this is the country, they'll be used to it."

"But I'll have to take my shoes off before going in. I can't walk around with muddy shoes on."

"Some people don't allow shoes on the carpet," he said, sipping his drink.

"Well, we don't know what they're like, do we? I'll have to take some in a bag or something. Oh, I don't know. I'm not used to all this big country house stuff."

"Don't worry, Deb. The thing about old money like that is that you are supposed to act like you know the rules, but that you don't need to follow them because the rules follow you."

"Ha, yes, I suppose you are right. Now, finish that and get washed and changed. I'm going to have a Babycham and listen to some music before we go. Oh, and I need to tell you the most interesting story I heard today, before we leave. Let me know when you are out of the shower and I'll tell you about it when you're getting dressed."

"How intriguing."

"It is. And, well, sad too. Now, off with you. Time to get ready. I'm nervous. I don't want to be late. It's not a great way to start."

"Yes, indeed!" Peter called as he left the room. Deborah started towards the kitchen, "plus I am sure you don't want to miss anything that you might want to put in your next letter to your sister!"

"Oh, of course! She'll be desperate to know!" Deborah shouted to her husband who was almost at the top of the stairs by now. *This is definitely going to be an interesting evening. In one way or another,* she mused. Deborah opened a bottle of Babycham and poured herself a glass. She looked out of the kitchen window into the darkness and fancied she could see a light on from the manor house from where she stood. She put on Radio 3. A Schumann Piano Quintet was playing. Deborah recognised the mournful second movement and got lost in the long lyrical sections. She listened and sipped her drink, all the while looking into the night time, waiting for Peter and anxious to finally go up the hill to the Manor House.

CHAPTER 6

"Here we are," Bernard Bingham held out a silver tray, "an Old Fashioned for you…" Deborah took her drink, "… and a whisky and soda for you, Peter." The empty tray was placed on a lovely wooden sideboard and Bernard sat down with his own drink, a Tom Collins. His wife, Diana came in with her own Tom Collins and a tray of nibbles.

"Cheesy-pineapple anyone?" she asked, smiling a big pearly white grin at her guests. She looked wonderful. Deborah couldn't take her eyes off her when she first arrived at Querney Manor House. Diana Bingham was older than Deborah, by five years perhaps; definitely in her early forties. But she radiated classic beauty in her white halter neck dress, gold arm cuffs and gently clinking bracelets. Her nails were a brilliant red and perfectly manicured. Her blonde hair was stylish and not a follicle was out of place. Pushing her own bushy brown hair behind her ears and brushing her green floral dress across the knees, Deborah thought Diana wouldn't have been out of place on the cover of a fashion magazine. Both she and Peter took a cocktail stick to eat from while Diana passed the rest of the grapefruit hedgehog round to the other guests: another married couple from a neighbouring village, a Mr and Mrs Flintrop - Ernest and Nancy. Deborah noticed how very pretty she was too, but not quite as much as Diana Bingham; the husband had his eyes at a permanent half-mast.

"It's so lovely to have you here and to meet our new neighbours properly," Diana continued as she sat down, sipping her drink. Her voice was velvet and she spoke beautifully. Like a real Lady of The Manor.

Music floated gently from a record player in the corner of this large, decadent drawing room. The windows were grand, there were comfortable seats and sofas offering views over the grounds, though it was dark outside and therefore it wasn't possible to see them. A huge fireplace with a mantelpiece homed several antiques including an ornate golden clock. Candles were lit all around the room. The atmosphere was welcoming, but, in Deborah's mind, stiff. *Not at all like my lunch with Theresa today*. She took a drink and coughed, the strength of the bourbon in her old fashioned taking her by surprise.

"This drink is good," she said, trying not to let her eyes water.

"Oh, thank you," Diana replied, stretching out her long, delicate arm, "Bernard is the real cocktail maker in the house. I open the champers and he stirs up all our other drinks. It's good to have our own part to play in the running of things I always say!" she laughed in a girlish way, and put her hand on her husband's shoulder.

"Got to have something I'm good at, eh?" he replied, shifting his seat on the large brown sofa.

"Hear, hear," joined in Ernest Flintrop.

Deborah looked sideways at her husband, wondering what he was thinking. He was looking around blankly, taking another cheesy pineapple on a stick, impossible to read.

"You have a beautiful house," Deborah said, trying to make conversation, "so many beautiful antiques."

"Oh, are you a collector?" asked Bernard.

"Oh, not really, we are appreciators aren't we, Peter?" he nodded in reply. *Why isn't he talking?* Deborah frowned. *He's leaving it to me*. "We have picked up some lovely pieces here in the village and around the county as we've worked on the house."

"And what a lot of work you'll have had to do," Diana said in sympathy, lighting a cigarette and offering some around. "I'm so glad that old place got sold off and is now being cared for. It was unsightly, wasn't it Bernard? Of course it belonged to - or was paid for by, is that right? - anyway, Bernard's family kept it for years and then it got sold off a while back. If the family still owned it it may have been kept better. As it was, it just fell into such disrepair. I feel for you, I really do. I saw the kitchens there a while back. And the gardens!" she snorted.

"Yes, it's been a lot of hard work. But we are getting there. It was the old police house, wasn't it? People in the village rather enjoy telling me every time they see me."

"People in this village love to talk about anything vaguely interesting,

I'm sure you'll have found," Bernard looked at Deborah and Peter as he spoke. *Is he talking about what happened here? I'm sure we shouldn't mention it.*

"Well, you know," Deborah said, coughing. "This music is lovely," she added quickly. *Someone was murdered here.* Her mind shifted to thoughts she'd been avoiding. *I wonder where it was.*

"Oh, this?" said Diana, "Astrud Gilberto. Do you like her?"

"I do, yes, I've not heard much but I've enjoyed what I have," Deborah sipped her drink.

"I met her at a party years ago, in the States when I was out there working."

"Goodness. What were you doing?"

"Oh, well, it's sort of embarrassing. Nancy and I used to do a bit of modelling, didn't we, Nancy?" Her friend nodded and sipped her snowball.

"Modelling, how exciting," Deborah replied.

"Well it was just a bit. You see, Nancy and I went to the same boarding school. When we left we wanted to go to London to have a fabulous time and meet interesting people. Our parents helped us get a flat in Knightsbridge. Do you remember those days, Nancy?"

"Oh yes," smiled Nancy.

"We had a lot of fun. We both joined this wonderful school for young ladies. A 'charm school' it was called. We had to learn lots of different things. You could also do secretarial skills too. We both did it, but I," she stopped to giggle and put hand on Nancy's, "I was terrible, wasn't I Nancy, darling? I passed but I was more suited to the other things. We both got jobs at a bank. Which is where we met Bernard and Ernest. Funny that, isn't it?"

"Gosh," said Deborah, "you two must have known each other -"

"Oh, yes, years. Far too long!" Both ladies giggled.

"So how did you get into modelling?"

"Well, as I was saying, I worked for a little while at the bank where Bernard and Ernest were based. They were in investments. But I was awful at it. Really awful. My shorthand was a complete mess, wasn't it Bernard?"

"Utterly disgraceful," he laughed.

"The other thing this school did was modelling. I handed in a portfolio - in fact I made you do it with me, didn't I Nancy? - Well, we handed it in and we were offered work!"

"Did you do it long?"

"Well I did it for years. Even after the children were born I dabbled a little. It was a wonderful way of seeing the world and meeting people and going to parties. At first it was only little photoshoots but eventually I got bigger things. I haven't done it in a while now. Far too old," she smiled wistfully.

"Oh, gosh not at all," Deborah tipped her head to one side. "How about you, Nancy? Did you do it for long?"

"Oh, well," she said a little timidly, "I did it for a little while but stopped when I got married. I didn't want to keep going like Diana. I was never as good as she was. Never got as far. But it was fun while we were young," she giggled.

"How exciting. Isn't that exciting, Peter?" Deborah gently nudged her husband.

"Oh, yes, yes," he said, sipping his drink. "And what were you doing in banking?" he addressed the husbands.

As the men started talking about investments and funds and other such things, Deborah observed the room more. The house was lovely, though now she was looking closer it had a shabby look to it. Some of the plush curtains were frayed at the tops, and the material on the cushions and sofas were threadbare. As she tuned back into the conversation, Deborah could hear they were talking about Peter's work.

"So you're in criminal law, are you?" Ernest was asking.

"Yes, on the Queen's Counsel. Up at the Old Bailey most of the time."

"So you handle the big cases, do you?"

"Yes, yes, some high profile stuff I suppose. I've done a lot on organised crime and fraud. And murder. That sort of thing."

Deborah looked around. *Murder*. The word hung around in the air. Or was it just her imagination? She cleared her throat.

"Oh, you boys and your work talk," interrupted Diana, "you'd go on forever if you didn't have us ladies around." Diana stroked her husband's arm. "I shall just go and check on dinner. It shouldn't be long."

When she left, conversation flowed back to what the men did in the city all day. Nancy hardly said a word and Deborah was left feeling uneasy. *I wish Theresa hadn't told me about what happened here. What if the woman who died is in any of the portraits around the house?* She looked around trying to see any family resemblance in any of the women in the pictures. Most of them were of men on horses and with hunting dogs. Diana Bingham returned after a few minutes and stood at the door.

"Dinner is served," she said, gesticulating with her slender, bejewelled arm.

The party made its way across a large hallway to the dining room. This place was also draped in finery that on closer inspection Deborah could see was moth-eaten. There were a few chips in the wooden sideboard as well. But the crystal decanters were spectacular and the candlesticks grand. In each seating place were little name cards and Deborah found herself seated between Peter and Ernest. Nancy was next to her husband and Bernard, who was seated next to his wife, Diana. At once a young woman entered, dressed in maid's clothing. She was carrying plates with what looked like a solitary apple on top. By the time everyone had theirs, Deborah was intrigued. *An apple?* Then she saw the top had been cut off but replaced.

"I hope you all like Waldorf Salad," said Diana, taking the lid off her apple and scooping out the chopped salad inside. The other diners copied her.

"How clever!" Nancy clapped her hands together.

The salad was clever, Deborah thought. It was quite fresh with apple, crunchy with walnuts and extremely rich with mayonnaise.

"Did the apples come from your garden? I hear you have beautiful grounds up here."

"Oh, well, it's something we enjoy. The garden is very old isn't it, Bernard?"

"Yes," he replied, "the family worked on it for hundreds of years. It became a lot to maintain though, especially without a gardener. In my father's day we used to have a team of them of course, but not these days. We gave it over to the National Trust a few years back."

"It's open to the public isn't it?" asked Peter.

"Well, yes... yes," he said, after swallowing. "From spring to the end of autumn. Well I say open to the public, most of it is. We still have a little private bit just for us, thank goodness."

"It's still our garden though," Diana interjected, "The National Trust just runs it and helps with maintenance and such. Are you interested in gardening, Deborah?"

"Oh, well. Sort of. I'm interested in Botanists."

"Botany?" Ernest asked.

"No, Botanists. I'm a historian really. With an interest in female botanists. I suppose over the years I've learned a bit about botany along the way. But it's the careers and the lives of the women doing it which fascinates me. I'm writing my post-doctoral thesis on two particular women. No one has heard of them but me, but I find their work interesting," she shook her head.

"Goodness, an academic," said Bernard, staring at her.

"Oh, I don't know how you do anything like that, how clever," Diana added, poking her mostly untouched salad with her fork.

The conversation moved onto activities around the area, which Nancy and Ernest seemed to have little to talk about until it came round to golf and the local links. Deborah noticed his eyes open beyond half closed for the first time in a while as he grumbled about handicaps and holes to Peter and Bernard. Nancy and Diana settled themselves to talking about being golf wives.

"Aren't you lucky that Peter doesn't play," tittered Nancy over the noise of the husbands, and sipping on her white wine.

"Bernard's off every Sunday," interjected Diana. "I must say it's nice to have the time to myself. I think men just need that sort of time with each other, doing that sort of thing. I dare say a lot of business is done on the green as well," Diana nodded at the other ladies, lighting another cigarette and placing it in a long, golden cigarette holder.

"Oh that's beautiful," Nancy leaned forward to look at it.

"It was an anniversary gift from Bernard," Diana smiled and looked up as the plates from their salad were cleared.

Deborah tried to listen to the men but they were being so loud it was almost impossible to tune into it.

Wine was refreshed and talked about. The Binghams had picked up a few bottles from their last trip to The Dordogne. Deborah listened to Nancy talk about their latest trip to Brittany and extol on how the French were simply insufferable and the food was worse. Ernest said little except to occasionally snort in agreement. As they were talking Deborah stared at them; Nancy in her pie-crust collared blouse and Ernest in his bulging suit. She looked back at her hosts, Diana and Bernard. They were better dressed, certainly. And there was an air about them that Deborah couldn't quite put into words. But she knew she didn't like it. As the main course came in, her eye turned to the paintings on the wall. There were gaps where some portraits had hung in years past. The red and gold wallpaper was faded around large squares. There was one picture of a woman whom Deborah thought might look a little like Bernard. *Could she be the lady who was murdered? I wonder if he knows what happened? I mustn't ask. I know I mustn't.*

Cloches were lifted from their plates to reveal a pinky-orange liquid with lumps of what looked like chicken in it and some green pepper slices, served on a bed of rice.

"This smells wonderful," Deborah smiled at Diana, "what is it?"

"Oh it's a little thing. Chicken paprika. I had it in a fabulous restaurant in London a few months ago and then saw a recipe for it in some magazine or other. I called the head chef at the restaurant - he's an old friend - and checked if it was right and he gave me a few pointers. He is *such* a darling."

"So you made all this, not your maid?" asked Deborah.

"You mean Lucy?" Diana asked, her face flushing.

"I wasn't sure..."

"Lucy is from the village. She comes and helps sometimes. I made the food and told her what to do to serve up," Diana forked her food and took a drag on a cigarette.

Oh bugger. I don't know the rules. Must remember not to talk about the help.

"Well, it's really delicious," Deborah looked down and focussed on her food.

"Oh yes, I must get your recipe, Di," Nancy coughed.

"Diana likes to try new things, don't you darling" Bernard smiled at his wife. "I do enjoy it, but I'm afraid I'm much more of an old bore than she. Though I'm glad you make me try these modern dishes from time to time. Or I'm sure I'd just eat whatever they served at the club," he laughed heavily.

"You men, you're all the same. Boiled beef and roly poly puddings," Diana took a large drink and seemed to smile a bit more again.

"Hear, hear," Ernest added, "delicious."

"Do you like to cook Deborah?" Nancy asked.

"Oh, um," Deborah cleared her throat, "yes, I do. A bit. My mother loved to cook, nothing fancy really. But she passed a lot of it down to me."

"Oh, that's nice," Nancy replied.

The conversation lulled. Eventually Bernard coughed again and began asking Peter more about his work in London and where he stayed when he went in. As the main course cleared, dessert wine was poured and a wonderful looking peach and almond tart came in. Deborah was starting to feel rather full and more than rather tipsy. *I need to slow down. These people can really drink.* She looked around. Ernest's eyes were almost closed now, his nose was a scarlet beacon and his cheeks matched. Nancy looked prim, with only a light flush to her face. Bernard and Diana were still going strong, apparently unaffected by several cocktails and even more glasses of wine.

"So," Diana turned to Deborah, "are you both feeling settled in now? To Querney life, I mean."

"Getting there, aren't we darling?" Deborah turned to Peter.

"It must be very different from London living," Nancy turned her head in sympathy.

"Oh, just a little," Deborah smirked behind her glass. "I've met a few nice people though. And the area is very beautiful."

"Good, good," Bernard topped up his glass and the rest of the table. "It's a little place, but we like it. We're proud to be from here and proud of our history of caring for the village over the years. Times have changed from the old days though. In my father's day..." he trailed off.

"I saw a portrait of a young man in your lovely drawing room," Deborah interjected, "was that your father?"

"Yes. Is."

"Sorry. He's still alive, isn't he?"

"Oh yes, still around. Strong in mind. Less so in body. He lives in an annex of the house with a nurse to help in the day."

"Oh I'm so sorry," Deborah wondered if she had made another blunder.

"Don't be. He's seventy-two now. As I say, he's still sharp as a tack in many ways."

"Does he not join you on these occasions?"

"No, no. It's too much for him these days. He likes the quiet. I'm sure he would love to meet you both some other time."

"Of course," Deborah smiled. "What about the rest of your family? You have two children, don't you?"

"Oh yes, Robert and Sylvia, both off at boarding school at the moment," Bernard replied.

"You must miss them, I'm sure," Deborah addressed Diana in particular.

"Oh yes," she replied, "very much so. But still, it's the best thing for them really. I had a wonderful time at boarding school. Sylvia has followed in my footsteps and Robert in Bernard's. Robert has nearly finished there now. You don't have children do you?"

"No," Deborah said back. "We never really got round to it, did we Peter?"

"No, though my mother still wishes we would," he laughed.

"I'm sure you still have time, Deborah," Diana said, "you're still young enough. You must want them, surely? I suppose living the life of an academic is very busy is it? Perhaps when you're done with all this botany research you could try?"

"Maybe. Yes. Probably not though. We like our life. And I'm not that young, really!" Deborah tried to laugh but her embarrassment was too much. Her cheeks burned and her eyes began to water. *How dare she.* Feeling almost bold Deborah pushed her feelings down and cleared her throat, "What about other family? Any nieces and nephews to dote on, Bernard? You'll have lots of cousins too I'm sure."

"Sadly not. We're not a large family. Just the one cousin."

"And where are they?"

"Um... She is in New York, I believe. Moved there with her father long ago."

"Oh, that's a shame. You must miss her. Where is her mother?" *I'm tripping close to the wind here. I know*. Even Peter turned to look at her with eyes widened.

"I'm sure the gossips of the village have informed you a little," he stood, getting a decanter and glasses from a silver salver on the sideboard. He poured three glasses of whisky and handed one each to Peter and Ernest.

"Not really, no. We've not heard anything, have we, darling?" interjected Peter who was eyeballing Deborah. The maid brought in coffee and collected the dessert things.

"I'll do the coffee, Lucy," said Diana. "You can clear up and go home, thank you."

"Yes, miss," the young girl nodded and made her way out, closing the door behind her.

"It's okay you know," Bernard gulped his drink and poured another. "We know it's about the only interesting thing that's ever happened here. I said to Diana earlier that I was sure it would come up. We have nothing to hide. It's just a great tragedy, really. My father couldn't bear to talk about it afterwards however. People gossip though, so we might as well own the truth of it."

I shouldn't have brought it up. A dam broke and guilt flooded Deborah.

"It was a horrible tragedy, wasn't it?" Nancy said, putting sugar in hers and her husband's coffee.

"Well, that's what murder is, isn't it?" Bernard stared off at the painting of the woman Deborah had noticed before. "That's her. My aunt, Eleanor. A robbery gone wrong, it was. My father found the body."

"Oh, how awful. I'm so sorry," Deborah leaned forward, the steam of her coffee helping her sober up.

"It *was* awful. Her daughter Mary was only a few months old. We don't know why Eleanor was walking in the grounds so early in the morning. That's when it happened. That was quite a mystery. My father said she was always quite, um, flighty, you know. Always doing things that were exciting. It was said she was returning from a party somewhere. It was scandalous for the family to be honest. First she married some New Yorker against all the wishes of her family. He was a rather rich investor to be sure. But, in those days... a foreigner, you know?" He grimaced. "Very coarse man, by all accounts."

"Have you not met him?"

"No, no. After my aunt died he went back to New York. Took the daughter with him. Signed away any claim to anything with the family."

"Yes?"

"Yes, well, you see, my aunt was the elder. She was in charge of the house. My father worried about her constantly. Unfortunately, Aunt Eleanor didn't really have a head for business, I've heard. When she died, had she written a proper will, it would have gone to her daughter and her husband as a protector until she came of age, but my brother couldn't allow that, could he? Got lawyers onto it so he could never have anything to do with the estate."

"But what about the daughter, Mary? Does she not get anything? Does she not want to be part of her family?"

"Not sure of the particulars. I think her father didn't want her to. Or something like that. I've only met her once or twice. A bit off the wall, so to speak. Perhaps she's taken after her mother."

"Your father did well, you know," Diana squeezed her husband's hand, "to fix the issues that your aunt Eleanor caused, didn't he?" "The family may have fared better in the last few years if he'd been able to help look after things sooner. Apparently she was very insistent on keeping him out and doing things herself. I mean, can you imagine? She was a party girl. A flapper, apparently. What she thought she could do, I don't know." Diana snorted delicately.

"Still, it's terrible what happened to her," Deborah said, kindly.

"Absolutely. An end like that? Awful," Bernard took another gulp of his single malt.

"Your poor father, finding the body," Deborah shook her head and sighed.

"Yes, he was out for a walk with a friend in the gardens and there she was. The friend noticed her first, I think. Then father saw her. He was sick with grief. They may have had their differences but he was utterly cut up by it, my mother told me years later. Devastated."

"I can imagine. How sad."

"Makes us all feel grateful for what we have, doesn't it?" Nancy said. Deborah smiled at her and saw that Ernest was asleep. *Perhaps he's heard this story too many times before.* Deborah sipped her coffee and felt it would soon be a good time to leave and think over everything she had heard tonight.

They soon finished up and thanked their hosts and Deborah promised they would have them over soon. Then she turned to Nancy and a barely conscious Ernest to say it was lovely to meet them and the usual end of evening pleasantries. The rain had started again and Deborah and Peter walked home in silence. Deborah was unable to speak as she ran through the evening in her mind. Peter opened the front door and held it for his wife.

"Well," he said. "That was rather interesting."

"Indeed," Deborah replied. *Very interesting.*

CHAPTER 7

When Deborah pulled back the curtains the clouds had already hidden the sun. She was up later than usual for a Saturday. Rubbing her head and reaching for a glass of water, Deborah looked at the other side of the empty bed. Peter's half was made neat, hers a crumpled mess. He will have been up hours ago, she knew. *A little thing such as a late night after a row and a hangover won't stop him from getting the papers at his usual time.* She threw a couple of aspirin down her throat with a gulp and a dressing gown over her shoulders. *Time to face the day.*

Downstairs smelled of eggs and coffee. Deborah heard Peter clear his throat, and the sound of a newspaper rustling. He was sat at the kitchen table. Whether he knew she was there, Deborah could not tell. *He's hiding behind his Times. He bloody well is.* Crashing about the kitchen, she made herself some toast and a cup of tea and sat opposite her husband.

"I got you The Guardian," he said from behind the Money section.

"Thank you," Deborah replied, gritting her teeth. *He's pig-headed enough to buy me the paper anyway. Bastard.* She didn't move to pick it up.

"Would you like me to pass it to you?" he asked, not moving.

"I shall read it later. After I have dressed."

Deborah drank her tea. She ate her toast. Peter drank his coffee from the other side of his paper. After drumming her fingernails on the table, Deborah scraped her chair and took her things to the sink. She washed and dried making as much clatter as she could. Peter cleared his throat and rustled the newspaper once more. Retrieving some beef from the freezer, Deborah clanked it onto a plate to defrost.

"Is that the beef?" Peter asked, turning a page of his paper.

"Yes. I'm stewing it for dinner tonight. Unless you have objections. Tomorrow we are at your mother's. I am taking a chicken to roast."

"I'm heading back to London after that, so we shall have to leave her promptly at three."

"Tomorrow? But it's Sunday."

"I'm aware of that. Big case starting first thing on Monday. I want to be at the chambers' flat and doing last minute prep by the evening."

"Right. Well. You didn't tell me."

"I'm sure I did. Last night."

"Maybe I didn't hear you while you were prattling on at me."

"Oh not this again," he finally folded his paper up. "Can't we move on?"

"You haven't apologised."

"What for?"

"What for? How can you say that?" Deborah banged a cup down on the side and filled the kettle loudly. "After everything I said about how you didn't stick up for me last night when they grilled me about not having children, how you barely said a word in general, and left it to me to make all the small talk. *And* how you only spoke to the men. That's not like you Peter! And let's not forget you lecturing me on 'proper behaviour' as well. I'm so sorry to have embarrassed you in any way. I guess I don't rub in the same haughty circles anymore, so I've forgotten how to behave around people."

"I'm not going into all this again. You were unkind to bring up that stuff about the murder," Peter stood up. Deborah gesticulated and made noises in protest. "You were. Don't pretend like you weren't. It wasn't the done thing. You should have waited for them to talk about it - *if* - they had wanted to. Which they may never do."

"Even so, you were a bore last night. You never used to be. Golf this, club that, city this. Blah, blah, blah. You were much more fun when we lived in London."

"Oh don't blame this on country living! Come on. It was a different situation than our usual friends over for supper. Also I'd told you I'd had a difficult day and didn't feel that talkative. Not everything is about you, Deborah."

"I've had enough of arguing. I'm going up for a shower. Then I'm driving to Bourton to do some shopping."

And so she did. It was aimless shopping, sought mainly to get out of the house and not have to talk to Peter again for a while. There were department stores in Bourton, with counters and ladies selling silk scarves and make up. Deborah bought a few dresses and a hat, and stopped for tea and cake before realising she wasn't having as much fun as she'd like. *I wish I was here with someone. A friend. Anyone.* She drove home in the late afternoon as the sun struggled to push its way through grey clouds. Peter was sitting in the living room, reading and listening to The Carpenters on the record player.

"Good trip?" he asked.

"Yes, fine thanks."

"Listen," he said, following her to the kitchen. "Please let's just move on. Let's just agree that I was a bore and that maybe - *maybe* - you could have had a little more tact. Can we?"

"I suppose I could agree to that. If you are definitely admitting to being a bore."

"I am. I was a bore. I apologise."

"Well, good. And I… I suppose I'm sorry too. I'm sorry we argued."

"It's six o'clock somewhere. How about we open a nice bottle of plonk and play scrabble." Deborah smiled and got out some wine glasses.

The next day they sat through church in Peter's mother's parish. Going back to hers for Deborah to cook them lunch while they reminisced and talked about Peter's school days. Elspeth talked several times about friends in the area who had just had children, Deborah couldn't help but notice. When it was time to go, Deborah and Peter went home and she dropped him off at the station with his briefcase and a suitcase of clothes for the next few days.

Back home Deborah stared out her kitchen window and watched drops of rain fall against the pane of glass. She sighed and decided it might be an idea to work through some of her books, or at least clear the ones that were not currently needed but were taking up a more permanent residence on the dining table. Sifting through a few, her eye was caught by the papers she had found in the attic so recently. She read them again, as she had done so many times in the last few days. She knew them almost by heart. *Oh, wait. Why didn't I think of it?*

Deborah paced up the stairs and made her way to the attic once more. *How much more could I find? There may be more stuffed in the walls, but what about the drawers and cabinets? Some of them would be rubbish, but what if…?* It wasn't hard to find where she had previously ripped things out of the wall cavity. She stuck her hand further into the hole, trying not to make it bigger. *Yes!* There were more. She pulled and pulled at reams of lined paper with the same cursive handwriting on it. There were other papers too, with different scribblings on as well. When she was certain there was no more in that particular space, she looked in the old wooden cabinets and on shelves. There were letters addressed to Coppers End, some things that were typed up and looked important and then, after an hour of looking… there it was. A folder.

Querney Manor House

The name was written on the front. It was a thick file. Deborah opened it and saw documents pertaining to some stolen pigs and then further in the words: *murder... body found... Eleanor Forrester...*

Grabbing everything together, Deborah made her way downstairs to the kitchen to put the kettle on and began to read.

CHAPTER 8

The crunch of leaves under his feet was cacophony. The wind swirled a number of them into his face. Sergeant Cooke did not want to be here. For the second time this year, he was up at Querney Manor House because of a dead body. This time it was no poorly maid, passed away in peaceful sleep. This time it was murder. There had been a call not ten minutes ago and he and Constable Smith had put their cups of tea aside and rushed straight there. They were shown to the gardens by Mr Carter and Mrs James. Her eyes had been puffy, her face pale. He was business-like as usual but with a definite shake in his hands that, in Cooke's opinion, belied the truth of his shock. As they made their way further into the woodland, Cooke could hear someone retching. Another person uttered inaudible words of comfort. As the party of four turned into a small clearing Cooke could see that the person retching was Mr Rupert Bingham, brother of the deceased. A man Sergeant Cooke did not know was standing near him, looking concerned.

"I stationed Bird here, Sergeant, to see that nothing happened to, uh, to the body," Carter said, nodding at the boy standing by who was trying not to look at the mess on the ground near him.

"Stand down, Bird," Cooke said, not unkindly. "You've done a good job. Thank you."

The boy looked at him gratefully and turned to look at Mr Carter who nodded at him before clearing his throat.

"Bird," Carter caught his arm, "go to the kitchens. Make sure the urns for tea are all on. We shall all need some. And we shall need plenty of sugar."

"Yes, Mr Carter, sir," Bird looked back at the body but turned his heel quickly and walked away towards the house.

Sergeant Cooke looked at his Constable and approached the corpse. It had been found under a great tree; a monstrous thing with the vines of another parasitic tree, wrapped all around it. It was grotesque. The branches all twisted and shooting this way and that. The leaves left on it were shades of orange and yellow, giving the appearance of flames. *If there was a gate to hell, this tree would be it.*

"Come now, Constable, let us examine the scene," Cooke said, knowing this was the boy's first murder case. Not his first dead body, but such a violent death would be a great deal for Smith to take in.

There was a lot of blood. The woman had been gashed across her abdomen a great number of times and her clothing was soaked red. Her face was untouched, however, and a genteel, delicate look was about her. *If you only saw her face she would appear to be sleeping. Lost in dreams,* Sergeant Cooke thought to himself. He made his way to the brother, who was sitting on a nearby log, wiping his mouth with his sleeve.

"Mr Bingham, sir. Please first of all let me offer you my deepest sorrow and condolences if I may be permitted to do so. This tragedy will be inspected with the full force of the law and I shall have whosoever has committed this heinous act. Be assured of that, sir."

"I am sure you will, sergeant," Rupert Bingham replied, making eye contact for a split second before rubbing his forehead with his flattened palm. The man was pale, a thin layer of sweat on his face, despite the cold. "Who?" he began, "who could do this? Why?'

"That is what I shall ascertain, Mr Bingham. Someone shall hang for it, I am certain," Cooke responded. "This has been a shock to you and the whole house, I am sure," he looked at Mrs James who was waiting nearby with Mr Carter, "but I will need to question you and the rest of your household very soon to find the meaning of these events. May I ask you a couple just now, while it is fresh and while we are here?" he indicated the woods in which they stood.

"Of course, of course," Rupert Bingham stood up tall and put his hand on his hips.

"These are your woods, are they not?"

"They are, sergeant."

"Is Mrs Forrester accustomed to walking in them?"

"Sometimes. She liked to tour the grounds most days."

"You found her like this, did you?"

"Yes," he said, turning to the body and flushing pale. "Just here. Just like this. How...?" he trailed off.

"She was dressed this way? Have you touched the body at all?"

"What? No. Of course not. You find everything exactly as I did. I found her with Mr Holcomb. He is a friend of mine, here for a visit," Rupert pointed to the man whom Sergeant Cooke had seen offering words of condolences. "We had our breakfast and decided to take a walk ourselves."

"Thank you. Does she normally do her tour of the grounds dressed this way? And this early in the morning?"

"What do you mean?"

"She appears to be in finery. Evening clothes. No coat. The dampness in them shows she may have been here some time. Overnight most likely. Can you explain any of this?"

"I don't see how what she's wearing is pertinent to the case, sergeant," Rupert Bingham pulled himself up tall.

"Well, it helps us piece together what she was doing. It is unusual for someone to walk in the woods so late, without a coat. And this October has been very cold. I am simply trying to get a picture of how she has ended up here this way. Forgive me."

"No. No. It is I who needs forgiveness. You are trying to do all you can and will have many questions to ask I am sure. I..." he trailed off again, looking at Carter and Mrs James. "Carter," he addressed his butler, "I am sorry. You and Mrs James have no need to be here right now, do you? Do they?" he turned to Sergeant Cooke.

"Not yet. But I shall need to question everyone in due course."

"But not at this moment. Good," he turned back to his servants, "you must go back to the house. Ensure the staff are well and there is no panic or upset among them. Your duty is to the house. Will you go and see things still run smoothly? The last thing we need is for everything else to fall apart."

"Of course, sir," Mr Carter nodded, taking Mrs James's arm and walking away.

"My apologies again," began Rupert. "It is better not to have too many staff around in such times as these. I trust Carter and Mrs James with my life, but stories and gossip always has a way of spreading and this... it would be too much to shame my sister this way."

"I'm not following, Mr Bingham," Cooke turned his head to his constable who got his notebook out at once.

"My sister... Eleanor," he rubbed his chin. "She was... how can I put this? She was... modern. She enjoyed going out to parties and listening to Jazz and... I believe domestic life bored her. I have chastised her and argued with her, to try to make her see sense..."

"My apologies, Mr Bingham, I still don't understand."

"You see why I did not wish the servants around. Although I am sure they must be aware of it all, they know everything about us, all our little habits, I am certain. But it wouldn't do to bandy about any reputation she may have."

"Reputation?"

"She would sneak out. Eleanor would. After dinner. Say she had a headache. Or some such thing. I knew what she was doing. It worried me and... now look at her."

"Where did she go to these parties? Could she have met someone there?"

"Oh, well, I couldn't say. When we argued about it, she always said she was never indiscreet. And I tried to believe her. She liked the nightlife but I don't think she would ever have been stupid enough to step out with anyone other than Bennet. Her husband. Mr Forrester. As to where she went, I can only guess. There are some nightclubs in Bourton. And there are hotels that have late Jazz evenings and singers and such like. Of course sometimes her friends would hold parties in their houses. I have been led to believe that sometimes she would catch a train to other places entirely." Rupert took a breath, "I'm not saying she was a bad person, or lacking in morals. She simply enjoyed dancing and music and didn't want to be stuck at home all the time. I knew she came back late from whatever gatherings she had attended. I suppose she must have done it last night."

"It would seem so, Mr Bingham. It would seem so." Cooke nodded absent-mindedly. "How did she travel to these nightclubs and parties? If she took one of your cars then it would be known instantly where she had been."

"I fear she was in the habit of walking and getting handsome cabs where she could. She was very secretive about it."

"If you don't mind me asking, how did you come to know about these habits?"

"Well, I'm her brother, sergeant. I've known her... I knew her. My whole life…" his voice broke and his upper lip began to tremble. Sergeant Cooke thought it best to look away for the man's sake. Bingham coughed. "It's hard to miss certain things. Things only a brother would know. We kept each other's secrets. As siblings do."

"Naturally, Mr Bingham. Naturally. And where were you last night and early this morning?"

"With Mr Holcomb. We ate dinner with Eleanor and Mr Forrester. Afterwards, Eleanor made her way to bed. So she said. *He* played cards with Mr Holcomb and I, but then retired to bed because he was expected in London the next day and would be getting an early train. Mr Forrester left Mr Holcomb and I playing at around ten thirty. We stayed up till after midnight. And went to bed. Is that about the gist of it, Holcomb?" he turned to his friend.

"That's right. That's the stuff of it," Mr Holcomb replied.

"Right. Thank you. I shall needs check on everything with other members of the household. You too, Mr Holcomb. You have no plans to go elsewhere soon, I hope?"

"I had planned to be off by tomorrow but if I can extend my stay then I will be yours for questioning," Holcomb replied.

"Of course you can extend your stay, man. And sergeant, the household is yours to talk to as you see fit. We must know what happened here."

"Indeed we must. Uh, is Mr Forrester still in London? Has he been informed?"

"We phoned and left a message with his secretary in his London office. He will only just be arriving there. I imagine he will be on the first train back here as soon as he hears. Poor devil."

"I should like it, if I'm not still here on his return, that someone should inform me of his coming home so I can speak with him too."

"Yes, sergeant. I shall make it known among the staff."

"I expect the medical examiner to be here any moment, Mr Bingham. He should be able to shed more light on the time of death and the particulars. Your sister will have to be autopsied, I am sure, so that we can ascertain as much as we can from her body."

"Gosh. That's cutting her up, isn't it? Does it have to be done?"

"It will give us much information about what happened here. It may be all the answers we need."

"Yes, yes. I just hate the thought… It seems gruesome. More violence for her."

"Simpson is a professional, sir. He will treat her properly."

Rupert Bingham drew breath, "This is murder, sergeant," he began. "Murder has not come to The Querneys before today."

"I understand. It is a great shock, but Simpson will help me solve it," he turned, "and here is the man himself. Dr. Simpson, thank you for getting here so quickly."

"Of course, of course," said the stocky coroner, heaving his bag onto the ground near the body of Eleanor Forrester. "Nothing to be done in these tragic situations. Got to get to the bottom of it." The cold autumn air had made Simpson's face ruddy, his nose red. "Well, I shall do my initial examinations, but I'm afraid, Mr Bingham, I will most likely have to perform an autopsy."

"Yes," Bingham replied, "we were just discussing that."

"So what do you think so far, Simpson?" asked Cooke. "And Smith, make notes of anything he says. Anything."

"Yes, sergeant," Constable Smith responded, snapping his notebook even wider open than before.

"Well, well..." the short, older Simpson said, "multiple stab wounds. I'd bet my life on it that that was the cause of death. Not likely to survive something like that! Ha!"

"Ahem, yes..." Cooke turned his eyes to Rupert Bingham apologetically, "it would seem not."

"Time of death? I'd put it down to... oh... six to eight or so hours ago. Between midnight and three in the morning I should say."

"Any signs of a struggle?"

"Well, some. There is dirt in her fingernails, not too many defensive wounds."

"Perhaps she knew her attacker?"

"It's possible. Certainly possible."

"She seems to have died here. The blood patterns and the sheer amount spilled on the ground," Cooke knelt down to point to what he was talking about.

"I shall be able to ascertain more after an autopsy but I should definitely say blood loss from these stab wounds was what did it for her."

"Just as I suspected. Thank you, Dr Simpson."

"Not at all, not at all, Sergeant. I shall finish making preliminary findings and have the body taken away."

"I shall come and see you tomorrow by ten to hear your report."

"Yes, yes... of course."

"Mr Bingham," Sergeant Cooke turned to the brother whose face was almost as pale as that of the victim, "I will talk with Simpson some more and see what else we can discover here. Then I should like to speak with your staff. Constable Smith and I will interview them and see if any of them has much to say that will shed light on your sister's death."

"Naturally," Mr Bingham assented. "I shall show you the way from the gardens to downstairs. I am sure Carter or Mrs James will happily give up one of their rooms to you so you may conduct your work in privacy."

"Thank you. You do not need to stay here while we work, sir. It may be hard for you."

"No. I must. I may not bear to look much, but... I do not wish for her to be without someone who loved her."

"Of course. Come, Constable, let us examine her some more and then make our enquiries."

Half an hour later Cooke and Smith were settled into Mrs James's sitting room and a long stream of servants came to tell them all they knew of the night before.

"It's not much is it?" Constable Smith said, after the seventh person came in to say they would have been asleep by then and heard nothing.

"Not yet," Cooke sighed, "but someone may yet know something. So far we have only spoken to people who spend most of their life downstairs and have almost nothing to do with backstairs or upstairs life. It is more like that we shall hear something from someone like Mrs Forrester's lady's maid. Or Mrs James or Carter himself."

More maids and servants made their way through the interview process with nothing helpful to offer. Then came Elsie Grable.

"Miss Grable?"

"Yes, sergeant," she said.

"Miss Grable," continued Sergeant Cooke, "you were Mrs Forrester's lady's maid were you not?"

"I was. For the last six months or so. It's just so awful, sir. Just last night I was..." the woman wiped tears from bloodshot eyes into a handkerchief.

"Yes, yes, I realise this must be hard to speak about."

"It is, sir. I was only her lady's maid for a short while. But I've been on the staff here for a few years. It is strange and horrible to think of murder come to The Querneys."

"It is. It is. May I ask why you were only her maid for a few months?"

"Well, there was another who was in my place before me. But she died. I think I saw you on the day when you came here. Sarah Miller was her name. Died after a short illness, I believe."

"Yes, I remember that," Constable Smith looked up. "We were here, sergeant."

"I didn't remember she was Mrs Forrester's lady's maid. Had she done it long?"

"Around two years, sir. She was very good. Taught me some things about hair and fixing clothes. It's awful though, isn't it, sir? To think that the both of them are now dead? One with a sick heart and the other taken from us so..." Elsie buried her face once more into her handkerchief.

"Constable, would you get Miss Grable some water please?"

"Of course, sergeant."

Once Elsie Grable was settled once more, with a cold glass of water and a cup of sweet tea that Constable Smith had insisted on bringing, they began to talk once more.

"Miss Grable, what was Mrs Forrester like to work for?"

"I - uh..."

"This is a police investigation, Miss Grable. It is not being 'indiscreet' if that is what you are worrying about. Anything you say could be useful in catching whoever did this to her."

"Well, it's just... we're not supposed to talk about family stuff, are we? Mrs James and Mr Carter are very strict about all that."

"Of course. But this is different. So can you tell me anything about Mrs Forrester? I would like to establish what her life was like and if anyone had a motive to do what they did."

"Well, she was ever so nice. She was a good woman, you know? She helped me if I got things wrong. Seeing as I hadn't been a lady's maid long. She was, um, modern, you might say."

"Modern?"

"Yes, independent. Enjoyed being in charge of the estate. Good with her daughter, too, as far as I was aware. And enjoyed, you know... Modern stuff."

"Can you go into any more detail on what that means?"

"Well, like, she would talk about politics sometimes. And try to find opportunities for me. And encourage me to have fun. She said that women shouldn't feel ashamed for enjoying themselves or wanting things like what men have."

"Did she go out much? And live by those principles?"

"She did. Sometimes. And... sometimes perhaps more than I realised... I... I shouldn't say."

"You really must, Miss Grable. You could say something that helps us find her killer."

"Well... okay. But... things for me to wash and fix were always left in a little basket in her room. Sometimes there were clothes in there that I hadn't dressed her in. Like she had changed into party clothes after saying goodnight to me. I always thought it was queer, but I never liked to pry."

"Did you never tell anyone or ask about it?"

"It's not my place to, sir. I washed what she wanted and kept her private affairs private. It's not my place to judge. And she worked so hard around here. If she was going to the odd party or jazz club - which is what I assumed - then I... pardon me for sounding so bold... but I think she deserved to enjoy herself."

"What about her husband? Would he not have noticed her absence?"

"They do not share a room, sir."

"Are they close?"

"I... I'd say they got on well, sir. There was a friendliness between them that I admired. But he was often in London on business and I believe they liked to keep separate lives a lot of the time. Do you promise I shan't get in trouble for speaking this way?"

"I do. You are obliged to help me in my investigation, Miss Grable. I dare say your information has been very helpful to the case."

"Oh, I hope so," she sipped her tea and sniffed.

"I need to ask where you were last night between midnight and three in the morning."

"Asleep. Or at least, I was definitely in my room by midnight. I had stayed up late to fix something for Mrs Forrester and... oh gosh, I've just realised I will be out of a job."

"That may not happen, Miss Grable. I'm sure you will be looked after," Cooke leaned forward to look at her kindly. "You say you were in your room."

"I was. I share a room with Ruth, the head maid. I went up a little before half-eleven. She was fast asleep. I washed and got into bed and fell asleep straight away. I didn't wake until morning. I was up by six as usual, I ate some breakfast in the servants' hall and got ready to take Mrs Forrester's breakfast tray to her for eight o'clock."

"And did you?"

"I did. She was not in her bed."

"Has that ever happened before?"

"From time to time, sergeant. Her bed looked like she had been in it, however. Only it had been neatened up. I assumed she had gone down to breakfast but not told me. She would do that if there was lots to do that day."

"I see. Thank you. One final question. Do you have any idea of who might want to do this to Mrs Forrester?"

"I'm sure I don't, sergeant. We are none of us popular amongst everyone we meet, sir. But to murder someone? You need to really hate them, don't you? I cannot see that anyone could have hated Mrs Forrester in such a way."

"Indeed. I think you have the right of it, Miss Grable. You may go now. Would you be able to send for Mrs James and Mr Carter for me?"

"Of course, sir." Elsie nodded politely, looking between the sergeant and his constable. Holding her tea cup she took her leave.

Once they were alone, Cooke and Smith looked at one another.

"What do you make of all this, Smith? A married woman of good place in society, a mother, living a secret life as flapper or whatever they call them, being murdered in the night in the grounds of her estate..."

"I can't say I know, sergeant. At the moment I can't make head nor tail of it."

"Me neither. I'm starting to get an idea of the people around here though, aren't you?"

"I am sir, I am."

The door opened and they stopped speaking. Mr Carter and Mrs James walked in and took their seats.

"The both of you know this house and its goings on better than most I'd imagine," Cooke began. "What do you say has happened here?"

Mr Carter looked impassive and cleared his throat, "I am at a loss, sergeant," his voice broke gently as he spoke and he coughed once more. "A loss, that's what it is. A loss all round."

"You must have known Mrs Forrester well."

"Since she was born. I have worked here almost all of my life, you see."

"That is why what you might be able to tell me could be vital to finding out what happened to her. How would you describe Mrs Forrester? Her character, say?"

"She was... clever. Modern. Sociable."

"I see. And you, Mrs James, how would you describe her?"

"I have not known her as long, so my information may not be as helpful. I have only been the housekeeper here these past ten years."

"Still, I should like to have your opinion."

"Mrs Forrester was a good employer," Mrs James continued. "She was firm but fair. She involved herself in the running where she needed to, but also left me to it when she didn't. I liked her company."

"You have given her an excellent reference, but what can you say of her character?"

"Forgive me sir," she looked sideways at Mr Carter, "I may be being bold but I'm not sure it is relevant to her murder what her character was like. Surely we should be thinking only of the man who did this?"

"You may have a point," Cooke replied, "but at the moment it helps me to establish her world, what she did, where she went. I can decipher more easily who this man, or woman, might have been."

"Well that information seems more relevant," she agreed. "As Mr Carter says she was sociable. But private. She did not take confidences easily, I do not believe. Her lady's maid would have more information about her personally, I am sure. All I can say is that, yes, she was modern. In her thinking and her ways. She spoke of women's freedoms, and at times I… I am afraid to say I heard her argue with her husband about them."

"Thank you, that is very helpful information. Do either of you think Mrs Forrester had any enemies?"

"Enemies?" Mr Carter gaped. "I cannot imagine -"

Mrs James smiled, "She was human, was she not? I am sure there were people who did not like her. Being a forthright woman is not always like to win you friends. But I dare say she had them."

"Indeed," Cooke replied, stroking his chin. "And what of her social life, can you tell me much about that?"

"I know she liked to go to parties from time to time," Mrs James replied.

"From time to time?"

"Yes. And I am aware she enjoyed the theatre in Bourton and London, and the occasional dinner and dance with friends."

"I see. Just occasionally was it?"

"Yes. Of course I do not keep her diary, sergeant."

"No. Indeed. Can you tell me of both of your movements yesterday and last night? What was happening in the house?"

"It was a family dinner," said Carter, "apart from Mr Bingham's guest. The men played cards after. I believe Mr Forrester left them to it because he had to get an early train to London. The house was cleared, everyone went to bed. It was a normal night in every sense."

"Anything to add, Mrs James?"

"Not especially, no. Grable undressed Mrs Forrester as usual. Got on with some cleaning and mending for her. I went up at my usual time."

"What time is that?"

"Eleven. Or soon after. Elsie was in the servant's hall darning something for Mrs Forrester. I told her not to be long. And I'm sure she wasn't because I heard her close her door about twenty or thirty minutes later."

"And what about during the night?"

"Well I'm sure I don't know. I'm not used to night wanderings. And I'm sure no one else here is either."

"I only meant that it passed as normal, Mrs James," Cooke replied, gently.

"Well yes, there were no disturbances, were there Mr Carter?"

"None."

"The first maids are up to do fires. They do bedrooms last," continued Mrs James.

"Ah, I see. Would the maid who had done that not have seen Mrs Forrester was not in her bed?"

"I always instruct the maids to be quick and make no fuss when they do it," said Mrs James, bristling. "It is not her place to look in on the bed. She should merely enter the room, go to the fireplace and set about her work quietly and then leave."

"Thank you. I will speak with this maid who made up the fire also." There was a knock on the door.

"Come in," said Cooke, loudly. In came the small and round form of Dr Simpson. "Ah, doctor, all done?"

"Yes, sergeant. I have finished looking at where she now lies. I am going to have her transported to my dead-room in Bourton. I have been looking at her personal effects too and it seems her purse is empty. Her brother has also informed me that her wedding and engagement rings are missing. Perhaps this was robbery? Opportunistic?

"It would certainly look that way. Though why a robber would take those things and then kill her in such fury… I'd like to know," Cooke shook his head.

"We shall get to the bottom of it. I shall begin the examination later today."

"I shall be with you in the morning then."

"Good. I shall take my leave." Dr Simpson doffed his bowler hat and left the room.

"And now," began Cooke, "I would see Mrs Forrester's room. Will you show me the way?"

"Of course, sergeant," replied Mrs James.

"With me, Smith. Let us find out more."

CHAPTER 9

Settling at her dining table with a hot cup of tea, Deborah had read and read until her tea was hot no more. Some of what she had found had nothing to do with Querney House and had simply been put in the wrong pile of papers. Other things were half ripped up pieces of policeman's notepaper, that she decided she should attempt to put together as soon as she found the time. Several things were of interest, however, including notes taken from statements by several people. Constable Smith had painstakingly authored full written statements that bore the signatures of people from long ago. Including that of Sergeant Cooke. Her finger traced the ink on the paper wondering about these names. Who they were. If they were still alive. Where they may be now. As she read her heart beat so hard she felt it in her fingertips. Sitting back in her chair for a moment, she stared at the ceiling.

"I need a drink," she said out loud. Leaving the records on the table she went to her drinks cabinet and poured herself a large glass of Peter's whisky. She shuddered as the heat of it made its way down her throat, warming and burning as it moved. "Oof," she said. "Another one will be necessary, I think."

What a violent way to die, she thought. *Seventeen stab wounds. Seventeen?* She downed her second drink. Taking a third small whisky, Deborah went back to the dining room and set about looking through the preliminary coroner's report again.

Cause of death: haemorrhaging. From puncture wounds made to the abdomen and legs (seventeen in total).

Deborah sipped her drink, reading those words for the fourth time. More things caught her eye.

Evidence of sexual intercourse. Possibly violent. Very few defensive wounds on body. Blood work requested.

SEXUAL INTERCOURSE. Possibly violent. What does all that mean? The family never said anything about that. But I suppose they wouldn't.

"I need to talk to someone about this," Deborah said to herself, standing up. "I need to call Lissa." Deborah looked at her watch. *It's not that late.* In the hallway she dialled a number on her avocado green telephone and waited. And listened. The phone rang and rang without answer. "Oh, Lissa, where are you?" she said, putting the receiver down.

Deborah paced to the bureau in the living room and took writing paper and a pen out and began to compose a letter instead.

Coppers End
The Querneys
Bourton
April 2nd 1973

Dearest Lissa,

I have just tried to reach you on your telephone but to no avail. In my last letters I have alluded to something but not found the time to tell you. You know this old house I now find myself living in? You remember it was a police house? Well, you will know that last night I went to Querney Manor for dinner. It was a fascinating thing, but not because I was overawed by the genteel classes. It was something else. I also mentioned in that same letter that I was seeing another person in the village earlier on the same day. It was over lunch with her that I was told a story: the story of murder in The Querneys.

About fifty years ago it happened. The sister to the current 'Lord of the Manor' was found dead. While I was at dinner with them, they told me about it all. It is very tragic, Lissa. I feel so sorry that something like this could happen to a person. But here is the twist: my Coppers End. You see, this old place still houses the files of the Sergeant who ran this place at the time. I found them in the attic. Yes! Complete madness. It doesn't seem real. But there some of them were, stuffed into the walls for insulation by a previous inhabitant. There must be years and years worth of ledgers and papers up there, all pertaining to this place, the people in this village and any crimes they committed. It is the most amazing piece of living history I have ever found. And you'll know how exciting that would be for me.

This afternoon, left alone by Peter who has returned to London for the best part of a week, I have been back up to that attic and discovered even more in old cabinets and drawers. I am now in the possession of official documents related to the murder of this Eleanor Forrester. I don't know what to do with them. Should I tell the family? I feel I should. But... there it all is in front of me. There are statements about her from servants and her husband. Apparently their marriage was just a convenience; she required money and he required standing in English society. I have deduced that he was the first suspect. They always think the husband did it, don't they? It wasn't him, you'll be pleased to know. I already know that. Apparently it was a robbery gone wrong by a local tramp. The worst part of it is that the tramp died pretty soon after and so no real justice was ever done. Makes the whole thing even worse, doesn't it? She died for absolutely nothing. Her infant child left motherless, for what?

Oh, there is so much I want to talk to you about! Eleanor Forrester was apparently a bit of a fast woman. A flapper, it says. With a secret penchant for dancing and champagne. So you'd have liked her (I jest). That's why they thought the husband might have done it. He could have found out and got jealous or something. But he said he never knew. It's written, right there, on his statement. Signed by him. I tell you I am so torn between sadness and shock, and excitement about the fact I can look upon this man's signature. I can picture him. He was a fashionable American investment banker so I imagine him in suits from Saville Row and carrying beautiful cigarette cases. Steam trains to London. Cocktails before dinner. I feel like I'm reading a real life Agatha Christie.

I know I am rambling. I'm finding it hard to get my head around what I have found. Medical examiner reports too! The one I have seen is covered in hand-written notes, by this Sergeant Cooke I believe. Question marks, wonderings, doubts. He didn't seem to like this Doctor Simpson much by the looks of things and he didn't agree with a few of the conclusions. Something to do with testing her blood, amongst other findings. I feel I would like to put it all together. Like a book. So I can see this whole history for myself. Oh, I don't know what I'm thinking. I should just hand it in to the family, shouldn't I? Plus I have so much to do for my own thesis. And doing up the house. I know that. But... I confess I have felt less interested recently in many of my old pursuits. I am not sure why. Finding these old papers is the first time in a long time I've felt that jolt of excitement in anything much. And it's research. Which is always a favourite with me, as you know!

I will send this letter to you, but I may end up (I hope) speaking to you on the phone before you receive it. I have so much I could add that I don't think I've included here. I wish you were with me to go over it and put it all together.

I have also just seen the time and I realise I was supposed to take something over to Peter's mother before it is too late tonight. So I will go. But next time I call, pick up your bloody phone!

Love you to pieces.

Deb xxx

CHAPTER 10

"You can see there is light bruising on her arms where she has been held hard. And there, that's where you can make out the shape of the perpetrator's hands, holding her at an upward angle, most likely from dragging her," Doctor Simpson pointed at the corpse on his table.

"But she was not killed and then moved, that was evident from the fact we found no other blood in the area. Just where she lay," Cooke rubbed his chin.

"Correct."

"So it appears she was dragged to her final resting place and stabbed there. Are there signs of a struggle?"

"A little. Some defensive wounds on her hands. Here," Simpson pointed to bruising, "and here."

"Why so few defensive wounds, I wonder? Had she been hit and made unconscious?" Cooke looked at the ceiling of the white cold morgue. *There is much about this I do not like.*

"No signs of a head wound at all. You can see the stab wounds all about her abdomen. Some are higher up than others. One is at the top of her right thigh."

"There seems to be such a frenzy in this attack. Smith, are you making notes of all this?"

"I am, sir," the constable replied. His voice was verging on inaudible.

"Are you quite all right, boy?" Simpson said gruffly. "You have gone grey. Sergeant, your constable needs a stronger stomach."

"Be easy on the lad. 'Tis his first murder. First dead body so ill used.

To be honest, this is the first murder I have seen in a long time. And the first of someone I had reason to be acquainted with. It is not easy for any of us."

"Yes, yes... ahem," Simpson cleared his throat, "I count seventeen stab wounds in all."

"What sort of instrument was used? Can you tell?" Cooke peered closely at them.

"Yes. Something about six inches. A dagger of sorts. Sharp. Very sharp. This attack was, as you say, clearly frenzied. In cases such as that I would expect to see more jagged wounds, nicks here or there. They are clean and smooth. Hence why it is my belief that the implement must have ben very sharp and well kept."

"Hmmmm, I see," Cooke shook his head. "Anything else?"

"On examination I can see that she had recently had intercourse. There is semen inside her vagina - oh come now constable, these are anatomical terms, no need to blush!"

Constable Smith looked between the floor and the tiled ceiling several times. "Sorry doctor, sorry sergeant," he said.

"Do go on, Dr Simpson," Cooke tried not to smile at his constable.

"Well, as I was saying... There is semen inside her. There is some evidence that this may have been an assault. I am uncertain. There is some bruising inside and a tear. The stories I have since heard about some of Mrs Forrester's, ahem, habits, make me wonder if coitus was... uh... ahem, coarse by choice."

"We cannot know that. It is possible it was part of the attack."

"Or before it."

"Are there any marks to suggest rape?"

"Well as I said there are these defensive wounds, here. But I would normally expect to see more. Any woman would fight to get away in those circumstances, wouldn't they?"

Cooke said nothing. He studied the naked corpse in front of him. Her arms at her sides, her legs a little apart. He could see light bruising on her breasts, her wrists, a large one on her neck. The holes from where she been stabbed were cleaned up and neat now. Even so, it was an awful sight. *What a thing to happen.* Cooke took a handkerchief from his pocket and dabbed at his head.

"Anything under the fingernails?"

"Mud, mainly."

"And in her blood?"

"What about it?"

"Are you not testing it?"

"Well, I could smell alcohol on her. No need to test for that."

"Yes, but what else might be in it?"

"We can see the cause of death, right there. Seventeen gaping cuts all over her body," he looked at his pocket watch.

"Do you have somewhere to be, doctor?" Cooke asked, standing up to his full height and turning to look Doctor Simpson in the eye.

"Well… I… as a matter of fact, yes."

"Surely nothing could bring you away from this murder of one of the patrons of our county? What could be more important?"

"I would have you know my expertise is needed and required in many places," Simpson blustered, "I do not need to share my personal diary with you."

"No, Simpson, but you are required to help me find out the reason that this young woman, this young mother died in so horrible a way. You will take samples of her blood and see if there is anything to discover within them," Cooke's face hardened.

"I am not accustomed to being ordered around in this manner."

"Be that as it may. I am the investigating officer and I require to know what is in her blood."

"Fine. As you wish," Simpson frowned, "but it will take time."

"This woman is going nowhere soon. Her family and those of us who knew her will thank you for taking that time to discover what happened so that justice may be served. I think especially of her daughter, who will grow up without ever remembering her mother. Come, Smith. It is time we went back to Querney Manor and spoke to Mr Forrester. He returned yesterday and should be in a fit enough state to speak with us." Cooke walked with Smith to the door, as he was leaving he turned, "Thank you, Dr Simpson. I look forward to your *full* written report." Shutting the door , he made his way along the dark green, sterile corridors of Bourton Hospital with Smith at his side.

"There is more colour in your cheeks, constable, now that we have left that dead room," he turned and smiled at Smith.

"Yes, sergeant. My apologies. It was just…"

"It's how you learn. No need to apologise. I must tell you there are many things I am not happy with in this case. Things that do not make sense. All these clues tell a story but it is one I cannot read as yet." Smith said nothing. "What do you think of what Simpson said about defensive wounds? Why so few?"

"I can't say, sergeant. Though he said he could smell alcohol on her breath. Perhaps she wasn't fully in capacity of herself for the drink, sir."

"Yes, perhaps. That might explain why she didn't fight off whoever attacked her as much as one would expect. Though I cannot believe this idea that there was not some sort of sexual assault. The bruising. The tearing. I think this Simpson has funny ideas, do you not?"

"I wouldn't like to say sergeant."

"No. No. Smith, it has been a long time since I have had to deal with this sort of crime. The war was brutal but it was a different sort of violence. This murder, and most likely assault of a sexual manner, disturbs me. I simply hope I am up to the task of it."

"I'm sure you are, sergeant."

Twenty minutes later, Cooke and Smith were parking their car round the side entrance of Querney Manor house. They were brought through the servant's hall and through the backstairs up to the library. The footman, Bird, brought them tea and after a moment's wait their next subject for interview had arrived.

"Good morning, sergeant," Mr Forrester said as he entered the room. Cooke took the man in. He had seen him a few times in the village at official things, but he had never had cause to behold him so closely and with such purpose. Bennet Forrester was taller than Cooke remembered. A man in his early thirties, his hair dark, and with what he would be sure young ladies would call handsome features on his American face.

"Good morning, Mr Forrester," Cooke stood up and tapped Smith on the shoulder to make him do likewise.

"You have been brought tea I see. Good," Forrester tried a smile and sat down. The man's eyes were puffy.

"Let me start by offering you condolences," Cooke began. "I am sorry to be speaking with you about something so tragic. This is a very difficult time for you, I am sure. Especially with your young daughter."

"It is, sergeant. It is," Forrester stood up and walked to the window. "How is it that things look so ordinary out there? My daughter has no mother. I have no wife. And yet things go on just like normal."

"Ahem," Cooke coughed, shifting uncomfortably, "I cannot know what you must be feeling now, sir. However, I am afraid I must ask questions of you. It will help me greatly in bringing to justice the person who did this, which may go some way to helping you with the loss you have suffered."

"Of course," he replied, "Of course you do," Forrester turned away from the window and returned to his seat by his bureau, sitting opposite the two policemen.

"Where were you on the evening before last?"

"At home. I had dinner with the family, played cards with Rupert and his friend, and left them to it. I was first to bed out of the three of us because I had an early train to London."

"Can anyone confirm this?"

"The servants. My valet. Our driver who took me to the station. But I slept alone, so I can't provide a witness to that part of my evening," he sighed, tapping the table and shifting in his chair.

"You and your wife have been married nigh on two years now. Is that correct."

"Yes, just a little more than that. But yes. Two."

"And, forgive my asking, but was it a happy marriage?"

"What are you insinuating?" Forrester sat forward on his chair, looking directly at Cooke.

"I insinuate nothing, Mr Forrester. These are simply lines of enquiry I must rule out."

"Because the husband always did it, right?" he scoffed.

"Not always, sir. But it has been the case in the past."

"I thought all you Brits loved the idea that the Butler did it. But now you presume I murdered my wife? Why would I do that?"

"I am not saying that, sir. But I must be allowed to ask the questions. A woman of good standing in this country has been brutally murdered. And I would find her killer. So I must ask you about your marriage. How would you describe it?"

Mr Forrester breathed in deeply, looking at Cooke in the eye. He softened his gaze, "How would I describe it...? Well. It was a good one. As far as I knew. I know in Great Britain there is no requirement of your ruling classes to love their spouses. Certainly not at first. And yes, that may have been the case for us. And perhaps I was not in love with my wife in a romantic sense... but I greatly esteemed her. She was... clever. Funny. She was the mother to my daughter. I believe we had both grown to have a certain kind of love for one another. We are - we were - good friends," Forrester took a pocket square out and dabbed his eyes with it.

"That is good to hear, sir. Were you close in other ways? Did you share secrets, for example?"

"Secrets? What do you mean?"

"I only mean, did you have absolute confidence in one another?"

"I... don't know. Probably not. There are always things a husband will keep from his wife, matters of business et cetera, and there are certainly things a wife will keep from her husband. Womanly mysteries and all that. We did not share every aspect of our lives with each other, if that is what you are asking."

"You said you slept alone. You did not share a room with Mrs Forrester, did you?"

"No. We had adjoining rooms, however."

"So you would not be aware if she was ever up and about at night?"

"Why would she be?" Mr Forrester's brow furrowed.

"I am trying to discover just this. There has been some suggestion that Mrs Forrester had, uh, certain habits. She liked going to parties and dancing to new Jazz music."

"She did. That is no crime is it?"

"Of course not. It has been put to me that on occasion she would leave the house without telling people and make her way to Bourton and other places to dance and enjoy herself. Would you know anything about that?"

"I am sure it's not true. Who has said this?" Mr Forrester stood up again. His mouth pursed in an angry frown.

"I cannot share that information with you right now. It is part of an ongoing investigation."

"You will tell me, sergeant," the man shouted. "Who is accusing my wife of being some sort of flapper, and a floozy?"

"As I said, I cannot tell you," Cooke could feel Smith tensing up next to him. It was becoming difficult for him to remain calm, he knew. "But you do not think there is any truth in what they have said?"

"No. Of course not."

"Mr Forrester, are you aware of how your wife was found?"

"I have been given some information, yes."

"She was discovered by her brother -"

"I know that."

"And she was in clothes that I can only describe as evening-wear. Very decorative and beautiful garments. There was alcohol on her breath. It seems she had been out for the night and there is some evidence that this wasn't the first time she had done it."

"I… I cannot believe it," he sat down again, staring out the window onto the park estate.

"I'm afraid it is true. Her purse had been robbed and her wedding and engagement rings removed, it would seem."

"So this was a robbery?"

"Perhaps. It looks to be. But also, and this is more awkward, were you and your wife intimate on the night she died?"

"I do not see how that is any business of yours."

"A yes or a no will suffice." Cooke stared at the man. He hated the question but it had to be asked and answered.

"No. We were not."

"I must check, however, exactly what you were doing between midnight and three o'clock in the morning?"

"I told you I was sleeping, goddammit!" Forrester slammed his fist on the bureau. "I had dinner last night with the family. I played cards with Rupert and his friend, Holcomb. I went to bed because I had to be up for the first train to London. I tell you, I didn't budge from my bed."

"And there is no one who can corroborate that at all?"

"Um. No. Of course not. I was alone in my room. Asleep. My valet helped me to bed just after ten-thirty. I stayed there. I was awake at five forty-five to make sure I was on the six-thirty train to London."

"Okay, Mr Forrester. Thank you. I will be in touch if there is anything else I need to ask."

"Like if I murdered my wife?" Forrester scoffed.

"I hope not, sir. I do not believe I will. I would reassure you, however, that I will do all I can to find her killer. I met Mrs Forrester a number of times and I always found her impressive. A good woman and a good example to many in this county."

"She was, wasn't she? That's what makes what you have said about her so hard to believe," Forrester stood up again, and sniffed. "I must take my leave. Business must still be attended to and I have a daughter who must needs be cared for without her mother."

"Of course. Thank you again, Mr Forrester."

Cooke and Smith took their leave of Querney Manor and went back to Coppers End. The car journey was short but quiet, both men pensive. Once back inside the police house, Smith made tea and they sat at their small kitchen table in silence.

"Sergeant," Smith spoke first, "do you believe Mr Forrester's story?"

"I should say I do. I've met many a liar and I do not believe he is one."

"He was very angry, sergeant."

"His wife has been murdered. If that is not reason to be angry, I do not know what is. Yes he was emotional, but he is American, isn't he? I am not sure there is any motive for his killing his wife. Unless he discovered her secret behaviours and murdered her in a rage. But… he does not seem the man. He is more like to divorce her. Americans do that, do they not? All accounts of him from the servants have been that he was a good man. And he spoke true, I thought."

"Yes, sir. I did not think him a man who did not speak truthfully."

"Then we agree on that much."

"You did not go into detail about the sexual assault on her person, sir."

"No. I did not see the need just yet. Sometimes it is good to keep some details private for reasons that it can bring out hidden truths from some, but also because there is doubt in my mind and I did not wish to burden him further with my belief that his wife was also raped before she died so violently."

"Of course, sergeant."

"We must set to writing this all down. I would have all our statements, notes and evidence written up so that we may peruse it at will and see each part of the story come together. This puzzle will be solved, Smith."

"Yes, sergeant."

"Well then. Let us get to work."

CHAPTER 11

rieg's *Lyric Pieces* played out on the record player once more. Deborah knew these pieces so well she hardly heard them. Nonetheless, they were soothing.

Coppers End
The Querneys
Bourtonshire.
April 13th 1973

DEAREST LISSA,

It was so lovely to chat the other day. The boys sound like they are really growing up. How is that possible? Soon they will be big grown men and out in the world. It makes me feel so old!

My project on this murder is coming together nicely. I work on it whenever Peter is away. He'd call me mad, so it's best that way. Luckily he is in London right now, so our dining room looks like a paper merchant has just exploded. I've really only just started putting it all together. There's just so much. I've got nothing new to tell you about the case. I've read and collated a little chunk of what there is but already I'm seeing the picture of it more clearly. There were loads of ripped up, hand written notes which I have managed to put together again (mostly), and I've matched them with the corresponding typed-up and signed statements. What's fascinating is that there are minor differences between them in places. I cannot fathom if that was by design or mistake. Not major things really, just precisely what time someone was somewhere, or when they went to bed. That sort of thing. This young constable, Smith, took all the notes in a pad and then presumably wrote everything up to be signed by all witnesses. I must say I really like this Sergeant Cooke as well.

Sometimes I feel like it's just a story I'm reading about. But then I remember. They were real people. Their smudges adorn ink on paper. What makes the whole situation more queer is that they lived in this house and some in the manor house I went to for dinner only a while back.

....

DEBORAH WAS ROUSED from writing her letter by the sound of a knock at the door. She looked up from the bureau in the living room and out of the window, only to see Theresa Slate's smiling face.

"Cooee!" the woman shouted, a large grin on her face. She was waving with one hand and holding a tin in the other. Deborah smiled to see her. They had bumped into each other in the village a few times and Deborah was sure the woman could not fail to cheer up even the most miserable of people. *Even Peter had to admit she was a lovely lady,* Deborah smiled as she opened her front door.

"Theresa!" she exclaimed, "what a lovely surprise! Come in!"

"Well," the woman started, "I won' stop, just popped in to see if you were doin' okay or needed anythin'? Plus we wanted to invite you both for a bit o' supper one time, or Sunday lunch, that sort of thing."

"Oh that would be lovely. Although it's definitely my turn to have you. You cooked for me last time."

"That was just a bit o' lunch! That wa'n't cookin'!" Theresa laughed, walking through the hallway. Deborah saw her peering around through the glass doors on one side that led to the dining room with all its mess, and the glass doors opposite which led to the living room.

"Come and sit down in the living room, I'll put the kettle on for some tea," Deborah took Theresa's coat and began to walk towards the kitchen. After a moment she realised the other woman was following her and had taken a seat at the kitchen table, putting her tin down in front of her.

"Oh, you've done it up nice in here. Last time I saw it it was a righ' mess."

"Last time?"

"Well, when we knew it had been sold we all took a nosey round didn't we. It was in a shockin' state."

"Yes, it was."

"Yes, yes. You've worked hard. Nice wood. And I like all your little knick-knacks and pots and things. All the stuff in our place I got from my mum. Who got it from her mum. It's all broken and battered but I can't face gettin' rid of any of it. Dennis thinks I'm mad."

"Well that's so charming, isn't it? I have lots of things from my mother. She loved to cook and be in her kitchen. Peter likes some of the more modern things and has got a number of gadgets for in here. I do miss her kitchen though, and the way she had it. Our old flat in London was her place originally, you see."

"Oh, that must have been lovely for you. A treasure to be where she loved to be."

"It was. Now, about you coming over - no I insist - I really want you to. We can't really do Sundays because we always go to Peter's mother's... unless I can persuade her to come here. She's such an old so-and-so though and set in her ways... gosh I shouldn't have said that!" Deborah laughed at her own candid behaviour. Normally it was only Lissa she complained about Elspeth to.

"Yes, yes. Oh, mothers-in-law are a piece of work the world over, I am sure. Dennis's mother is impossible to please. Impossible! Loves the children, mind. Accordin' to *her*, I'm not raisin' them the way she wants and I don't cook anythin' right either."

"What!? That's madness. You are a brilliant cook. I'm almost nervous to make anything for you."

"Nonsense. Now, speaking of which. I've got you a wee thing here," she pushed the tin closer to Deborah who was taking a seat with two hot cups of tea.

"Oh, well what is this?" Deborah opened it and was greeted by the warming smell of spices and ginger. "Oh, mmmm," she said automatically.

"It's just a bit of parkin. I suppose I should say Yorkshire, but I'm not from there, so it's Bourtonshire Parkin," she laughed, and took a sip from her tea. "Ooh, good brew that is."

"Oh, I love parkin. Thank you. That is so kind."

"Well I know Peter's been away a lot. An' sometimes you just need a cup of tea and a slice of something scrumptious with it. That's the best medicine for bein' somewhere new an' without your normal comforts, I say."

"Well, it's wonderful," Deborah felt an ache in her heart. *This is the first kind thing anyone has done for me in a while.* "Let's have some now," Deborah stood up and got old china plates out of her cupboard, feeling grateful to have a moment to pull herself together. *Come on, Deborah. Sort yourself out. No tears over parkin.*

"What's this music you've got playin'?" Theresa asked.

"Oh, it's Grieg. Lyric Pieces for piano. It's my favourite," Deborah turned and put the plates on the table.

"Oh, well then. I don't know much about that sort of thing, though I must say it sounds very nice. Peaceful."

"It is. It brings me comfort. Much like this cake will."

The two ladies sat in the kitchen and gossiped for a while, and Deborah found herself laughing harder than she had in weeks. After two slices of parkin each, and another cup of tea, Theresa declared it was time for her to be getting on before the children were back from school. Once she had her coat on and they had made their way into the hall to say their goodbyes, Theresa poked her head in each of the doors to the other rooms as she went past. At the living room she made appreciative noises and 'oohed' at the lovely furniture and the drinks cabinet. Crossing to the dining room she saw the disorganisation all around. Peter's law cases were on the floor and in the window seat, all wrapped in their official red ribbon. Then there were chairs filled with Deborah's doctorate research, and the table was covered in old police files from Coppers End.

"Got a fair bit going on here, haven't you?" Theresa asked. "Work is it?"

"Yes. It's a bit shameful isn't it? Some of it is Peter's, some of it is mine for my PhD. I've also started a local history project as well. Umm.. About the village. Just as a hobby. Sort of thing."

"Oh well, there's plenty of that here. That's for sure. There's lots of records at the library in Bourton and at Querney Manor you know."

"Are there?"

"Oh yes, loads of stuff about the village and the local area. The Binghams have always kept stuff. I suppose it's because they were the main hub of the place for so long. I don't know if they've given any to the National Trust, you know, history about the gardens, that sort of thing. But you should take a walk up there. Have you been to the gardens yet?"

"No, no I haven't. That's actually a brilliant idea. I think it will really help. Seeing the gardens."

"Will it?"

"Oh, yes. Well, because someone from the Trust may know some history or where to look for it."

"Oh yes, yes. Well, go and do that, I suppose. Anyway, it's been lovely to see you."

"You too! And I can't wait till you come over for dinner in a couple of weeks!"

Once Theresa had gone, Deborah started pacing. *The gardens. Why didn't I think of it? That's where she was found.* She walked to the dining table and found the description of where Eleanor Forrester's body had been discovered. *Some monstrous tree, apparently.* After a moment she had it. And a description of how to find it. *I'm sure they had cameras in those days. I wonder where any photos have gone...* she shuddered at the thought of seeing a dead body though. Within moments her coat was on and Deborah was out the door. She was warm quickly, the early spring sun shining down on her through little clouds. At the public entrance to the gardens she took a map after paying her penny, and began to explore.

The house appeared very different in the daylight. It was grand, with beautiful brickwork and a few wings, like something from a painting. It was only once she had studied the map that Deborah realised quite how extensive the grounds were. There were cultivated areas, a lake, a couple of small Grecian-style temples, huge woodland and parkland stretching far into the countryside. *No wonder it was too costly to maintain by themselves.*

The air smelled wonderful. April was bringing out colours and flowers and scents. Birds were flying from tree to tree and singing to the sunshine. *If I lived here I would walk here everyday,* she decided. There were National Trust signs explaining the work going on to maintain the place, and over a little hill, Deborah could see a few Victorian glasshouses, and behind them were walled kitchen gardens. Her work often took her into the world of botany, though it was not the plants she cared most about, but the women who discovered, toiled, and put all their curiosity into them. They were the ones whom Deborah had spent so much of her life so far digging for information about, attempting to get their work recognised and celebrated.

It was so lovely to walk among the shrubberies and planted paths, that for a while, Deborah forgot why she had originally come to Querney House Gardens. Checking the map once more, she began to make her way to the woods. It was a winding path, leading away from the house, past a car park for the paying public, and behind a number of dilapidated outhouses.

The description set out by Smith as to how to find that particular tree was imprinted into Deborah's memory. She knew she had to head north and west from the house, and that the body was found on the western edge of the centre of the woodland. There would be a path to follow and a clearing to get past as well. Deborah had thought it would be quick and easy. She hadn't counted on the sheer size of the parkland. *I've obviously never taken in the grandeur of this place on any map. I've never been interested enough.* Once she was among the trees, the light started to fade as the foliage blocked it from above. The ground was still muddy from all the rain they had had, and Deborah's footing slipped a number times as she made her way through. After twenty minutes of no luck and feeling quite lost, Deborah decided the best thing to do would be to walk the perimeter and make her way slowly in, looping her way round and covering as much ground as she could to find this huge tree. *Unless they got rid of it... I'd definitely think about doing that if someone I loved was left dead beneath it.*

For what felt like miles Deborah walked, roaming as much of the wood as she could, feeling more hopeless as time went on. She cursed herself for not thinking sooner that they may have dug up or cut the tree down. Though part of her still hoped, even if it was the smallest hope, that in the very least there would be a great hulking tree stump. One that was so obviously cut down in recent years that it would have to be the one she was so desperate to find. Then she spied something. *That must be it.* She walked faster, getting closer. *It's got to be...*

She had never seen anything like it. There was a normal tree trunk somewhere deep down in the depths of a huge cloud of branches belonging to another. It was hard not to feel sorry for whatever was growing inside. It was engulfed. The parasitic tree was wild, its branches flailing and growing this way and that, without care for beauty or for what it was choking within. And it was enormous. *It has to be this one. It has to be.* Deborah walked around it, thinking that when autumn came, as it had been when Eleanor Forrester was found beneath this tree, it must really look like something from hell. All reds and oranges and yellows. All fire.

Deborah sat down in front of it, not caring about the mud and wet seeping into her clothes. It was too interesting not to want to stop and take it all in. *This is where you were found, Eleanor. Here. This is where you died. I am sure of it.* At that moment, Eleanor felt so real to Deborah. In her mind's eye, Deborah could see this gorgeous woman, a brunette, with fashionable hair and clothes, listening to Jazz and talking about suffrage, or other such things. She had read about the woman before, but only what had marked her for death, the causes of her demise, and the tidbits of her character as told by those who knew her and worked for her.

Deborah shivered and looked up to see the clouds moving in through the treetops. Whether it was the long walk this afternoon or the relative lack of light in the woods around her, Deborah's eyes felt heavy. Leaning against the tree, she closed them for a moment.

When she opened them she was standing a little away from the tree. Gone were summer flowers in the ground and leaves on the trees. The floor was no longer dark with mud and green with grass. Leaves the colour of burning embers, fiery reds and earth browns carpeted the landscape. The crackle as Deborah walked upon them burned through her head. A breeze lifted wisps of fine hair and swirled flora around her feet. A bronze leaf caught on top of her head and as she pulled it out she could see the twisted curve on each blade; so fragile, so beautiful. Deborah let it go and as it tumbled across the air, it floated in circles and danced gracefully, before landing on something that didn't belong in the forest. A glint. A sparkle. Deborah moved closer. An elegant, jewelled buckle, attached to something. A black, heeled shoe. There were two of them, both adorned with the glinting buckles. Someone was wearing them. The owner was lying down, hidden behind that gruesome tree. Deborah stared at the buckles, hardly noticing the smears of mud and how one had snapped away at the strap. A closer look. One step further. Deborah shivered and stood back. There was a woman. Blood all over her petite body. Her dark hair a mess. Deborah stooped down, an urge to tidy it up. *She wouldn't want it like that.*

A noise (or was it some movement?) distracted her. Deborah looked away from the body. Men were crowded together, deep in discussion, but she could not hear their words. Two of the men were in dark uniform. *I think I know them,* she looked from the younger man to the older one. Another man, short and stout, with a large brown leather bag talked while waving his free hand round. *I don't want to be here,* Deborah's chest thrummed. Her attention was drawn to the body again. *She needs someone. Why aren't they looking after her?* Deborah kept surveying the men, outraged that they were ignoring the body so close to them. *She needs you,* she tried to call out but she had no voice.

A blink. Someone was near her now. One of those men. In the dark clothes. An older man. An officer of the law. He had lines around his eyes that told Deborah stories of laughter and worry and care. *I know you. I'm sure I do.* Her heart became quiet, no longer banging a reel inside her head. *He is here now.* He looked at Deborah, drawing her eyes to his. They both looked down at his hands. In them was a hempen rope. Again. It was thick and grey, rough and frayed with age. The gentleman stared at Deborah in mute appeal as her stomach convulsed.

His eyes shifted back to the corpse and Deborah followed his gaze, feeling drained. Placing her hand on the tree to steady herself, Deborah looked again at the older policeman's eyes. They fixed upon her. Repulsed, Deborah realised the rope that had once been in his hand was round his neck. A shiver of fear ran through her and she turned away from the horror of it. Holding her eyes tight shut, Deborah willed herself to wake.

Eyes open. The men had gone. So had the fallen leaves. And the body. The body. *The body.*

The air was different. Spring had returned once more. The ground was green and fertile and alive. Deborah sighed.

Up she stood, brushing mud off her clothes. Deborah's arms were all goosepimples as the fading sun was lost to the trees. *It's time I went home.*

Once out of the woods, Deborah felt warmer. She crossed the gardens, heading for the glasshouses and where she knew the path out of the grounds would be. Now she was closer to the house, Deborah heard voices she recognised from behind a hedge. She knew Diana Bingham's ice cold laugh from anywhere. Stopping close-by to listen in, she could hear Diana and Bernard discussing an up-coming party. In June by the sounds of it.

"Hopefully the weather will be better by then, Bernard. All this rain has been far too awful," Diana was saying. Deborah heard a lighter flash and the woman take a long drag from her cigarette. They must be very close by. Deborah took a step back.

"Absolutely. We can get a marquee put up of course. We always do."

"Yes, but it's not the same. Sitting under a marquee in the bloody rain. All crammed in like sardines, eating sandwiches and vol-au-vents."

"Well, I can't actually do anything about the weather, darling. We'll just have to see what happens and plan for all occurrences."

"Of course you know what that means, don't you?" Diana asked.

"No. What's that?"

"You'll have to open those purse strings of yours. If we want to plan for eventualities, that is. I know how much you enjoy doing that..."

"Diana..." Bernard took a deep breath in. Deborah waited behind the bush nervously, wondering if and when she should move. "You know how it is. Things aren't great at the bank right now. We will do what we can."

"You say that all the time."

"It's true all the time. But you must -"

Deborah was pulled from the conversation by a tap on the shoulder. She jumped.

"Hello," a young man said to her.

"Oh gosh, I was just admiring this, bush here, the ummm…" Deborah looked around. At once a set of eyes was peering at her from over the greenery.

"Ah! Deborah! What are you doing here?" Bernard was smiling and affable.

"Oh, I was just taking a walk in the gardens. I haven't been yet and I've heard so many wonderful things…" she turned to look at the young man who had only just made himself known to her. He was grinning.

"I see you've met Robert, our son. He is home for the holidays."

"Hello," she said, looking Robert in the eyes for the first time. He looked familiar somehow.

"Come on in and say hello, Robert will lead you round."

"Oh, no, I mustn't," Deborah protested.

"Of course you must," Robert said. "I've heard much about you and the house you moved into. Come on, let me show you in. It's time for an early cocktail, don't you think?"

Deborah looked at the time, "Quite early, really."

"Well, who's watching, eh?" he said as he led her gently round the back of the house and through a large gate. They walked a little more and came to a very grand lawn, hidden from the rest of the public. It was rather lovely; someone had taken the time to care for it, even if it wasn't quite as splendid as the gardens outside the hedges.

"Is your sister at home too?" Deborah asked.

"No, Sylvia is staying with some friends near to school. She often does. Makes it easier for her to study, she says."

"Oh, well that's nice for her. To enjoy working and academia."

"Yes, father told me you were an academic."

"Did he?"

"Yes, a historian? Or a botanist? He was confused. Father often is," Robert smiled conspiratorially and Deborah couldn't help but return the look.

"I'm a historian, yes."

"I'm hopefully bound for history at Oxford. Either that or in London. Just got to get these blasted exams out of the way."

"Well, if you want any help or to chat, do let me know. I'm more than happy to come to the aid of a fellow enthusiast. Though my subject is very narrow these days. But I'm sure I can just about do the basics!"

"Thank you, I may just take you up on that. Ah, here we are. Don't you think you should fix Deborah a drink, father?"

"Bit early, Robert, don't you think?" Bernard said, standing up. He and Diana were sitting at an ornate wrought iron table, painted white. She looked as splendid and as beautiful as Deborah remembered. Her hair was perfect and her clothes so trendy. *She could have walked right off the front cover of an Italian magazine.*

"Don't be silly, Bernard. It's six o'clock somewhere in the old Empire. Make us a batch of martinis won't you?" Diana flicked her cigarette. Bernard nodded and headed into the house through large French windows. "How are you Deborah? We've not seen you since our dinner party." Diana was all smiles, Deborah could see. But only the corners of her mouth moved. Her eyes were placid pools of cold blue.

"We are well thank you. Peter is in London at the moment."

"He's a barrister, isn't he?" Robert asked.

"Yes, he is. Criminal Law. Queen's Counsel."

"Goodness. He is in London a lot, I suppose?" he replied.

"He is, these days. Over the summer things shut down pretty much. So I'm sure he will be here all the time then. It's the way things are really. Thank you for inviting me in. I do feel like I'm imposing on family time."

"Nonsense, it's great to meet the neighbours, isn't it, mother?" Robert was so affable, it was hard to see how Diana could have raised such a friendly boy. *Perhaps Sylvia is more like her mother?*

"Oh yes, absolutely," Diana put another cigarette in her golden holder and lit it.

"Mother, you must stop this," Robert leaned over to Diana lovingly. "I'm always telling her to quit this smoking stuff. She never listens to me."

"Robert worries about these things," Diana said, rubbing her son's cheek with one hand. "Don't you, darling?"

"Here we are!" Bernard was at the French doors once more with a large jug of martini and four glasses. "Only a small one for you, Robert. You've got exams to study for."

"I've worked all day!"

"Go on, Bernard, don't be a bore!" Diana said.

"Fine, fine. Far be it from me to think of the younger generation, eh? Right, one for you, Deborah, and Diana," he poured out the drinks and handed them to each person. "Cheers!" he said, sitting down. Everyone clinked their glasses together and sipped. Deborah's eyes watered.

"We were just talking about our annual summer party, weren't we, Diana," Bernard started.

"Yes, we love throwing it every year. It's such fun," Diana took a large gulp of her drink.

"You and your husband must come," Robert said.

"Oh yes, you must," Bernard agreed.

"We wouldn't want to, you know -"

Robert laughed, "If you were about to say 'impose' again, then I shall have to call you a simpleton, Deborah. She is far too polite for our family, don't you think?"

"Ha ha!" Bernard laughed. "Everyone is welcome. And so are you and Peter. It would be great to catch up with the man. See how's tricks."

"Ernest and Nancy will be there of course," Diana nodded.

"Oh, not those bores," Robert laughed. "You didn't subject them to the Flintrops did you?"

"Robert!" Diana cackled. "Really! Such a thing to say."

"I don't know," Robert sipped his drink. "He's always half asleep and she never has anything to say," Robert looked sideways at Deborah, smiling. She couldn't help but like Robert.

"I'm sure it will be lovely to see the two of them again," Deborah drank gently, trying not to go too fast. Diana was already finished and pouring herself another from the jug. "And meeting more people, of course. I'm sure your parties must be wonderful."

"Well, yes. The summer do is always lots of fun," Robert replied. "Tell me," he leaned back in his chair. "Are you working much on your thesis right now? I'd be fascinated to learn more."

"Oh!" Deborah laughed, "I'm sure you wouldn't. I think it's likely there are only a very small number of people interested in my subject. Very narrow field indeed."

"Still, I'd very much like to see what someone doing a PhD in history writes about."

"Naturally you're very welcome to come over and see," Deborah smiled.

"How do you work?"

"What do you mean?" she asked.

"Well, do you work in the morning? How much research have you had to do? Do you need silence? That sort of thing."

"Robert," Diana shook her head, "I'm sure Deborah doesn't need to answer these questions right now."

"Oh it's okay," Deborah thought for a moment. "I do work best in mornings. And I often listen to music. Mainly Grieg. But sometimes the radio. I like other music of course, some pop stuff, but I find I can't work when it's on. I've been very distracted from my work recently though. The house and moving and, well, other things. Luckily I have two more years till I have to submit everything!"

"Two more years, gosh," Bernard finished his martini. "That's a long time to work on something."

"I started two years ago."

"Good grief!" he exclaimed.

"That's PhD life, father. Isn't it amazing?' Robert drained his glass. "Anyone want an olive? I fancy some. Mother? Father?" Robert's parents shook their heads. "Deborah?"

"No, no," she said, drinking the last of her martini. "I really must be going. Peter is back tomorrow so I must get a few things ready for him and get some work done too. Thank you for this," she indicated her empty glass. "We must have you over for cocktails soon." Deborah stood up, wobbling slightly with the gin.

"Robert, show our guest out will you, darling?"

"Oh, there's no need, -" Deborah began to protest. Before she knew it, Robert had walked round the table and held her coat for her. "Thank you. That's very kind."

"It's nothing. Let's go," he said.

He led Deborah back to the gate into the public gardens and began to head further towards to main gate.

"Oh, there's no need, I can get home from here," Deborah smiled.

"And what sort of gentleman would that make me?"

"Honestly, I'm fine. But thank you very much. I meant it when I said you would be welcome to come by and talk about history and your studies though. Feel free, especially while you are on holiday."

"Thank you. That's really very kind of you."

"It's nothing. Just a favour from one historian to another," she smiled at the boy and Robert grinned back. "Come on, back you go. Your parents will wonder what happened to you."

"Okay, well then. Hopefully I shall see you soon."

"Of course."

Deborah waved at him as she walked down the lane and out of the grounds of Querney House. For the first time she was looking forward to the solitude of her home at Coppers End. She put the kettle on for strong coffee and sobered up over another slice of Theresa's parkin and thought only of the tree she had sought out and found today. The grotesque nature of it contrasted starkly with the warmth she then received from Robert and Bernard (and nearly from Diana). She put all thoughts of it out of her mind as she turned to the dining room. *Time to find out what happened next.*

CHAPTER 12

"It's time we went to the medical examiner again, Smith," Sergeant Cooke said as he stood up from his desk.

"Yes, sergeant. Jus' coming," Constable Smith ran the last few paces through the hall and put his coat on quickly.

"Let's hope he's done what I asked him -" the phone interrupted Cooke as he spoke. He sighed and picked up the receiver. "Coppers End, sergeant speaking."

Smith stared hard at Cooke for the few minutes he was on the telephone. The man hardly spoke, nodding his head, making noises of understanding and looking grim. When he replaced the receiver he looked over to his constable and scratched his chin.

"Well, constable. It looks like we have double the reason to visit Simpson today."

"Why's that, sergeant?" The boy's face was puzzled.

"They've picked up a vagrant. Dead. In Bourton. You may wonder what that has to do with us. As did I at first. It seems that this homeless man had about his person the missing possessions of Mrs Eleanor Forrester, as well as a bloodied knife. We must rush now to see what Dr Simpson has ascertained and to follow up with the questions I had from two days ago."

"Goodness, sir. I… I can't quite believe it."

"What can't you believe, constable?"

"Well, it seems we may have the answer to our problem right there."

"Yes. That may well be. That may well be…" he put on his hat, "but does the answer fit the questions I am required to ask?"

Once they arrived at the morgue it wasn't long before Cooke and Smith were looking at two bodies in Dr Simpson's dead room. One was known to them, the other not.

"Let's start with this new body shall we?" Dr Simpson asked, looking over his notes and walking to the man lying naked on a slab. "We have no identifying items for him. I can tell he was a man probably in his forties. Though often with vagrants they appear older than they really are due to illness and style of living."

Cooke scoffed, "I hardly think homelessness constitutes a *style* of living, doctor."

"Well, in such cases as these, I find the people themselves often seem to choose it. They do nothing to help themselves and take part in activities and pastimes which will only make their lives worse. Drink. Illicit substances. Criminal behaviour. That sort of thing."

"I see."

"His body is of little interest to the case, I am sure -"

"How did he die, doctor?"

"Ah, well. On first examination I was hard pressed not to find a range of issues with his health. His lungs showed advanced pneumonia and there were tumours in his liver, as well as signs of excessive alcohol consumption. I would have thought this man did not have long for the world given the state of him. Though what I believe actually killed him was the cold. The temperature these last few days has been low, and a man in this kind of physical condition, without shelter or medical assistance would have been very vulnerable to exposure of any kind."

"Are you sure? Exposure? It's not the middle of winter here, is it?"

"No, you are right. But as I said, he was not a well man. There was also a weakness in his heart valves. Any prolonged cold could have finished him off. He had only threadbare clothing on. We are in coats and hats out of doors. We would not feel it quite as keenly as someone such as him.

"What about the items on his person? Is it possible that they connect him with Mrs Forrester over there."

"Yes, yes they do. If you will follow me..." Doctor Simpson took the two men over to a drawer where a number of items had been locked away. "Here is some money which was hidden in his trousers. It has blood on it, which I have ascertained as a matching type to that of Mrs Forrester. There is a ring there. Seems to be an engagement ring to me."

"It does. Constable, may I see the description of the ring that was missing from Mrs Forrester's body?"

"Of course, sergeant." Smith leafed through his notebook to find the relevant page and handed it to his superior.

"Round of little diamonds, round cut sapphire in the centre on a gold band..." Cooke spoke as he fingered the ring in front of him. "It seems to match. We will have to get the official documents kept for insurance purposes, of course. Check it against them. I know that Mr Forrester was getting those for me. But at the moment it does look like we've got her ring. But no wedding ring. That's curious, don't you think?" He looked at the woman's body as he spoke. *Have we really found your killer?* "All these things he could have found somewhere else though, a chance thing. Does anything pin him to her murder?"

"Well, there are his clothes, and the knife," Dr Simpson replied.

"Show me," Cooke rubbed his chin as Simpson pulled out another locked drawer.

"Here is his shirt. It has blood on it. It's not his. I have tested it and it matches the type of Mrs Forrester."

"I see."

"And here is the knife he also had on him. It matches the type of wounds on her body. And there are bloody fingerprints on it too. Looking closely at them, they are his. And it's her blood."

"So we have her possessions on him, a shirt that he was wearing with her blood on and a knife with her blood on and his fingerprints," Cooke summarised.

"Correct. Looks like we have found our killer. I'd say it's fairly conclusive, wouldn't you?"

"Quite likely..." Cooke scratched his chin again. "I can't fathom why though. What was he doing on her property? And why so many wounds to her person?"

"Huh. Well. He's a vagrant. Who can say? When one lives like that, one often lacks for morals. He most likely wanted money, or something he could sell. He probably went onto the property with a view to stealing, met Mrs Forrester on the way back from wherever she was. Perhaps she stopped him and they argued. He robbed her and it ended in tragedy. Although, I am no policeman," Simpson looked grimly at Cooke.

"It is certainly looking like your theory might be the best though, Simpson," Cooke walked over to Mrs Forrester's body to look it over once more. "I want to know why he had a knife like that. That's a very sharp, very ornate knife. Where did he get it?" Cooke asked as he looked at Eleanor Forrester's face, wondering if she knew the answers. He turned to the doctor once more, "Were there any results from her blood report?"

"Ah, yes. Alcohol, as I suspected. And trace amounts of a barbiturate."

"A barbiturate? Do we know if she was a user for medical reasons? Is there anything on her notes?"

"Yes..." Simpson looked over some notes. "Yes... she was prescribed some last year for insomnia."

"But that was last year."

"That's not to say she used all of it. And didn't use it recreationally at these parties she was said to go to. It's not uncommon, unfortunately."

"No. Indeed. Was there a sufficient amount to affect her during this attack?"

"What do you mean?"

"I mean, was she conscious? How high was the level in her blood?"

"Not very high. Though a lot depends on her constitution and how used to taking it she was. That amount for a small person like her could have been enough to render her unconscious, I suppose. Though as she had used it before makes me think it likely she had a certain tolerance to it. Especially if she used it more often than simply for getting to sleep. If you catch my meaning."

"I do, doctor. I do."

"It'll all go in my report, sergeant. And I will give it as evidence at the inquest when it happens as well," Dr Simpson strode to his desk and sat down to sign some papers.

Cooke was quiet all the journey back to Coppers End. He let Smith drive so that he could focus his thoughts on the case and sat in the passenger seat, staring out of the window. From time to time he would clear his throat. Other times he would rub his chin with his forefinger or thumb. Once inside Coppers End, he placed his hat and coat on the stand in the hall, told Smith to put the kettle on for tea and went into his study, overlooking the front of the house, and sat at his desk. Every so often, he wrote a word on the paper in front of him.

Knife - why? Wounds? Blood
Defensive wounds
Barbiturates - level? Shirt, money, rings.
Character?

When Smith brought in the tea, Cooke was so lost in thought that he jumped at the sound of the tin mug being placed in front of him.

"Well, constable. What do you think of it all?"

"Me, sir?"

"Yes, you. Do you see another constable with me in the room?" His voice was sharp. " My apologies," he said, softening his look and indicating that Smith should sit. "I should like your thoughts on this case. It would please me to hear what you think before we must venture up to the Manor House and tell them what we have found today. Which must be soon. They cannot be left waiting much longer."

"No, sir. They can't."

"Well then, constable. And tell me what you are thinking."

Smith took a seat with great care and stuttered. "W-well, sergeant. It seems fairly cut an' dry to me. This man has been found with her possessions. An' a knife with her blood on an' these fingerprints. That's all pretty incriminatin' to me."

"Yes, it is. All very incriminating." *So why doesn't it sit well?* "I have a few questions and ideas that I want you to consider with me while we drink this tea. Yes, this vagrant certainly appears to be what we are looking for. Tell me this, why did he stab her so many times? The maid had it right, you have to really hate someone to do that, surely? If it was a robbery and he needed to incapacitate her, why not stab her one or two times? Why all over her body in a frenzy? Did they have a connection we don't know of? And why did he have that knife? It is ornate and incredibly sharp. Someone cared for that knife. Did he steal it? If so, where from? Were they sexually intimate? If so, why? Did he assault her too? And what about the barbiturates? Did she really use so much that she would be used to it? People said she was modern. Perhaps she was. I was lucky to meet her a few times. She always appeared sensible to me. Not a party girl at all."

"But sergeant, you've said before that people can surprise you. That deep down we never know the real person. You've often told me you're shocked at the private lives of people you've had to investigate. Especially when you were working in London all them years ago."

"Yes... You have the right of it there. I suppose I didn't really know her. Who would have done so?"

"Her brother?"

"Yes. True. Anyone else?"

"Her husband?"

"Hardly. Well, not that well anyway. It sounds like they were on friendly terms but didn't have all that much to do with each other, if he is to be believed. Ah!" He stood up quickly. "The steward. He worked with her closely."

"I asked abou' him but he was in London when it all happened. Has been for ten days."

"Has he not returned? His employer has been murdered."

"I don't think so, sir."

"Well we must ask when we go up to the house later."

"Is it relevant to speak to him, sergeant? Given tha' he wasn't there when she was killed?"

"Possibly not. But I should like to see if I can speak to him all the same."

"May I… may I ask why, sir? It seems to me we have the killer."

"I am not sure I can explain it. It's instinct, I suppose. Copper's instinct. Just wanting to make sure I have all the facts and have joined all the little pieces together before I settle on something."

Cooke finished the dregs of his tea and walked to the hat stand once more, indicating that Smith should do the same. The boy came running.

"You may be right, Smith. And I hope, for the sake of all this, that everything is exactly as it looks, and we have found our killer. I am probably just an old man, looking too hard into things that aren't really there. Either way, the whole thing is a sad affair, and one we must now disclose to the family in Querney Manor. Let us go."

They walked up this morning, rather than taking the car, Cooke and Smith both grateful for the fresh air. The walk was brisk and easy. Once they were at the house they were shown immediately to Mr Carter's study and given tea. Mr Forrester and Mr Bingham were summoned and brought to the library upstairs, where Cooke and Smith were escorted to attend to them.

"Gentlemen," Cooke started, before sitting down. "We come with news."

"Well, what is it, man?" Mr Forrester asked loudly, his eyes red and tired.

"Ahem," started Cook. "The body of a man was found in Bourton in the early hours of this morning."

"Another murder? Surely not?" Mr Bingham looked aghast.

"No. No murder. He was a vagrant. Died of natural causes. It appears he had Mrs Forrester's engagement ring. And money with blood on it that matches hers. As well as a knife that matches her wounds and has his fingerprints on."

"You... you found him?" Mr Bingham's eyes were wide. Mr Forrester stared out the window.

"Yes, it seems so. I should very much like to check on your insurance documents for the ring we found, to ascertain that it was that very one, Mr Forrester."

"Of course," he turned. "Of course. You must. Do you... do you know why?"

"What with her things on his person, it seems it was a robbery. Most likely she caught him on the property and he tried to rob her. It must have become violent."

"That's saying something," Mr Forrester's hand shook as he rubbed his forehead. "Will we, ahem, will we be able to bury her soon?"

"Once the inquest has taken place, Mr Forrester. I doubt that will be very long."

"And you are sure?" Forrester asked. "That this is what did for Eleanor? A, a... a tramp who wanted her things?"

"The evidence makes it appear that way. I have a few things I want to find out. Just to make sure all the dots and crosses are done. Speaking of which, is the steward, Mr Barnatt available for me to speak to?"

"Oh, Barnatt?" Bingham spoke up, "he's still in London. He's finalising business there for us. And um, I don't think he will be returning here."

"What? Ever?" Cooke was nonplussed.

"No. You see, he is completing some sales of our London properties for me. I am going to manage the estate myself now. He has been with us a few years, but it seems it is necessary for us to economise where we can in the current climate. We no longer have need for a steward."

"I see. Perhaps I can have an address for him? I should like to contact him if at all possible."

"Of course, I shall give you a forwarding address as soon as I have one for him. I believe he has taken new lodgings in Richmond, that's west London way."

"Thank you. I am sorry to bring news about your sister," Cooke nodded to Bingham, "and your wife," he nodded to Forrester, "but it looks like we have our man. I will let you know when the inquest is. In the meantime, we shall take our leave and let you go about moving on." Both police officers moved to leave the room before Cooke stopped and turned. "Before we go, I've remembered I wanted to ask you, Mr Forrester, did your wife take barbiturates of any sort on a regular basis?"

"What?" the man looked irritated, "Well, I mean, I don't know. Never in front of me. Why would she?"

"Uh," Mr Bingham interjected, "actually I think I can help with this."

"You can?" his brother-in-law asked. He gripped the back of a chair tightly.

"Yes, I can. I believe about a year ago she had a small problem with not being able to sleep. She got some to help with that. I imagine she's been using it on and off since then."

"I see," Cooke said, straightening up. "Do you think she may have used any recreationally as well?"

"I really couldn't say," Bingham replied.

"I could," Forrester's voice was loud. "Of course not. I think I would have noticed something like that, don't you?"

No one spoke.

Cooke cleared his throat, "I'm not trying to imply anything. I just need to ask questions. You also weren't aware of your wife's proclivity for going out to parties as often as she did. It's possible you weren't aware of other habits."

"Yes, well, I'm not even sure that she really did go out all the time. I just… I can't picture it. Will this come up in the inquest? I would hate for her to have her name ruined. You know what the press is like. And she has a daughter. Mary will have to grow up thinking her mother had a reputation."

"I will have to present the evidence I have been given, Mr Forrester. And inquests are always public. I'm sorry to say. I shall try to be as discreet as possible, naturally," Cooke tried to look sympathetic. Forrester grunted and turned away.

Cooke and Smith were shown out via the servants' hall, where the news had impossibly already spread. They said goodbye to Mr Carter and Mrs James and left the house.

"Do you know what I think we need, constable?"

"What, sergeant?"

"A pint. And a pie. It's been a long morning. Let us go to The Horse and Cart and seek sustenance. Goodness knows I have need today." Constable Jacob Smith nodded as they made their way to East Querney and away from Querney House.

CHAPTER 13

There it all was. On paper. Deborah put down the file she had found and sighed deeply.

"So that was the inquest," she said aloud.

It had been a few hours since she'd started reading. The records were kept perfectly. They had been found in a drawer and had yellowed with age, but they were a brilliant artefact of history. It was all there: the evidence given by Sergeant Cooke as investigating officer, members of the household, Mrs Forrester, and the doctor who had examined the body. There were several mentions of Eleanor Forrester having a 'modern life' several times, and enjoying a certain lifestyle. Both Sergeant Cooke and her brother, Rupert Bingham said it. Interestingly Mr Forrester had seemed sceptical of that in his evidence, but had conceded it was all possible given the way they carried out their life together. The sound of a key in the door caused her to jolt.

"Bugger!" she exclaimed, throwing all the papers together as quickly as she could and placing books and newspapers over the top of her Coppers End folders. Deborah looked at her watch. It was just after six-thirty. Peter was back later than usual but she also wasn't ready for him to be home. *Bollocks. No dinner ready, nothing.*

"You're home!" she shouted from the dining room, running into the kitchen to start putting something together for the two of them to eat.

"I am!" he called back from the hall. "Had to get a slightly later train, I'm afraid. A meeting ran over." He appeared in the kitchen, putting his briefcase on the orange formica table. "I hope I haven't messed up dinner plans."

"Well, actually, I've been working and lost track of time. Only just stopped. So I hope egg and chips is okay for you tonight. We may even have some sliced gammon in the fridge if you'd like that too."

"Perfect."

"Great. Well, go and get washed up, it'll be ready for when you're down."

They ate a quiet supper together and afterwards Peter went to the living room to read the paper as Deborah washed up. She joined him when she was done.

"Want a drink?" she asked, heading to the drinks table and pouring herself some Beaujolais from a half-drunk bottle.

"Scotch would be lovely," he said, not looking up from the Sport section of The Times. Deborah looked at the sight of the back of his newspaper.

"How was London?" she asked, bringing his drink over.

"Same old, same old. Just work and staying at the flat."

"I bet it's nice though," she took a deep gulp of her wine.

"Well... you know..." Peter turned the page of his newspaper.

"Someone is coming tomorrow afternoon about the living room, remember?"

"Yes..."

"Peter, can you look up for a moment please? I've not seen you properly since Monday morning."

"Oh, yes, of course," he folded up his paper, placing it gently on the coffee table in front of him. "What were you saying?"

"I was saying someone is coming about the living room tomorrow."

"Why?"

"Because it's next on the list. Not a major refurb like the kitchen. Just a decoration job. A few other bits and bobs. And especially to sort the fireplace out."

"It's April. What do we need with a fireplace?"

"Well, if you remember, it smoked a lot in winter. It wasn't very good. We need it replacing. I'm going to get one of the modern electric ones. It will need quite a bit of work to block it all off et cetera."

"Huh, well. Good thing I'm here to make sure they don't try to sell you things you don't want or need."

"Oh yes, *a very good thing*," she rolled her eyes and laughed. "Speaking of ridiculous notions, we've been invited to a garden party in June at Querney Manor."

"Have we? How interesting."

"Yes, Bernard and Diana asked me today."

"Oh, did you see them?"

"Yes, I took a walk in the gardens and sort of bumped into them."

"How lovely for you."

"Well. Yes. I suppose. It really is very large. And I must say, very well kept. On that subject are you going to do some work on our garden now you're back for a long weekend? You've done a good job weeding. But we may want to clear some of the other mess and plant something."

"Yes, yes. I'll do what I can tomorrow. Got a little work to be getting on with for next week but I shall try and fit it in."

"Well. I hope you will try." Deborah finished her wine and stood up, "I think I will go for a bath and then head to bed."

"Okay, see you upstairs shortly," Peter picked up his paper again and resumed reading.

The next day, after breakfast, Deborah left Peter to his work at the dining table, glanced out of the kitchen windows to their neglected garden and reminded him to try to get something done there. Then she got in the car and headed out to Bourton Library.

"Local newspapers from the nineteen-twenties," she requested of the librarian.

The woman who helped her was very enthusiastic about showing Deborah to the old newspaper cuttings and clippings, and explaining how to use the machine to study them. Deborah was used to this sort of thing from her PhD but didn't have the heart to tell the old lady. Once she found the correct year, Deborah began searching in earnest.

There was lots in there about a local war memorial being erected for the local boys who had died in The Great War, as well as adverts for jobs in shops and local factories and articles about farm shows and prize pigs. And there it was.

'Murder At The Manor House'

The headline ran. An article followed about Mrs Eleanor Forrester being found dead on her property. It talked of her many good works in the area, the jobs she had provided, and how tragic it was that her life was cut short. As Deborah scrolled on she could see further reports on it.

'Body of Vagrant Found with Murdered Woman's Possessions'

Below the headline it read:

'Vagrancy to blame for biggest criminal investigation in small village's history, as a man, now dead, has been discovered to have the missing possessions of beloved local benefactor, Mrs Eleanor Forrester. Police have refused to comment on the findings. However, a source has disclosed to us at The Bourtonshire Times that they have been confirmed as Mrs Forrester's and would therefore place this man in top position for being found guilty of her brutal murder. We ask the question, therefore, what can be done about people who blight our local area and how our local councillors can...'

Deborah scrolled on further, scoffing at the article which was quickly becoming a complaint about the pestilence of homelessness and what efforts those in power might go to to rid the county of people such as would dare to be poor, and without the sense not to be. The another article caught her eye.

'Secret Life of Murdered Woman Revealed!'

'Our reporter stationed at the inquest into the murder of Mrs Eleanor Forrester can reveal to our readers, that she was no innocent and perfect lady. Though appearing outwardly proper, we are shocked to learn that Mrs Forrester had nocturnal habits akin to modern flappers. Evidence was brought to light, to a room packed with locals and those with interest in her death, that Mrs Forrester often left her house after dark, to attend parties at local places and further afield, coming home in the early hours. There were also suggestions that she regularly used alcohol and barbiturates for her pleasure. Once thought to be a pillar of the community, our reporter was shocked to hear that this wife and mother was believed to be returning from one such party when she was murdered by a local vagrant, a man whose name is still unknown. It appears he robbed her for money and jewels before killing her in a frenzied attack with a knife it seems he most likely stole as well. Evidence was inconclusive about whether they had engaged in improper relations beforehand, or if Mrs Forrester had acted with another person that evening. Her husband confirmed in his evidence that it wasn't with him, however. No doubt this scandal will rock the family and they will try to distance themselves from it. Her husband, Mr Bennet Forrester has already stated his intention to move himself and his daughter back to his home in New York. We are left asking ourselves a number of questions, why did such a woman live such an immoral life? And how did she get away with doing it so secretly for so long? Continued on page three...'

Deborah felt a tap on her shoulder.

"Oh! Robert!" she clutched her heart. "You made me jump. I, uh," she looked back at the paper she was reading and blushed red. "I was just looking at local history, this just came up... Um..."

"It's okay. You're not the only one interested in it. I'm sure it gets looked up many a time," he smiled.

"What are you doing here?" She looked at her watch.

"Just here having a gander at some books. My exams start in two weeks so I took father's car and drove out here for a bit of study. And a bit of fun," he held up a large square, plastic bag.

"Ooh, what's in there?"

"New record. It's just come out."

"I see."

"Yes," he lifted it carefully from the bag. "Pink Floyd. Dark Side of the Moon. Do you like them?"

"Actually, I do. Peter's not such a fan. Bit of an old fuddy-duddy when it comes to new music. But I do quite like them."

"Maybe I can bring it over and we can listen together?"

"Oh, maybe. But you wouldn't want to listen to it with a boring old lady like me. You should be hanging out with your friends."

"Ha, you're not old. And you're very interesting. I'd love to chat more about your -"

"Sssh!" came a loud sound from one of the librarians. Robert and Deborah smiled guiltily at each other.

"Would you like a cup of tea?" he whispered, "I was going to say I am interested in your work. It might be nice to chat."

"Oh. Um. Yes. Of course," she whispered back, "let me get my things."

They left the library together in silence and laughed once they were out of the building.

"I've never liked the fact you have to be deadly silent in a library," Robert said. "It feels unnatural. So much shushing as well. For a noise that's supposed to induce quiet, it's bloody noisy."

"Ha," Deborah laughed. "You're right. Though I quite like the silence of it all. Libraries are hallowed places. I think of them as almost religious. I'm struck with reverence and awe. People are hushed by the godliness of so much knowledge and information in one place. All bound together in beautiful books."

"Well, gosh. I never thought of it like that. Here, there's a nice tea shop round the corner. It's after ten. I think it's acceptable to have tea and scones, don't you?"

"Oh, absolutely. Is it ever not?" The two of them laughed as they walked and came to a very quaint place, every surface covered with doilies and lace.

"My mother hates these kinds of places, says they are old fashioned and belong to a previous world we need to forget about," Robert smiled.

"Oh, I quite like them," Deborah said, sitting at a doily-laden table and looking at a plastic menu, "old fashioned, yes. But charming. Usually they have character and a great slice of cake."

"Well you're correct there. This place has excellent cake, and tea."

Robert had been right, Deborah reflected as she drove home, speeding a little to make it on time for the decorator and fireplace specialist. *The scones were wonderful,* she thought. It had been nice to chat to someone new as well. They had discussed Robert's exams and his hopes for studying history and what he wanted to do next. He had asked her lots of questions about her work. *What a nice boy he is,* she concluded as she pulled into the driveway, just before a van followed her in with the decorator.

Once inside, Deborah put the kettle on for herself, the decorator and Peter.

"Four sugars, please," the workman called from the living room where he was inspecting the place.

"So," Deborah said, handing him his sweet tea when it was done and sipping her own, "shall we talk about the work?"

They spoke for half an hour about colours and plaster work, how long it would take and how to incorporate whatever would need to be done on the fireplace. He promised to get back to her with a quote by early next week and left his half-drunk tea on one of the coffee tables.

"Well, that went okay, didn't it?" Deborah asked Peter who was having a break in the kitchen. "He did our kitchen and dining room, and this is a much smaller job than the kitchen. I can't wait for him to start work, can you?"

"Yes, yes, he's very competent," Peter replied, "I must get back to this brief before the next one comes. When is that?" he checked his watch.

"Well, now actually, I can see him pulling in in front of the drive."

"Blast. I really want to finish what I'm doing. I need to if I'm going to get anything done in the garden like you want."

"Don't worry," Deborah said, following him out into the hall but heading to the front door as he went into the dining room again. "I am sure I can do this by myself. I handled the whole kitchen, didn't I?"

"You did, you did. And marvellously too," Peter added. "Thank you," he mouthed as she opened the door and he put his glasses on and went back to work.

"Come in!" Deborah shouted to the fireplace man, as he got out of his van.

"Thank you," he shouted back.

"Would you like a cup of tea? The kettle boiled only a short while ago. I can make you one as you take a look at the fireplace in question, uh, David, isn't it?"

"That's righ'. An' a tea would be lovely. Three sugars please. And milk. Thanks."

She showed him to the living room and went about making more tea. Once it was done, she returned to David and found him on his knees with his hands up the chimney.

"You've definitely got a blockage up here. If you want the fire working properly you've got to deal with that in the first instance," he said, standing up and accepting the cup from Deborah.

"Well, actually I want to replace this old thing with a new electric one."

"Okay, tha's a differen' job really. Though it will still need to be cleared out. There's somethin' stuffed up there. It could be a dead bird. It usually is." Deborah screwed up her nose. "I can try and get it out now if you like," he continued. "It seems to be big. Could be an owl. Have you got any equipment for cleaning it out?"

"Oh, um, I don't know. We didn't bring any. And I haven't found any yet. There are some pokers by the fire, if that helps?"

"Could do." He bent down again and used one of the tongs to pull at something wedged behind the back of the fireplace. "It's moving. I think. Looks like it's gone over the back part here." He pulled and pulled and there was the sound of something crumbling. He stopped. "Shall I keep going? It's already all damaged back here, I don't think I can make it much worse."

"Yes, I think you should."

Deborah leaned into to see what was blocking the chimney. David pulled and directed Deborah to the fire poker and asked if she could hook it from behind and push. Diligently, they worked together and all at once, a cascade of feathers from a dead pigeon, whose body then followed, came pouring from the chimney piece and settled on the hearth spreading dust and cinders everywhere. After that came a thud as a leather-bound book fell to the floor, once again throwing dirt into the air. Deborah leaned down to pick up the book, wiping her eyes of filth. She looked at the cover and used her skirt to get rid of a layer of grime. It was a journal. She opened the first page and saw a name in a beautiful script she knew all too well.

Diary of Sergeant Cooke 1920

"What's that then?" David, the fireplace man, asked while wiping his hands with a dirty handkerchief.

"Oh..." Deborah flipped through it and her heart skipped, "it's um, just looks like an old book," she said, her face warming and flushing. She could see entries from a whole year, the words of someone who lived in her house, someone whose life had been here before her, someone who had investigated the murder that had fascinated her so much in the last few weeks.

"Well, I'm not much of a reader," he replied, lifting up the body of the dead bird and placing it in a sack.

"It's funny," Deborah said, a thought occurring to her, "I've found papers in the walls, they'd been stuffed in there -"

"Yeah, that was quite common as a way to keep the houses warm. You find all sorts when renovating."

"But a book in the fireplace. That wouldn't be for insulation, would it?"

"No, not unless you're burning it, ha," he laughed. "Though that was stuffed right at the back, behind the main chimney. So it wouldn't likely burn. Looks like this bird here," he began picking up loose feathers, "nudged it a bit, you can see where the smoke's got it on the edges, like," he pointed to where a few of the pages were blackened around the sides.

"So someone put it up there on purpose?"

"Most likely. Can't think why. It's not got a treasure map in it, I don' suppose?" David laughed again as he tied up the sack with the pigeon and the feathers.

"Can't see one. Just words," Deborah smiled, holding it tight in her hands, her heart beating, wanting David to go as soon as possible. "So, um, what now? With the fireplace?"

"Well, you want to replace it don't you?"

They discussed plans to replace the coal fire with a new electric one, went over timeframes and quotes before saying goodbye. Deborah held onto the journal the entire time. The soft, slightly burned leather in her hands. Once David was out the door, Peter came through from the dining room.

"All well?' he asked.

"Yes, yes. Pigeon in the chimney. All cleared. Plans made for getting an electric thingy in."

"Are you alright?"

"Yes. Fine. I'll start on dinner soon."

"Okay, what's that?"

"Oh, nothing. Just a thing I picked up in Bourton this morning."

"Good. Well, I'll do a little work on the garden before dinner."

"Great. Thank you. When do you go back to London?"

"Sunday. After lunch with mother again, I'm afraid."

"Not a problem. I'm getting used to it now."

"Well, it'll be summer soon. And you'll get sick of me being around," he laughed. "And then we will be heading north to The Highlands."

"I'm still hoping we can at least stop off to see Lissa on the way?"

"Yes, yes, of course. I'm sure that'll work..."

Peter headed out the back door and Deborah passed behind him, going through to the kitchen. Her whole body ached to read what was in the diary, but she knew there wouldn't be enough time before Peter got bored and came back in. Deborah placed the book in a drawer, underneath clean tea towels, before getting on with chopping onions and wishing desperately for it to be Sunday evening.

CHAPTER 14

"Thank you, Smith," Cooke smiled at the young man who had just placed a cup of dark, sweet tea in front of him.

"I'm glad that's done, sir," he said, sipping from his own cup.

"You and I both, Smith."

"If you don' mind me saying' so, I thought you spoke well, sergeant. You were clear and concise and gave the evidence that we gathered well. I hope that if I ever have to do that, that I can do it half so well as you, sir."

"You'll be fine, Smith. It's no more than sharing a statement."

"In front of a coroner and loads of people, sir. That's the bit that concerns me most."

"Just tell the truth, Smith. The truth as you know it, anyway."

"What do you mean, sir?"

"Oh," Sergeant Cooke looked out the window over his desk on to the street outside. The lamplighters would soon be doing their jobs and illuminating the way. "Nothing. Not really. Just a feeling you get sometimes as a copper," he paused and drank deeply. "Well, 'tis done now anyway. The coroner has listened to all the evidence available and made his ruling. That unnamed vagrant has been found guilty of Mrs Forrester's murder. And that is the most likely thing based on all the evidence given."

"But… you're not sure?"

"I don't know what I am, Smith. That's what's concerning me. I cannot decipher it quite yet but I confess I feel a little ill at ease. But that can be any number of things. Perhaps I am simply getting old and my guts are telling me so." Cooke looked out the window, letting out a short, bitter laugh. "It does not sit right with me that the man found guilty was unable to speak his corner. Of course, there were a mountain of clues that pointed to his involvement. But we cannot speak to the dead and hear what they would say. Speaking of which, neither did I ever get to interview the agent of the house. Dismissed from duties very quickly."

"He wasn't there at the time of the murder, sergeant. He had nothing to do with it. He was only given notice because Mr Bingham had said that had been the plan all along. Once Mr Barnatt had seen to the sale of the London house he was to go his own way."

"Yes. Still, he was part of that house. He could have spoken as to the character of Mrs Forrester in the very least. He had worked closely with her and known her for years."

"Yes, sir."

"I also do not like that we never recovered or discovered the whereabouts of the wedding ring. Lost, it is said."

"Her killer was livin' on the street, an' a drunkard, sergeant. He could 'ave sold it or mislaid it in any number of ways. The coroner said so. You said so, sir."

"I know I did, Smith. I know. It was the only evidence I could give as regards to the ring. There is a part of me, deep down, that feels as though I wasn't allowed to do a thorough enough job, constable. I mislike the feeling." He paused and sipped his tea. "It shall pass soon, I am sure."

There was a heavy knocking on the main door. Both men looked up from their tea and Smith stood to answer it. Cooke placed his drink on the table wondering what small emergency would bring someone to his door today. *Another drunk? Petty theft?* He looked up and saw the portly shape of Dr Simpson entering the hall. *Give me strength.*

"Dr. Simpson," he exclaimed, "to what do we owe this pleasure after seeing you only an hour ago?"

"Ah, yes, probably sick of the sight of me," the man snorted in laughter. Smith and Cooke remained straight-faced. "Right, yes, just came to drop off the final paperwork before I make for home."

"Thank you," Cooke stood up to receive it. He looked expectantly at the doctor who was eyeing the cups and pot of tea currently on the bureau to the side of the room.

"Ahem, yes, well. Sad case," Dr Simpson said, sitting down on one of the chairs. "Glad it's done and dusted now. Big crowd today, wasn't there?"

"It was a high profile case. Someone like Eleanor Forrester being murdered. And a scandal about her person to boot. The newspapers have been covering it for weeks. Smith, do pour Dr Simpson some tea," Cooke said, looking at his constable.

"Well, thank you. Don't mind if I do," Simpson said, shifting his large buttocks. "I dread to think of the papers tomorrow, now that it's all out. The family will struggle with this for a long while I am sure."

"You think? Most of the time I find people move on to the next one and then the next. Today's news is tomorrow's chip paper, is it not?"

"Still. It will stick in a lot of minds. Families like that, they remember it all. A good marriage will be more difficult for Mrs Forrester's child, naturally. And Mr Bingham, perhaps as well. Though a man's reputation is never nearly so marred as a woman's. People will wonder whether the daughter will turn out the same way, won't they?"

Cooke nodded imperceptibly and continued to drink his tea. Dusk was beginning to fall in earnest and he wanted no more than to light his pipe and read his book with a bottle of beer. *That will have to wait.* He sighed.

"Of course," Dr Simpson continued, talking to the room, "I had occasion to spend time with the family a few times. At least three. I noticed Eleanor had a certain look to her then. I didn't say anything when we were on the case because it would be unprofessional of me. I saw a glint in her eye I didn't quite like. Rupert, her brother, he was always a funny chap. Plays the links too from time to time. Never played with him, as such, but I'd seen him about with his golfing chums at the club. I wonder what plans he has for the house?"

"He? Surely the daughter has inherited."

"I believe so. But he is to take charge of the place till she comes of age. I think. Lord knows these sorts of things can end in dispute. Families say all kinds of awful things to each other when the will gets in the way."

"Well, let's hope it does not come to that," Cooke replied, gravely.

"No, indeed. I'm sure it won't. Mr Bingham has always seemed a reasonable man to me."

"He has?"

"Yes, don't you think?"

"I don't know him that well," Cooke coughed. " But I've been up at the house a number of times. I was there for the summer fête in June. Judging the gardening competition. It was a great afternoon."

"Were you? Goodness. Well, I suppose you're part of the community more than I -"

"Yes, well. I saw Mrs Forrester there. And I met her before at the house when there were things to discuss. We had half-yearly meetings too. About the village. I always saw brains in her. She was professional. I liked her. Her brother? I saw him less. But he always had a smile on his face. Like he could see something funny that no one else could."

"He's not been smiling much since his sister's death, though."

"No, indeed, you are right doctor. Hmmm..." Cooke was lost in thought and then cleared his throat. "Ah, it seems you have finished your tea. I don't want to keep you from getting home. Smith? Shall we help Dr Simpson out?"

"Ah, thank you, yes, yes," the large man said, picking up his medical bag and a briefcase. Smith lead him to the door. "See you again soon, Sergeant!" he called, "And you too, constable," he said to Smith.

"Shall I lock the door?" Smith asked, as he closed it.

"Please do. I need five minutes of peace from any more madness in this village." Cooke sat down once more at his desk and began thinking about the day, the inquest and what he had said and all he had heard about the deceased and the accused. He looked at the last of the paper-work and felt a strange sensation in his belly once more. Putting the files away into a wooden filing cabinet, his attention was caught by the sudden appearance of light out the window. The street lamps were being lit. There was light in the dark outside once more.

CHAPTER 15

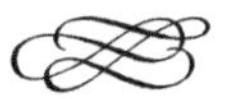

Coppers End
The Querneys
Bourtonshire
30th May 1973

Dearest Lissa,

I'm so glad we will be coming to stay with you on our way up to The Highlands. I tried getting Peter to commit to more than three days but he is determined to do this long walk through the lochs. On top of that his mother has managed to persuade him to visit some old relative. A long lost third cousin once removed who apparently inherited some castle. The old so-and-so probably wants to make sure the family is added in the will... Therefore we have an appointment up near Fort William that we must make. And then we are set to walk all the way to Dingwall where there is another connection to the family to be found. Family and whisky. That's what we have in store. I shall mainly enjoy the beverages and leave the rest of it to Peter. Even so! We shall have three wonderful days together in Auld Reekie.

There is so much to catch up on. I told you about that diary I found belonging to the old Sergeant who lived here. It's fascinating. His own words. His own thoughts. Everything is there. It's slow reading because I really am trying to get more of my own work done. Plus Peter disapproves for some reason. I finally told him all about it and he thinks I should have given it all to the family at the old Manor House as soon as I found it. I suspect he doesn't like that it takes me away from sorting the renovations out and getting his dinner on the table. Yes, you read that right. My Peter, becoming more caveman-like in his old age. Especially now he is living a gentleman's life in the country. So, I try not to read things like that diary until he is away and I have done the majority of my other commitments. I can't wait to tell you about it. It makes more mention of The Manor House than I thought it would do. There was the theft of prize pigs in the same year the lady of the house was murdered. Caused a huge stir. Over a few pigs! Apparently they never caught the culprits and the sergeant writes about how suspicious it is that the thieves knew exactly when to go, where to go and how to get them without raising any alarm. The whole thing meant the house lost a lot of money and had to sell some of their land. That was the start of the whole thing; the beginning of the end for Querney Manor. They had managed to keep it all together until that point. I've found out from the library that the following years more and more of it changed hands, got sold off, remortgaged etc. All starting with some missing pigs. Anyway, I am about half way through the diary. If I am brave enough I might bring it with me up north.

I am sure I will also be bringing gossip up with me as I shall only just have attended the garden party at Querney Manor. Am I looking forward to it? No. Not really. Whenever I see Diana Bingham around the village I always get the feeling she is a bit disgusted with the sight of me. I'm not glamorous enough for her perhaps? Who knows?

I simply cannot wait to see you. Only a few weeks and we shall be talking to the early hours like when we were little.

All my love,

Deborah x

THE LETTER WAS POSTED SWIFTLY SO that Deborah could get back to reading. It was a Friday and Peter would be home in a few hours so she'd have to put it all away. She opened the leather-bound book gingerly. The yellowing pages smelled of ash and ageing.

June 3rd

We were back late from yesterday's jollities. Smith overdid it with the ale and I've had to leave him sleeping this morning. People were mainly on their best behaviour for The Family so there isn't much for me to do today. I shall let him lie there till about nine and then wake him with fried bread and sweet coffee. I was proud of him all day. He held himself well and pleased the crowds greatly with his abilities at the coconut shy and the shooting gallery. His first Querney Manor House Summer Fête was a success. Of course I was therefore to be the officer on duty. The uniform kept me hot in the sun. Judging the gardening competition was an honour (though I confess I hardly know much about the activity myself, just the few alimentations we grow here in the vegetable patches). The winning marrow was a huge triumph. Quite literally. As were the beautiful roses grown by the gardener at The Manor House. It hardly seems fair that they win their own competition, but I am certain I never saw a finer bloom. Next year I hope I am judging the cake stand - though it is traditionally done by the lady of the house - I'd much rather sample slices of sponge than examine carrots and beets. It is a shame there was no pig show, but without the pigs, how can there be?

Mrs Forrester did a fine job of it this year. The whole affair was as excellent as the ones I attended when her own parents ran the show. I am glad of the revival. We haven't had a fête since before the war and the happiness felt by all was palpable. For the most part. I saw very little of the husband, Mr Forrester, and even less of Mr Bingham, the brother. I spoke to Bingham briefly in the food tents. He was a very inattentive conversationalist. Some might say rude. I would say distracted. Followed his sister about a lot. Seemed jumpy. Probably just all the folks hanging about his house. The villagers can be a rowdy lot at times and yesterday was no exception. The staff were on hand to *control everything though. Mrs James runs an excellent house and Mr Carter was discreet about making sure anyone making any sort of scene was escorted away or given coffee. But mostly it was laughter and joy. Especially from Mrs Forrester. She was in fine fettle and I enjoyed my conversations with her. Quite the smart cookie, as some are wont to say. She seems to have that house in hand. Too many great houses are being forced to sell up. The village would be sadder for it if she were forced to. All those people working at The Mill would lose their jobs. To the fried bread. Might even find a rasher of bacon for Smith's poor head. Ah, to be young.*

THERE WAS a knock on Deborah's front door so she looked up from the diary. Closing it she walked slowly to answer the caller, thinking about what she had read. *A summer party. Like this year's. It must be a tradition.*

"Robert!" Deborah saw the young man in front of her, struggling to stay dry. "How nice to see you. Come in, come in, out of the rain," she gestured to the inner hall and Robert followed gingerly.

"I'm so sorry, I know I must be disturbing you. It's not like me to call by without warning but I was walking past and saw you were in."

"Not to worry, it's nice to have company from time to time. Otherwise it's just me rattling around the place. Let me take your coat. Would you like a cup of tea?"

"Thank you," he gave her his wet macintosh and unslung a backpack from his shoulders. He carried it as well as the same large plastic bag he had the other day, following her to the kitchen."What is the lovely music you are listening to?" he asked, "Grieg?"

"Yes, it is. Well remembered," she smiled, putting the kettle on. "Milk and sugar?"

"Just milk, please."

Deborah paused at the mug cupboard and changed her mind, "Back in a sec," she said, walking to the dining room cabinet and retrieving cups and saucers and a matching milk jug. When she returned Robert Bingham was staring out the large kitchen window into the garden.

"It's a wreck isn't it?" she said.

"Not so bad as it was, I am sure."

"I try to get Peter to do things but he's ever so busy and gardening simply isn't my forte. Ironic really, considering my area of study," she laughed gently. "How are your exams going? Finished yet?"

"Two left. Both at the end of next week. Came home to study for the weekend. Lots of the boys who don't live far away from school do. It's a lot quieter and the food is better. No younger boys running around the dorms noisily disturbing you. It's the last hurdle."

"And then freedom," Deborah said, pouring water onto premium tea leaves she had reached for at the back of the kitchen cupboard. She poured milk into the jug as the leaves brewed. "I'm so sorry. We could sit in the dining room but the table's covered in work. I do have a study upstairs but, I confess, it's still full of boxes. The desk is completely hidden by them. I prefer to work down here for now. Don't know why."

"Strange."

"What is?"

"I believe your dining room was the old sergeant's study when this was a police house."

"Was it?"

"Yes. I think. There are pictures of it in some of the archives of the village in our house. Haven't looked at them in a number of years. Had to though. For a history project for school."

"Are the archives extensive?"

"Quite. I've never gone into them in detail but father enjoys having them I think. Grandfather does, certainly. He never likes to throw anything away."

"Let's go to the living room," she walked with a tray of cups and he followed with his bags once more. "You say your grandfather likes the archives," she repeated for him, setting herself down and moving the old diary of Sergeant Cooke away to another side table. Her mind flashed to the old papers about the murder of Robert's great-aunt in the dining room and she panicked. *That's all about his family. Bugger. Can I get away with moving them...?* She sat up straight, nervously playing with the pleats in her orange floral skirt.

"Yes, I think it reminds him of the good old days. I help him, you see. When I'm on holiday. He has nurses but he often gets me to do bits of writing for him here and there. Letters. Sometimes he fancies trying to write down his memoirs but he never gets far. Not sure why. He's as sharp as a tack. Just can't move so well. He's taught me so much about life though. He's a treasure trove of information." Robert's eyes glinted.

"It must be very hard for him. Memories are a difficult beast. Sometimes there are things we would prefer not to remember."

"Indeed." Robert looked off into the distance and then around the room at some of the pictures and paintings on the wall. "Say, you've got good stuff here. Whose taste is all this?"

"Mostly mine. Peter casts his eye about and has a few pieces that belonged to his father and other relatives. We do enjoy antiques a lot. I know it's not very fashionable but I suppose you can't help liking what you like. I also like more modern art too and Peter can't bear it. I sneak bits in here and there!" she giggled.

The record player stopped and the arm went automatically back to its resting place. Deborah stood to replace the LP into its sleeve.

"Any preference on more music?" she asked. "Or would you prefer none? I'm so used to working with it on in the background I hardly notice it. We have some more popular stuff here but I'm not sure what you are into or what's hip these days."

"None of that matters really, not to me. Though actually I brought this. Do you remember, I bought it the other day," he picked up the large, dark blue plastic bag and pulled out a record from inside. "I haven't had time to listen yet," he handed it to Deborah. The cover was dark, with a triangle in the middle and a rainbow off to one side, like light from a prism.

"Oh yes. Pink Floyd. Fab cover."

"I've heard it's very good, but father said I had to get more of my exams done before I could listen to it." For the first time since she had met him, the sound of his voice and look on Robert's face belied the fact he was only a teenager.

"Well, we can have a listen if you like. Might be one of the hippest things I've done in a long time, listening to a totally new album almost the minute it comes out," she smiled, thinking back to when that might have been. "I definitely got excited about The Beatles. And the Rolling Stones. But Peter really can't stand all the stuff. He's much more into 'Easy Listening'. Quite the old fuddy-duddy sometimes."

"Well, shall I put it on?"

"Be my guest," Deborah smiled.

The LP started clicking under the needle and both Robert and Deborah sat back to listen to the heavy beat and ticking clocks that began. And then the swearing. Robert looked at her and blushed and she waved her hand at him.

"I may be older than you," she said, "but I've lived. A swear word is nothing."

She was cut off by the sudden appearance of a voice and then gently strumming guitars. Deborah sat in her chair, sipping her tea, thinking it sounded like she should be consuming something much stronger to enjoy this music. At once she felt quite conscious that there was a young man in her room who might be mortified to be listening to this with someone nearly twenty years older than him, in her living room, over cups of PG Tips. He looked over at her and made only brief eye-contact. *He's probably more embarrassed than me, poor sod.* She stood up and turned the music down a little as it changed to a different track. Fast electronic sounds and drums played now.

"It's very good," she said, "very different, isn't it?"

"Oh yes. Experimental."

"Takes me back. When I was your age I would have been enjoying a gin and chatting to boys about the latest records. Not sipping tea with an old lady down the road."

"You're not old! How many times must I say this," Robert laughed. "Plus you're interesting. All the studies you have done. Mother and father aren't into all that academia. Mother wants me to go straight into law and become some high-flying city lawyer. But I want to study history first. Grandfather says a man should do what he wants when he is young."

"I have no children, but I'm sure your mother just wants what is best for you. I know my own mother did. She didn't like me going off. Thought I'd be murdered or something and found under the Magdelen Bridge."

"Did you do your postgraduate at Oxford too?"

"No. Just my undergraduate. Masters at London. And PhD there too. Wanted to be nearer home as my mother became ill. It was such fun. London in the sixties. When I wasn't at home with my mother I was studying or out having a good time."

"I can't wait to go off to university."

"You've been studying away since you were a young boy I suppose. What's the difference?"

"Since I was six, yes. It's very different. No school masters watching your every move. I don't suppose at Oxford they cane you quite so much."

"No. No they don't. I bet you were well behaved."

"For the most part. Got my fair share of scoldings from the house masters. I'm just looking forward to studying and getting out on my own two feet for a bit. I'll be home during the holidays to keep working for Grandfather, of course."

"Oh, right."

"Have you met him yet?"

"No."

"Well, you will. At the summer garden party."

"Oh yes. That's the weekend after next. Is everything ready?"

"Not nearly. Mother is having fits about vol au vents and crab sticks."

"I'm sure it will be just lovely. I hear it's a traditional do that's been happening in the gardens for years."

"Yes, that's right. It's changed a bit. Used to be quite a deal. Half the county would come in the old days, Grandfather told me. It's a bit smaller now. Canapés and cocktails. The odd stall. Nothing big and nothing compared to London in the sixties I shouldn't imagine."

"Ha, well. That was a while back."

"Did you ever... um... smoke pot or anything like that?" Robert asked, blushing.

"Once or twice, yes. Never had much effect on me to be honest. Much preferred a gin and bitter lemon." Deborah looked at her watch. It was half past three. She thought for a second. "Speaking of which. It's six o'clock somewhere. Do you fancy a stronger drink? Seems more appropriate than tea when listening to a new pop record like this one? No pressure. Don't want you to get in trouble, especially when you are supposed to be studying for exams."

"Oh no, mother and father don't mind. In fact, mother would be joining you," he laughed.

"What's your tipple?" she asked, walking to the drinks table. The sound of a loud bell ringing came through the speakers. Deborah jumped, laughing. "Good grief! Thought it was time to wake up!" Robert laughed too and walked over to the drinks to see what was there. The music became less loud at once and he looked over at Deborah.

"I know," he said. "I'm going to mix you something up. My grandfather taught me how to make it."

"Blimey," Deborah said, feeling nervous, "okay, go ahead. I'll be right back."

Deborah left the room and decided now was a good time to quickly move the papers pertaining to Querney House on the dining table. She was gathering them together as Robert entered from across the hall holding a cocktail glass filled with clear liquid with a dash of something orange at the top.

"Here you are, The Rupert Bingham Special," he said, offering Deborah hers and clinking their glasses together. They drank and Deborah nearly coughed hers up.

"Oh my, that's the strongest thing I've ever had," her throat burned. "What's in it?"

"Ah, that would be telling," Robert smiled. "What's this you're doing here? Not work?"

"No. Just clearing a project away. Been meaning to do it for ages and just remembered about it."

Deborah threw most of the papers into a large box and looked around for others. There was too much to tidy up successfully. She had to hope Robert hadn't noticed, or if he had, didn't know what it was all about. Or, at best, didn't care. She led him back to the living room to where the music was still going on and a woman's beautiful voice was singing out soulfully.

"Gosh, what a voice," Deborah declared. Her drink was going to her head with some alacrity. Robert, on the other hand, had got halfway through his and seemed just fine. *The drinking rich, I guess.*

"It's beautiful. Quite a record isn't it?"

"It really is."

"What time is Mr Gordon back usually?"

"Oh, please call him Peter. Well, it's a Friday. So that could be any time from now, if he's managed to get away. Sometimes he stays for work drinks though. So I'm not sure. He often rings to let me know. Not heard anything yet, so I suspect it'll average time of about six."

"It must be annoying. Hanging on for him to return like that. I know it used to annoy mother when father was in the city all hours."

"Well, Peter's got a busy and difficult job so..."

"Yes, sorry. Didn't mean to pry. It seems you are very busy here anyway."

"Exactly. Hardly notice he's gone most of the time."

She drank deeply from her glass and immediately regretted it. The song changed to the sound of cash registers and talk of money. Her head was swirling and she felt hot and she didn't feel good. Robert stood up and walked to the record player, picking up the sleeve to read it.

"Nice sax," he said, listening to it and swaying slightly with the music. Deborah wished he wouldn't. The room was doing that well enough by itself. The music then picked up pace and so did Deborah's nausea.

"This is strong," she said, standing with difficulty, "I'm going to make some coffee." She left the room, her legs like jelly. Soon Robert was following her.

"I'm so sorry, I shouldn't have assumed you'd have my family's tolerance to such things," he tittered.

Deborah was putting the kettle on and quickly retrieved the normal cups from the kitchen cupboard this time, holding herself up with the counter. Putting two scoops of Nescafé into the mug and stirring in hot water, she felt Robert's hand on her back. She jerked away.

"Truly I'm so sorry. Let me make this for you," he was smiling at her, taking the mug and spoon to stir it. His face looked friendly enough, but not his eyes. They were enjoying this. He was smirking, not smiling.

"I think you should get back home. You've got studies. I'll be fine," she replied, retrieving the mug of coffee from him and blowing on it. Deborah stepped back from him. "I'm not used to having such strong drinks. I haven't eaten since breakfast either. Very silly of me." She looked out into the garden. The rain had finally stopped. "The weather is better. You should get back." Robert joined her at the window. He placed a hand on her shoulder and turned to look at her.

"Are you sure?" he asked, "it's no problem for me to stay. I could keep you company until your husband returns. You can tell me about what you are looking into about this house. And mine." She looked at him intently. "I saw it when you were clearing them all away. It's no problem. The local history is quite interesting. What I can't work out is why you were trying to hide it."

"I wasn't. I… I just remembered I'd promised Peter I'd tidy up and thought he might be back soon. That's all."

"Of course. You're very good to him, aren't you?"

"Well, he's my husband. He'll be back in a short while and I need to get dinner on. I think you should go home and do some work. You'll not get into Oxford hanging around with me," she laughed weakly and began turning to the hall. The coffee and her unease was sobering her up quickly. His grip remained on her shoulder.

"I'll be fine. Exams are a formality really."

"Come on, let's get your record," Deborah pulled herself from his grip and went to the living room, pulling the needle off the vinyl abruptly. At once Robert's hands were on her back and moving down her shoulders.

"Stop it, Robert. I'm old enough to be your mother," she said, trying to laugh it off., and turning to face him.

"Only just. You're much more interesting than my actual mother. More beautiful too."

"I don't think so, she was a mo -"

At once his lips were on hers, his hands sliding clumsily around her blouse. She pulled herself back.

"Stop it, now! I want you to leave," she shouted.

"Come on," he smirked again. "We were having fun. Drinks. Music. I know you're a bored housewife, like mother. I know what she gets up to. Lonely afternoons with local boys and handymen round here when father's away in the city. We could do the same. You could prepare me for life at university. Teach me things you learned in your bedroom and not from the lecture hall."

"No, Robert. The whole suggestion is disgusting."

He pushed himself onto her once more, his grip on her arms hurting as his tongue clumsily pushed its way into her mouth. She slapped him.

"Leave now, Robert. Please don't call by here again."

He stood back, staring at her and rubbing his reddening cheek.

"You're kidding."

Deborah handed him his backpack and record and marched him to the front door. He followed slowly, grinning the whole time.

"You'll change your mind. I'll be here all summer. With Grandfather. He says that women just need help from time to time. You know. Realising what they want. When it comes to men."

"Not this woman. Goodbye, Robert."

He took his things and left the house. He waved at her, smiling, as though nothing untoward had just taken place. Deborah scowled at him, before closing and locking the door, and rubbing her sore arms from when he had held her. She walked to her kitchen and sat down at the table, in silence, waiting for Peter to come home.

CHAPTER 16

"Afternoon, sergeant," Mr Carter said to the man as they met at the main crossroads of the village.

"Afternoon, Mr Carter," he replied, falling into line with the man's long strides towards East Querney.

"Oh, it's my afternoon off, sir. Call me William," Carter smiled. "Well then, you must call me John."

The two of them walked towards the village pub, exchanged pleasantries with the boy behind the bar, asking where his father and mother were.

"Da's in the cellar, changing a barrel. Ma's in the kitchen, cleanin' up from lunchtime and getting the dinner on for tonigh'," he said, looking worried to be questioned by both the local police sergeant and the old butler from Querney Manor.

"That's okay, Stan, two pints of the ale for us?" Cooke looked over at Carter, who nodded.

"Course, sergeant. We got pork stratchin's as well. Ma told me you're partial to them. She made 'em fresh this mornin'," the boy looked pleased with himself.

"Oh, well, I suppose I had better indulge," Cooke smiled as he was handed a brown paper cone filled with salty, only slightly hairy, pork crackling. Placing one into his mouth he offered some to his companion who shook his head.

They supped on their beer and chatted about the weather. Carter was fiddling and shifting in his seat the whole. Quite unlike his usual iron-rod self. Half way through their drinks, Mr Donaldson appeared and made friendly chat with them before the sound of his wife yelling for him took him away again. When he was gone, Carter looked at Cooke and coughed.

"Thank you for meeting me, today," Carter said. His face was lines and worry.

"You've already said that, William. Twice. Is anything the matter?" Cooke tried to look entreating.

"Well, yes, you could say that."

"Oh yes?" Cooke leaned forward.

"Yes. It has been such a strange and distressing year." He sighed deeply. "I wanted to ask you how you feel the inquest went - I know it was a few weeks ago - and not just that," he paused, searching for words. "The whole business. I suppose my staff and I are still muddling through it all. And it looks like the year's upheaval is set to continue further."

"How so?"

"Mr Bingham," Carter looked around to see if anyone might hear them, "he is letting most of the staff go."

"Is he? Can he? I wouldn't have thought he had the right to?" Cooke also checked to see if they could be overheard. They were the only ones there so he continued, "I know nothing of the particulars of the will, but I would have thought the house and estate went to Mrs Forrester's daughter. With Mr Forrester as guardian until she comes of age?"

"Well, that's part of it. There have been arguments," Carter stopped himself. "I mustn't talk like this about my employer I know," he looked down at the table, "but it has been quite hard to ignore. And the way some of them are behaving," he shook his head. "I do not wish to worry Mrs James anymore about it than she already is. I cannot speak with her on the subject lest her nerves get the better of her. I must needs talk with someone with a sound, logical mind. One who will not repeat anything I say to anyone."

"You have my word. Let me get us another drink first." Cooke went to the bar and got two more pints of ale. Being careful not to spill them as he returned, he could see that Carter was staring out the window into nothing.

"Come now," Cooke said, sitting down and pushing Carter's drink towards him. "Things cannot be all bad. You sound very worried, William."

"I suppose I am. Well, not really. Merely thinking of the future of the house I have served for most of my life. I always do think about it.

Always. Whatever I have done I have only ever done for Querney Manor and its prosperity."

"Of course."

"Mr Forrester and Mr Bingham have been having the most frightful rows about money and the will. Mr Bingham feels the American should not have any part in running his family estate. I am rather inclined to agree on that. What would an American banker know of English country life? Of English traditions and values?"

"Quite."

"I think Mr Bingham wishes to pay Mr Forrester off with some percentage of profits from the estate. And take control himself."

"Do you know what Mrs Forrester's last requests on that matter were?"

"It's not certain. There were problems with her latest will. It seems she hadn't finished getting the paperwork done after her daughter was born. It was written up but finalising it had been delayed by one thing or another. I am not privy to all the information, and nor should I be. Either way, Mr Forrester is outraged. He said he's going to go to America as soon as possible with his daughter to fight the matter from there rather than 'from this rainy little hole in the armpit of the world', as he puts it. I shan't say some of the other words he used. It's all rather unpleasant."

"Naturally."

"And now Mr Bingham has come to me, saying that whatever happens, the house cannot keep all of its staff and that he will be drawing up a list of people he will be letting go. We are only weeks from Christmas. Mrs James is beside herself."

"Of course she is. Though, I must say, lots of these old houses are doing similarly. Things have changed since the war. Death duties and the like. I know of a number of houses in the county being sold off. Bit by bit. Auctioning their possessions. In fact, Mr Barnatt, the old steward of Mrs Forrester, was in London selling their house there when she was killed."

"I know, I know. You must think me foolish. I wish so much that we could continue in the old way when many people are unable to do so," Carter paused, licking his lips. "We are none of us immune to the progression of modern times. Mrs Forrester was all for innovating. Too much, perhaps..." he coughed. "Even so, I... I really hoped that at least the staff would be able to stay on. What will people do if all the big houses die? They are patrons of towns and villages. They bring jobs and prosperity."

"We will all have to change, William. I know that for certain. People are choosing to work in shops and factories. As a result, they have more money and leisure time now. Even Constable Smith and I cannot escape it. I received confirmation only the other day that we are to be absorbed by Bourtonshire Constabulary and Smith and I are to be redeployed."

"Coppers End is to close?" Carter's mouth opened and shut quickly. "The world is changing too fast for the likes of me."

"I suppose it is to be sold privately. The house belongs to the estate. And their patronage of us has long been threatened. I wasn't surprised at all when I got the letter."

"When does all this happen?"

"We are already packing the place up and we must be out of there by the middle of January. Smith and I are already clearing the place out."

Carter sat still. He looked into the middle distance and shook his head slowly.

"I am in shock," Carter sighed. "I cannot help but worry at what my place in this modern world will be."

"You must know that you are a vital member of this village and the running of Querney Manor. Your place will be honoured, no matter what happens, man."

"At one time, I could be sure of things. But we have lost so much. We lost boys in the war. The whole of the county. Husbands and sons. And now this. The loss of so much in my house. What happened to Mrs Forrester and the death of our good name. Now my master is preparing to rid himself of many of my staff and you? You will be gone as well. Coppers End sold. What will this little part of England look like in a few years? Or more. Fifty years may go by and it will be unrecognisable."

"Come, William," Cooke looked at him sympathetically as the Donaldson boy cleared their empty glasses. Cooke looked up at the boy, "I think we will need a brandy each, there's a good lad," he smiled and returned to the bar.

"We had best not, John. I cannot return to the house worse for wear."

"You shall not. You are far too professional. But these are exceptional times. 'Tis only medicinal."

In his own way, Cooke was fascinated by how much more animated and chatty Carter was after only a couple of pints of beer. *What might a brandy do?*

The Donaldson's boy brought them over small glasses of brandy and left them to their conversation once more. The smell of Mrs Donaldson's cooking was wafting from the back kitchens. Cooke found his mouth watering and his mind wandering to dinner later and whether he could get some from here, or if it would be more polite to see what Mrs Jennings might have brought for him and Smith. *Cold pork pie and pickles probably*. A tasty meal, but not the steak and kidney puddings Mrs Donaldson was serving tonight, laden with extra gravy.

Sipping his brandy, Cooke sighed and thought about what Carter had been saying. *What would this place be like in a few years? Or fifty? Or one hundred?* It wasn't like him to speculate about the future and it wasn't long before he gave up.

"The important thing to do, William," he said, swilling his glass, "is not dwell on what might be but deal with what we have before us. What do you know? What can you do about it?"

"A policeman's way, if ever I heard one."

"I am very sorry for your situation. And my own. Though I do not have to manage it all in the middle of squabbles and fights between two grown men."

"Indeed. I cannot fathom how they can bear it," he lowered his head and then his voice to a whisper, "it is not for me to speak ill of my employers, but it feels a wretched thing to have the tragedy of a young woman's death, and then spend so much time in this manner. Neither of them conduct themselves in a way which is becoming nor with the countenance and grace she had."

"Countenance and grace? I did not hear those words when I was investigating her murder, William. Nor were they said at the inquest. The words were 'modern', 'flighty', and 'interested in parties'." he looked at Carter, beseechingly.

"I feel I should have said so much more in my statements. About her. It's a funny thing, isn't it. How when one person mentions something, and then you find a little evidence here and there, how it is so easy to be swayed."

'What do you mean? Do you speak of my investigation?"

"Yes. And no. I speak of my feelings. And those of others with whom I spoke. This last year the things that stacked up against Mrs Forrester's good person grew and grew in number. She could not control her own property," seeing Cooke's inquisitive face, he continued, "you know. The pigs. Spending money on them and their new stye at the farm. And then what happened? Stolen. As easy as pie."

"Yes, that was such a sad business."

"Not just sad. Mrs James has said it was the harbinger of doom for our house. The insurers wouldn't pay. Some reason or another. Mrs Forrester lost the whole investment. And those pigs were supposed to be part of a recovery for the house after the war and the deaths of the older Mr and Mrs Bingham four years ago. The way Mrs Forrester was going about it before then made me feel she had her head screwed on. Even if, I must say," he lowered his voice further, the smell of the brandy sour on his breath, "I did not believe it becoming of her to do all this while with child. And showing! Mr Barnatt didn't seem to mind. The brother though..." Carter drifted off.

"What about him?"

"He didn't approve either. I heard him tell her a few times. Thought it wasn't lady-like," Carter stared off into the middle distance. "Told her she should leave it to him for a while. She didn't like that. Of course. Told him so. I suppose that's why people thought she was modern. She wouldn't kowtow to a man's authority. I - I shouldn't speak about my feelings on that matter." He paused. |And after all that? More bad things went round the staff about her," he looked at Cooke briefly and flinched, "I discouraged their gossip, naturally," he took a swig of his drink, "but there was talk. The things you heard. After that it was difficult to think of her differently." His voice faded away as he rubbed his forehead.

"It's natural for you to reflect on it. And you now what you say will go no further than me."

"Indeed," Carter half-smiled.

A thought occurred to Cooke, "When did you first hear that she was living this second, secret party life?"

"Oh, gosh," Carter's brow furrowed. "I'm not sure. Months before she died. Certainly."

"So you'd never heard that before then? Never had a suspicion?"

"No."

"And Mrs James? Do you know if she had any idea of it?"

"Well, all she ever said to me was Mrs Forrester's old lady's maid, Miller, said she would find other clothes to be washed that she knew Mrs Forrester had not worn to bed or to dinner that night."

"Miller, she was the one whose heart gave out?"

"That's right. Another sadness brought to our house. She was a young thing. Impressionable and sweet."

"And then she died. Her replacement also found such items of clothing. It was quite damning evidence against Mrs Forrester's character." Cooke thought again, scratching his chin, "You must have known Mrs

Forrester when she was growing up. Did she show any such signs of immoral behaviour then?"

Carter stared at the sergeant, "Well, it's not for me to say. But sometimes..."

"What is it?"

"I'm not sure I should say."

"No one will hear but me. You have my word," Cooke repeated himself.

"You see. What you should know is... Mrs Forrester was a mixture of parts. Flighty one moment, steady and staid the next. As a young girl she had a ferocious temper sometimes. Though only ever in private. I would hear things from the maids."

"Young girls can sometimes have changeable temperaments, can they not?" asked Cooke.

"True enough. But she had been such a happy thing when she was little. And something switched. And..." Carter paused. He looked around himself as though looking for an answer somewhere in the public house.

"What is it?"

"I can't... I mustn't."

"Perhaps what you say might change the outcome of the case? It could be important, man. Come now," Cooke was becoming impatient. The drink may have loosened Carter's tongue, but it was becoming clear there was a limit to how much his walls of propriety would come down.

Carter heaved a sigh, "In her teens. That's when it started."

"When what started?"

"Immoral behaviour."

"Go on..."

Carter finished his brandy. Cooke looked at the barman and tapped their empty glasses. They were refilled in moments.

"She," Carter began, his voice crackling. "She would flirt."

"Don't all girls flirt?" Cooke smiled at the man. *Is this all it is? A flirtatious young girl?* "She won't be the first and certainly won't be the last."

"This was different. It was lewd. And... with people she shouldn't... I was told. By him. He told me. Confessed."

"Who confessed?"

Carter looked into Cooke's eyes. *He is deeply pained by this.* The butler coughed and drank all of his brandy in one.

"It is of no matter," he said at once, his voice the same professional one Cooke was used to. *The shutters are down.* "Now I speak of it, it seems silly. I am sorry to have concerned you."

"No apologies necessary," Cooke studied the man in front of him. "If ever you do wish to speak to someone, you need only ask. It is good to remember the dead, even if we didn't think them perfect, we should remember them."

"We should," Carter assented.

Cooke finished his drink and both men took their leave of The Horse And Cart, thanking Mr Donaldson and his son for their hospitality. Cooke took one last deep breath in to let the smell of Mrs Donaldson's cooking send him happily home. He closed the pub door behind him and Carter. They said their goodbyes and Cooke made his way back to Coppers End, to Smith and Mrs Jennings's pork pie and pickles.

When he returned, Smith was in the main office, sorting through large folders of paper and ledgers.

"Good man," Cooke called to him as he removed his coat and hat in the hall.

"There's a lot to get through, sergeant," Smith responded, dropping a big pile onto a table and letting a great cloud of dust engulf him.

"Yes, yes, I know. I shall be there in a moment to help you. I must do something first. In fact," he said, looking at the now dirt-covered Smith, "why don't you go and wipe your face and put the kettle on for some tea. Once that's done we can settle into it for a couple of hours and then see what Mrs Jennings has left for us."

"Yes, sir."

While Constable Smith was gone, Cooke went to his own office at the front of Coppers End and opened a low drawer in his desk. Underneath some papers he pulled a leather-bound book out with '1920' embossed on the front. He opened it up to the last page he had written in and on the very next he inscribed the date and began to recall the conversation he had had with Carter this afternoon. It had concerned him, stirring up feelings that he could not quite fathom. He finished his entry.

Deep down, something is not quite right. I must find out what it is. Before I leave The Querneys and Coppers End once and for all.

He replaced his journal in its drawer. He then joined Smith in the main office where they toiled for over an hour to decide which things could be burned, which should stay and what they were not sure about.

It was not interesting work, but it flared up their appetites quickly. At ten past six, Cooke looked at his watch and declared it was time to look in the pantry for their dinner and call it a night on all the paperwork.

"Soon one of us will have to go on an evening patrol through the village, just as usual. See everything is alright," Cooke said.

"Yes, sir."

"But first, to the pantry."

They made their way to the kitchen where the kettle sat on the stove, blackened from years of use. Smith opened the door to where Mrs Jennings usually left them their evening meal.

"What is it tonight, Smith?"

"Cold tripe in vinegar, sergeant," he turned to Cooke, his face a little green. "With bread and dripping."

"Well, a bit of bread and dripping should see us right," Cooke reached in to get the food out as Smith's gaze lowered to the floor. Cooke could see the bread was stale and would need every drop of dripping to be palatable. *Poor lad,* Cooke thought, putting the food on the table and feeling in his pockets for anything that rattled. He was in luck.

"I think there's only one thing for it, Smith," he said.

"Sir?"

"We'll keep this for bread and dripping for tomorrow. I'll fry it for breakfast. But for now, I know there is a steak and kidney pudding waiting for us at The Horse And Cart. With extra gravy. Come on," Cooke said, pushing Constable Smith out the door.

CHAPTER 17

The first Harvey Wallbanger was very welcome. The second even more so. Deborah was nervous.

"Are you alright?" Peter asked as Deborah took sips of her drink and looked about, twiddling her fingers and clearing her throat.

"Yes, yes, just new people. Big party. Haven't been to one for a while. I'll be fine in a few moments," her smile was weak.

Her eyes scanned the lawn. People were milling and chatting. Horsy laughter filled the air. There were tall blonde women, clones of Diana Bingham, all wearing long, flowing dresses with, Deborah guessed, no bust support underneath. There were couples too: men in brown suits, which seemed inappropriate for the hot weather, walking around with women in frocks and large pie crust collars, pearls round their necks, pinched looks on their faces and the same large up-do teased into their hair. Music was drifting towards Deborah from somewhere: smooth music, a singer singing in a foreign language, possibly Italian. A bar had been set up by some large doors which lead into the house and a huge marquee had been erected further down the lawn. Inside it were trestle tables with pressed white cloths covering them and adorning those were plates of food and huge tureens of something Deborah hadn't yet discovered. She'd have to get closer to see inside. Croquet had been set up in a different part of the garden and a couple of people were playing. A man was explaining how to hit the ball with the mallet in a very intimate way, it looked to Deborah. The woman, a red-haired version of Diana Bingham, tall and willowy, utterly beautiful, if rather skinny, was laughing stupidly and making attempts to do whatever the man was showing her. Deborah snorted.

"Don't envy them a little flirting, dear," said Peter who had been watching them himself.

"I don't. I'm just feeling a bit sad that she feels she has to pretend to be so stupid."

"How do you know she's not stupid? And happy?"

"Oh, Peter. Do be quiet. I realise women's lib hasn't quite made it to the lofty walls of the Inner Temple yet, but it would be good if you could at least try for me?"

Peter sighed and gulped his drink. The couple moved on, walking through the gardens, seeing if there were any people they recognised.

"Let's not stay long okay, Peter? We're leaving early tomorrow and I'm doing the first leg of the driving."

"Of course. I can't imagine staying very late. We don't really know anyone. And it's an afternoon party."

Deborah coughed and straightened up at the sight of Diana, the hostess, walking toward them in a beautiful green and yellow maxi dress.

"Oh, I'm so glad you could come!" she yelled across to them, a huge grin on her face that didn't reach her eyes. Her fingers sparkled with gold rings and her arms twinkled with what looked like hundreds of brushed gold bangles. Diana was statuesque and graceful as she crossed the garden, past the beautiful tables and chairs that had been dotted about the place. Her hips swayed gently to the lovely foreign music. Her arms held out in front of her, she embraced Peter, adorning him with air kisses.

"Hello, darlings," she said. Moving over to Deborah, her smile flinched and returned, revealing her perfect white teeth. The woman did not embrace Deborah but placed her hands on her shoulders, producing more air kisses before sipping from her martini glass.

"Let me look at you," Diana said to Deborah, taking a step back. "What a lovely dress," she smiled, feeling the large collar on Deborah's blue, floral, sleeved maxi dress. "It's very you, isn't it? Laura Ashley?"

"Yes it is," Deborah responded.

"I thought so. I recognised it from the collection last year. Very nice. Well, I must introduce you to some people, and you must also make sure you get some food and play some of the games we've laid out." Diana lead them further into the gardens, which were encircled by the high hedges Deborah recognised from the other side, hedges that kept this part of the garden private from the bit where members of the public were allowed to roam. Diana went around saying people's names and that "you must meet..." followed by names like Hortensia, Lulu, Clairee, and also Lavinia, Bob and Simon. Very quickly, Peter had separated off to talk with a group of men all in suits of a different shade of brown. They offered him a cigar which he took, solidifying a new fraternal bond.

"Did you invite the whole village? I'm sure I heard that the family always does," Deborah asked Diana as she wound her around a group of women all talking loudly about their children.

"Oh, well, it used to be that way. But you know. The garden is smaller now," Diana's smile dropped for a split-second. "It's just not possible. So it's sort of just our friends now - Hello Madge, darling -" she waved at someone in the marquee, "and some people from the village. Like you. People we know and like. It would just be mayhem if we opened this little bit of lawn to everyone. It's a very big village now."

Deborah nodded, "Of course," she said. The 'lawn' was still a couple of acres of land, but she wasn't going to say so.

"You know Nancy, don't you?" she gestured to the woman Deborah had met at their dinner party back in April. Nancy was sitting at a table in the marquee, nursing a drink and listening to her husband, Ernest, talking to another man so fervently there was a large piece of spittle dangling from his chin.

"Why don't you go and say hello?" Diana pushed Deborah gently in that direction. As Deborah looked around, Diana was already gone, talking and laughing with another man and woman. Deborah made her way forward and cleared her throat.

"Nancy, hello," she said to the woman in the frumpiest summer dress she had ever seen. It was orange, with a high collar and long sleeves. Nancy looked as awkward as Deborah felt.

"Oh, it's Deborah, isn't it?" she asked, looking up and gesturing to Deborah to take a seat at their little table. Nancy went back to listening to her husband pontificate. A din was rising in the marquee as people came to get food in large groups and take seats in the tent and just outside. Deborah also realised this was where the music had been coming from. Large speakers attached to record decks were nestled in the corner. As more people joined in, the music became lost in the squawking of laughter, and only the faintest sound of the bass was audible.

"What a lovely dress you're wearing," Deborah said, leaning towards Nancy. The woman turned abruptly.

"Oh thank you. I like yours too," she said, smiling.

"Have you and Ernest been well since we last saw you?"

"Oh yes. Very well, thank you. Ernest has been in London a lot with work. And enjoying the extended playing hours at the golf club."

"That's," Deborah paused, "nice for you. And him. Peter still hasn't got into golf around here. Thankfully. He's in London a lot too. A different part of it than Ernest I believe. Although he's not that far away from the city, I suppose. A few stops on the District Line."

"Oh gosh. I've never really managed to get my head around The Tube map. It all looks so confusing. Ernest says I'd get lost in our bedroom. I'm hopeless," she giggled.

"I'm sure you'd get used to it if you had to," Deborah looked around. She was hoping to catch sight of some of the villagers she knew. Theresa Slate, or her husband. Some of the people in the shops perhaps. Instead of spotting any of them, Deborah found her husband Peter making his way toward their table with a large drink in his hand.

"Ah, hello Nancy, Ernest!" he said. His voice boomed. *He's already a bit squiffy*. Her shoulders tensed. Ernest stood up to shake Peter's hand and he turned to look at his wife.

"Oh, Deborah, didn't see you there," Ernest said, taking his seat. "Join us, Peter. Go on."

"Absolutely I will," Peter said, pulling a chair out.

"How about we get some food first, Peter?" Deborah asked, standing up, taking his drink out of his hand and placing it on the table.

"Oh, yes, of course. How about it? Nancy? Ernest?"

"I'll get some for you, Ernest," Nancy said, standing and starting to walk a couple of paces behind Deborah and Peter. When they arrived at the buffet, there was a grand array of interesting dishes.

"Diana must have worked hard to make all this," Peter said, getting himself and Deborah a plate.

"Don't be silly, Peter. She will have got catering in. It's a huge amount of food. It looks rather good, I must say. Doesn't it Nancy?" Deborah turned to hand Nancy a couple of plates.

"Oh yes, Diana uses London caterers for all her events. It's all marvellous," Nancy twitched her neck to one side and began choosing food for herself and her husband.

Deborah looked up the buffet and back, her eyes casting over huge plates of vol au vents, terrines, several aspics: chicken and egg, fish, and vegetables all set in different jellies. There were also whole salmon whose skin had been removed but carefully recreated with rounds of cucumber pieces, fashioned to look like scales. There were salads and fruit dishes. Each plate was decorated beautifully and delicately with other fruits and vegetables that had been carved into flowers of different varieties. There was beef galantine, chicken liver puffs, shellfish in mayonnaise, vegetable mousses, chicken mousses and fish mousses, ox tongues served with a watercress sauce and calves' livers with courgettes.

Peter took a little bit of everything, and a lot of ox tongue, which Deborah knew was his personal favourite. She was happy with the salads and very much enjoyed an aspic, so she took little bits of those. She added vol au vents to her plate and took a piece of apple that had been carved into a rose to add to her meal. After getting some salmon, Deborah returned to the table with Peter, Nancy following shortly after. Ernest looked up to receive his lunch from his wife and tucked straight in, starting with a large piece of the beef galantine.

Another couple joined them to complete their table and Deborah learned quickly that they were a husband and wife: he an insurance broker in the city (Peter and he had lots to talk about) and she an artist who also lectured at the local college. The party was finally picking up and Deborah felt her shoulders relax. The artist, named Cressida, was very forward about getting drinks for the table and Deborah was happy to stretch her legs from time to time and help.

As the savoury courses were being cleared away and desserts were being brought out, Deborah and Cressida walked to the bar up near the house, stationed by some double doors. The two of them strode, lost in conversation about academic study in the arts, when Deborah looked up and felt her stomach do a loop. Robert was by the bar, talking to the barman. They hadn't seen each other since he had forced himself on her a few weeks ago. Deborah had pushed it out of her mind, resolved not to be upset by it, nor tell Peter about it in case of any trouble it might cause.

"Hi there! Hello Auntie Cressida!" Robert shouted.

"Not his real auntie," Cressida said quietly to Deborah as they approached. "Hello Robert, how are you? Done with your exams?"

"Yes! I'm a free man!" he said, smiling at the two of them. Deborah's innards squirmed as she got closer. Once she was at the bar, she placed her hands on the wooden top and then back to her front and then she clasped them together. "Deborah," Robert continued. "Nice to see you again, as always. Let me guess, an Old Fashioned for you?"

"Oh, that's my favourite too," said Cressida. "Yes, make that two." The woman may have been an artist, but there was nothing flouncy about her, Deborah thought. There was a comforting solidness about Cressida that she appreciated in the moment. Latching onto it, Deborah coughed and let her shoulders drop once more.

"Thank you, Robert. An Old Fashioned would be lovely," she managed.

"Actually, while we are here, and while this very nice barman is making the drinks," Cressida gestured at the young man in a shirt and bowtie, sweating and making cocktails in the heat, "I'm just going to pop to the loo. It's just through here isn't it?" she asked Robert as she made her way in through the large french windows into a grand sitting room. It was very bright outside so Deborah could not make out many details but there seemed to be a few people sitting inside on beautiful orange sofas, large pouffy things with matching ottomans and armchairs.

"That's the garden room," Robert said, turning to Deborah. "Mother's favourite place to sit. She's recently redone it all. Probably because of this party, I should think. I know she was sick of the old stuff father had kept there for centuries. All in the attics now."

"Right. Well. It's very nice."

"Listen," Robert said, moving closer, "I know you're embarrassed about what happened, and you really needn't be."

"Embarrassed? I don't know wha -"

"I mean, you're probably twenty years older than me."

"Um, well -"

"I think we should just forget about it all and put it behind us, don't you?"

"Well, yes, but I'm -"

"I had to tell mother, naturally. She wanted to know where I had been. I was later home than I said I'd be, you see. She wasn't that happy with it, of course. She had thought you and she were friendly at the very least."

"We were b -"

"And then," he stroked her arm with one finger, "you went and tried to kiss me. She said it was rather desperate of you."

"Excuse me, what? Me? Tried to -" Deborah coughed and lowered her voice. "I did *not* and you know it. You were the one... who... behaved like a pig."

"Mother did wonder if you should come today. I told her it would be good to let water under the bridge. You're lonely without your husband around so much and without any real friends in the village. She agreed. But maybe I was wrong."

"I cannot believe what you are saying. Did you really tell your mother that I -" she lowered her voice even further into an angry whisper, "that it was *me* who tried to kiss *you*? How could you?"

"I suppose you told Peter?" he asked, ignoring her question. He passed her the Old Fashioned the barman had finished making.

"Of course not. It was disgusting and I didn't want him to come here and make a scene."

"Good girl."

"Girl? I'm thirt -"

"It's best if you don't mention it. The whole thing must be awkward and rather mortifying for you."

Deborah drained her drink and then picked up the one meant for Cressida and turned around only to walk into Diana.

"I think it would be good for you to stay away from my son," Diana said, a face like sharpened steel.

"Happily," Deborah replied, storming off into the house.

She walked past the orange three-piece-suite, past glass candlesticks and straight into something hard she couldn't see.

"Excuse me!" an old man's voice was at waist-height. Deborah looked down and saw to whom the voice belonged. He had been talking to Cressida.

"Ah, Deborah, drinks ready are they?"

"Yes, gosh I'm so sorry. Really wasn't looking where I was going," she said, looking at the wrinkled face in the chair in front of her.

"Happens often enough at these things once the sherry's been passed around," he huffed. "People forget the crippled man in the wheelchair. Just bang into him. Like he doesn't exist."

"Come now!" Cressida laughed. "It's not all that bad. Anyway, this is Deborah, a lovely person from the village."

"Oh. You're Deborah are you?" He pointed a bony finger at her."I've heard all about you."

"Oh yes?" Deborah tried to smile but it wouldn't crack across her face.

"Yes, from my grandson, Robert." His eyes bored into her. *He has the same eyes as Robert. Only older. And meaner looking.* Deborah tried to maintain a poker face, hoping her quick judgement wouldn't show.

"Deborah, this is Sir Rupert Bingham," Cressida finished making the introductions.

"Sir? Goodness, no one said," Deborah held out a sweaty hand which Rupert stared at.

"Yes. Sir," he said. "For services to King and Country in the second war. Gave the government our mill to make weapons."

"Well, the country thanks you for your service," Deborah's brow was now very sweaty and her face was going deep crimson.

"And the county, they thank me too. Or so they should. Helped bring in money for a lot of people. Hired women and all," he said, coughing. "What the blasted hell is this awful music? Bloody foreign nonsense," he asked, referring to the quiet sound emanating from a small, brown, vintage record player.

"Oh Rupert, you are awful. It's Demis Roussos. He's Greek. Diana and Bernard saw him perform live the last time they were holidaying in the islands. Brought back all his records."

"Huh, well, load of nonsense if you ask me. Bloody Greeks. No help in the war. None."

"If you'll excuse me," Deborah said, clearing her throat and wiping her forehead with a handkerchief, "I really must find the loo."

"And I must retire to my rooms before I start speaking in awful foreign languages," Rupert Bingham scoffed. "Also I think I am suffering from the ghastly things my daughter-in-law has seen fit to call food and serve up," he started to turn his chair.

"Hahahaha," Cressida laughed loudly, "you are so awful, Rupert. You old card. Let me help you back," she started to push the chair and turned to Deborah. "The loo is just through that door and it's the first on the right," Cressida said, taking Sir Rupert through another.

Deborah thanked her and went through the side door and finally recognised where she was. The dining room was right by here. She had used this cloakroom before at the dinner party. Once inside, she sat down on the toilet lid and caught her breath, sipping from the exceedingly strong Old Fashioned she had taken from Cressida without her knowing. Deborah was reeling from her conversation with Robert. And now, with the sound of music flowing from the garden room, the drink she now realised she'd had too much of, those vol au vents and the fish terrine, there were a number of decisions Deborah was thinking better of. Deborah stood up, lifted the toilet seat and vomited. Standing up she looked into the mirror and cursed herself for putting on more make-up than usual. *I wanted to fit in,* she lamented. *Why would I ever want to fit in here?* Splashing water onto her hands, she put a little on her brow and neck, trying not to disturb her eyeliner and blusher. Wetting her hands, Deborah tried flattening down her hair which had a tendency towards frizzy in hot, damp weather. She repinned it at the sides just above her ears, took her Old Fashioned and sipped it before making a face. Deborah placed the glass back down and this time used the loo for its original intent and had a wee that seemed to last for several minutes. Once she was done she poured the rest of her drink away, washed her hands and went back into the cool hallway of Querney Manor.

The place was quiet here. The people in the garden room were chatting to each other and Deborah could hear no other sound than their conversation and Demis Roussos crooning. Recognising the door to the dining room she poked her head round. The place was set up for a dinner, just as it had been when she had visited. Except this time the table was extended as large as it could be and the china looked a little finer, the candlesticks polished more. *Are they having guests? Or is this for show?* Deborah wouldn't put the latter past Diana. Closing the dining room door Deborah felt a jolt of rebellion against this showy, awful family. *Who does Robert think he is?* She asked herself. *And Diana? All her skinny modelling friends and horsey rich county toffs.* Making her way down the hallway, Deborah took in so much more than she had on her first visit. Perhaps it was the daylight, or just that she was less nervous and less in awe of this family.

The stairwell was huge and curved to the upper floors. Another door invited her to look inside. Deborah inhaled deeply when she saw the enormous room that could only have been a ballroom. Except it was very dusty. There were light fittings where chandeliers must normally have hung, but there was nothing there right now. They were on the floor, under groundsheets. *Perhaps for cleaning,* Deborah wondered. Everything in that room needed a clean. Some of the wall paper was peeling off more obviously than anywhere else she had seen in the house. On close inspection one of the tapestries here had a hole in and all the paintings were covered in a thick layer of dust. *Why so little care about this room?* Deborah wondered. *I suppose no one has balls these days. It could be used for something else, I suppose.* She left that room, quietly shutting the door behind her and checking no one else was in the house like she was. *If anyone asks, I'll just say I got lost from the loo.* She knew another door led into the drawing room they had been sitting in in April. There were others, one to a library, which led straight into a much less formal living room space. There was evidence of family mess in there and it was the first time Deborah could imagine anyone actually living in this enormous pile. There was a noise from upstairs, so Deborah ducked against the wall, passing the ballroom again and heading back past the dining room. Someone was coming down the stairs so she snuck into the dining room to let them pass without seeing her.

Deborah stood by the door, listening out for the footsteps going by. As she waited she looked once more at the portrait of Eleanor Forrester hanging there. Not having any idea of how like her it really was, Deborah did think she must have been a very beautiful woman. Deborah's heart broke now that she knew so much more about what had happened. Her eye was caught by photographs on the dresser as well. There were people in them Deborah didn't recognise, but then she saw Diana's face with Bernard standing on a yacht, champagne glasses in their hands. There was another of them both with two children; the boy clearly a younger Robert, he must have been about fifteen, and then a girl aged around twelve, who looked a bit like him, but with a scowl on her face. *That must be Sylvia, his sister.* Moving around the room, Deborah then came to a wooden screen. She had seen it in that exact place at the dinner party, only this time she looked behind it. The area hidden by the screen was a servant's staging area, where dishes and platters were kept. Decanters and glasses as well. There was a door to one side which, when opened, lead downstairs to where the kitchens must be located, Deborah presumed.

In front of her was another door, a door that looked slightly out of place. It was more modern than any of the others she had seen in the house. Curiosity getting the better of her, Deborah pushed it open and saw inside a large bedroom. The curtains were drawn so it was rather dim light. There was a musty smell coming from the place, like the windows weren't opened as much as they should be. The large bed in the middle of the room was made beautifully, with perfect hospital corners. There were chairs dotted about the place and a dark wood writing table to one side. Spurred on by her adventures around the house thus far, Deborah walked towards the desk and saw old photographs in silver frames. One made her gasp. It was Eleanor Forrester. Deborah recognised her from her painting. There was another of Eleanor with a man whose face looked very familiar. In fact, an older version of that face was wheeling itself towards her as she was looking. Hearing the wheels of the chair, Deborah turned and her feet turned to stone.

"I'm so sorry, I - I was lost," she started.

"Get out!" Rupert Bingham shouted. "Out! How dare you!" He grabbed his pictures from the table and snatched them from Deborah's hands. "How dare you touch my things!" He continued to pick up things, even items Deborah had not touched, a pen, some papers, a collection of drawing pins, and a small brown cigar box.

"I really am, I got lost and then, then I found myself here. I saw the pictures. I'm so, so sorry, really I am. I'm going, I'm so sorry," Deborah backed out of the room and bumped into a woman in a nurse's outfit.

"Who are you? What are you doing here?"

"I - I got lost. Sorry," Deborah pushed past her and out of the servants' staging area, into the dining room and back to the hall of the house. Taking deep breaths, Deborah tried to recover herself before going back to the party. *I'm an awful person.* Trying not to shake, she opened the door to the garden room and walked straight into a young girl.

"Sorry," she said, "I seem to be doing that a lot today," Deborah tried to smile.

"It's okay," the girl said, "I'm stepping on too many toes today as well. Apparently I can't help it."

"You and me both," Deborah took the time to slow her heart down. The face of the girl in front of her was familiar. "You're Sylvia, aren't you?"

"You are correct," the girl replied, her left eyebrow arching.

"We haven't met before, how rude of me. I'm Deborah. Deborah Gordon. I live in the village with my husband, Peter."

"Oh, so you're a real person then, are you?"

"Sorry?"

"Not one of mummy's fake modelling friends, or worse, one of the country club clones?" Sylvia smiled to herself. "If you're from the village then you must be at least a little bit more normal. Hang on, did you say you were Deborah?"

"Yes," Deborah looked at her quizzically.

"Oh. I heard mummy and Robert arguing about you yesterday."

"Well, I can assure you, whatever your brother has said -"

"There's no need to worry. Robert is a lying bastard. A creep. He tries it on with most of my friends from school -"

"But aren't you all only -"

"Yes, I'm fifteen. I told you he was a creep. It's why I hardly return during the holidays. I'd rather stay away from this load of weirdos. I'm only back for this awful annual party to pretend we all like each other and I'm leaving to go on holiday with friends in the South of France. Well, if you've riled him and Diana up, then good for you. Keep going, I say." Sylvia walked off into the main part of the house, leaving Deborah to make her way back out into the bright sunlight, to find Peter and get away from this place as soon as possible.

CHAPTER 18

The ballroom was jolly enough, but it was obvious to both Cooke and Smith as they entered the house that things weren't right. They exchanged glances as the frosty weather outside flowed into an icy mood inside. Mr Carter had welcomed them at the door, which was strange enough in itself, until Cooke remembered that the footmen had already been given notice and had gone.

"It's odd to use the front door isn't it, Sergeant?" whispered Smith.

"Indeed," he replied.

"I like seein' the house properly," Smith continued. "Not jus' up and down the backstairs and a quick walk from one part of the house to another. Feels like a treat, sir."

Cooke nodded. Tonight they, along with a few other people from the village, were guests. There were other visitors too, clearly friends of the family, come to join in some festive celebrations. Though there was holly up, delicate decorations over the fireplace in the ballroom, and punch being handed round in little silver cups, the mood was sombre. *And tense,* Cooke noticed. There was a large portrait of Eleanor Forrester up on one wall and several were glancing up at it.

Carter had a flustered look about him that Cooke had never seen before. *It's no wonder. He is doing several people's jobs.* It gave Cooke pause to consider just how many staff had been let go. Mrs James was nowhere to be seen. *Surely she is still around?* Cooke stroked his chin before realising that Mr Carter was still probably proud and old fashioned enough not to have allowed maids upstairs, even without any other help to hand from footmen.

"Mr Carter," Cooke said, walking slowly to the man who was currently holding a silver salver with drinks on. "Is everything okay? You seem to be doing a number of jobs tonight."

"Yes, sergeant. I am. Nothing to worry about, however. All is in hand."

"Are there so few staff left?" Cooke asked, turning to see if anyone was listening in.

"We have enough, sir."

"Of course," Cooke said. "What about Mrs James, and the maids? Is it not customary for all the staff to join in at the Christmas party? They are normally here."

"They will join us shortly, when they have undertaken and finished their normal duties." The front bell rang. Carter turned to put the salver down, and went to answer it.

Cooke took the room in proper and saw Smith talking to one of the doctors who lived in the village. His name was Jones and he was a nice man, who lived with his wife, Gertrude, 'Gerty', and their children in West Querney. Cooke moved around the room, recognising a few other people from that part of the village; solicitors and professionals all. There were a few of the shop owners from the main street in East Querney. The only people Cooke could not see were their hosts. Neither Rupert Bingham nor Bennet Forrester were in the room to meet or greet their guests. *Highly irregular*. It did not seem as though people were giving it much care however. Once the punch had been sampled guests were talking amongst themselves and making something resembling merry. *Still, something isn't quite right here.* Cooke shook his head. This wasn't the first time he hadn't been able to shake off his natural instincts as a police officer. *Not everything is a crime to be solved,* he reminded himself, laughing and walking towards Smith.

"Well, life is much more quiet these days," Dr Jones was saying.

"I would hope so," Smith replied. "D'you think we may get more of that Spanish Flu?"

"I should think not. It's always possible I suppose. It's most likely that we are over the worst of it, however. Which I, and Gerty, are most grateful for."

"I'm sure you are," Cooke said, joining their conversation. "She must have grown sick of not seeing you, and you leaving at all hours to tend to the sick at the hospital."

"Yes, and the hospital in Bourton is small. We were very often full to bursting when the flu was at its worst. Terrible. And so many young people claimed. Right after the war."

"Did you fight, Doctor?" Smith asked.

"Medical Corps. Stationed in Belgium for most of it." The man said no more on the subject but looked around the room instead. "I can't see our hosts anywhere. Can you, sergeant?"

"I haven't seen them, no. I'm sure they are simply busy sorting things out for this little get-together."

"Yes, it's good they have done this. After such a year. It mustn't be easy for them having lost Mrs Forrester. The house must be in disarray after her death and such a public inquest. You investigated it, did you not?"

"I did," Cooke replied.

"Must have been quite a job. I hear it was quite gruesome," Dr Jones lowered his voice. "And for what? A vagrant wanting some money for drink and nothing more," the man shook his head. "We should get the parish council to do more about these sorts. Here and in Bourton as well. Nothing but trouble."

"Yes, well. I'm not sure it is a crime to have no home."

"It is a crime to rob and kill, though. I would have thought you'd know that, sergeant."

"I do, I do. You may be right though, more must be done. I only hope it is in a Christian manner. I would like to think that we would reach out to those most in need and help them on their feet so they do not feel the need to resort to crime."

"Naturally," Dr Jones replied, nodding.

At that moment the door nearest to them opened and in came Rupert Bingham looking exceedingly smart with a beautiful young woman next to him. The friend who had been with him after Mrs Forrester's murder, Mr Holcomb, was with them both, and another man Cooke did not know. Another lady trailed in behind them. All of them were very fashionable and the room turned to admire them. Bingham was doing his best to grin, taking a glass of punch from a nearby table. Cooke watched him closely; the man smiled to his guests but spoke only to the friends he arrived with. He saw Carter make his way to the man and whisper something in his ear. They conversed and a look of annoyance flashed briefly across Bingham's face. However it wasn't long before his smiles returned as he shrugged Carter away and continued chatting to the lady-friend who had accompanied him. The party continued, people drank their punch and admired the Christmas tree. A pianist soon arrived and lead some carolling. Cooke looked over at his constable and saw him staring off into the distance as the group sang for their figgy pudding.

"What is it, Jacob?" Cooke whispered to the boy.

"Oh it's nothing, sir. Just being silly."

"I'm sure you aren't. I don't think I've ever seen you be silly," Cooke chortled, never having seen such a serious facial expression on Smith's face in their time in service together.

"Well, it's just. I feel," he paused, "It's going to be odd, sir, not working here together. It feels like an ending."

"It is an ending, Smith."

"I know that, sergeant. Don't mind me."

"I shan't. But you're right. It does feel -"

They were interrupted by the sound of clattering. All carolling stopped. The source of the noise was Mr Forrester and Mr Bingham with eyes locked, knocking some glasses over.

"Look what you did!" Bingham shouted, looking around at his silent guests.

Forrester scanned the room too and stormed out, Bingham following. Mr Carter stared at the room at large and then out the still open door. Cooke snapped into action and walked the few steps to where Carter was standing.

"You know what to do, Mr Carter," Cooke said, snapping into action. "Keep everything going here, I shall make sure nothing happens with those two. If you will give me leave, of course. I do not wish to pry, but as a member of the police I must make sure everyone is safe."

"Of course. Yes," Carter nodded, worry flashing across his face for a split-second. "Please do so."

Cooke left and followed the sound of angry voices into a room across the large hall. The first door he entered was a library and study area. The voices were coming from another door inside that room. It was open a crack and as Cooke started towards it, he heard more clearly what the two men were arguing about.

"You cannot take her with you. I won't allow it," Bingham shouted.

"On what grounds can you demand it? She is my daughter," Mr Forrester replied.

"On the grounds that she is my family. She belongs here, at this house. She is my sister's child. I -"

"You have some nerve, Rupert. You cheat her out of her birthright -"

"Me? Cheat her? How may I ask I -"

"You know exactly how. As if Eleanor had *ever*, not sorted her will properly. She was fastidious about such things. I know you did something."

"How on earth could I do something like that? Eleanor was flighty. She got bored with things and moved on. You heard the inquest."

"Oh, I did. I heard that fiction you dreamed up."

"Fiction? What on earth?"

"You see, I got to thinking and I can honestly say the Eleanor the police told me about just never made sense. I cannot believe it."

"Oh, like you were one to know. You were never here! In London on business. You and she never shared any love for one another. I know she didn't truly love you. How could she? She needed you for your money and that was all."

"You think I'm not aware of that? I know what you Brits are like. It is improper to *ever* talk of money and yet you all crave it so much. You hang onto it and pray for it and stop others from having it so you can keep it all. But God forbid we ever speak of it. Luckily, Eleanor was practical and she and I were always open with each other about what she needed to keep this estate going."

"She didn't understand any of it. Not properly. She had these ideas but she never got it. You sanctioned and empowered her. You and Barnatt."

Barnatt? The Steward? What does he have to do with this? Cooke stood in the doorway, knowing it was wrong to stand there listening. Even so, he could not bring himself to cough or loudly open the door.

"Eleanor was a capable woman," Forrester continued. "Another thing you English hate. And another reason I won't allow my daughter to be brought up as a simpering, whimpering, English drip. She is coming to New York with me tomorrow and will be raised by my own family."

"I will get lawyers onto you, Forrester. I want my niece." Mr Forrester started walking to the door and Cooke jumped back a few steps.

"You won't have her. You have stolen her inheritance. And what do you even want her for? What would you get out of it?"

"She is Eleanor's daughter. My sister's daughter, she..." his voice trailed away.

"Don't tell me this is about familial affection. I know you hated Eleanor."

"I did not!" Bingham's voice was louder than ever. Cooke started forward again, worried this may turn physical.

"She told me about you," Forrester yelled. "How you meddled with her. Undermining her plans for this place. Making her uncomfortable. Never leaving her alone."

"I didn't. I didn't hate her. I didn't," Bingham's voice sounded small. "Please don't take her daughter from me," he pleaded.

"We're leaving, Rupert. Tomorrow. Have fun with your guests, and enjoy the ruin you will bring on this house. With you in charge and without my money this house and its land have their days numbered. I give you five years before this place is on its knees or close to it."

Cooke heard footsteps and he panicked. If he stayed they would know he had been listening, but hiding was uncouth and improper. Instinct kicked in and he shuffled behind the door as Forrester came out of it, not noticing the policeman as he stalked off, slamming the library door behind him. *What to do now?* Cooke panicked. He heard Bingham pacing the floor in the other room. The man was muttering and Cooke couldn't hear a word. He stood, frozen, concerned that his feet would move in no direction at all. Not forward, not back, not out from behind the door. It was large and he was well hidden; it would be easy to stay there unless Bingham came out and closed it. Noticing an ornately carved Victorian room divider, Cooke managed to gain control of his legs and shuffle behind it until the coast was clear. He moved just in time, as Bingham came slowly out of the room beyond and into the library. Cooke spied him through some of the wooden scroll work on the screen. The man moved deliberately to a large mahogany writing desk and immediately to a cigar box. Opening it, Cooke saw Bingham take something small and silver out and put it to his lips. He breathed in deeply and sighed out, muttering to himself.

"I'm so sorry," Bingham whispered, as he replaced the small keepsake into the wooden box and left the library, closing the door quietly behind himself.

When he felt enough time had passed, Cooke drew his first breath in a while and walked out from behind the screen. Knowing there might not be much time lest someone return, he went straight to the cigar box to see what Bingham had been looking at. The box was almost totally empty except for a few letters and one, ornate silver ring. Cooke knew it immediately. He had studied it many times when investigating the death of Eleanor Forrester, and later when preparing evidence for the inquest. It was her wedding ring: the one that had never been found, the one the convicted murderer never had in his possession despite having her money and the engagement ring. His heart jumped into his throat and he put his hand to his mouth. Cooke knew every scroll and tiny gem from all the insurance documents he had been given after Eleanor's murder. He looked around, fingering his way through the letters too, but heard footsteps in the hall. Replacing the ring in the cigar box, Cooke decided to get out, in case he was found snooping. *If I am to investigate this, I need to do it properly. With grounds to search the place.* Gingerly, he opened the door and peered through a small crack. Mr Bingham was on the other side of the large hall, replacing the phone onto the receiver, with his back to Cooke. Cooke took his moment and slipped out of the room, staying behind Bingham as he returned to the party in the ballroom which would be winding down any moment. Cooke went through, manoeuvring his way around the crowd to where Smith was standing, talking to a pretty florist from the village.

"Do you have much mistletoe in your shop then?" Smith asked the girl. *He's in his cups,* Cooke shook his head as he approached and tapped the young man on his shoulder.

"Well, yes we -" the girl started, a coy smile on her face.

"Smith," Cooke interrupted. "I'm going back to the house. This is finishing soon but I want to get a small amount of work done to get the place ready for leaving."

"Oh," Smith said, his face going bright red, "do you want me, sergeant?" Smith was pained as he eyed the girl he had only just then been flirting with. Cooke smiled.

"No, no. You stay till the end. Perhaps walk this young lady back home? It's cold and dark out now. I shall see you shortly," Cooke nodded and turned away, waving goodbye to Mr Carter and leaving via the front entrance. He turned to look at the house as he wound his way down the drive, and shook his head.

The walk home was cold and to Cooke it seemed to take an age, his mind wondering what best to do. *How to proceed now... I must be careful.* He needed to set his thoughts down. Once back in the house, he made himself a hot cocoa and sat in his study, looking out of the window onto the main Querney street outside. *There is a murderer still in this village.* Opening a drawer in his desk, Cooke removed his journal and began to write. *This is how I'll know what to do next. It'll be in front of me then, but private.* He sat for over an hour, composing his thoughts and putting them in the right order. Once more glimpsing out the window, he saw a few people walking past. *They are leaving the party,* he knew. *Smith will be back soon too.* Dotting the page with a full stop, Cooke screwed the lid of his pen back on and blew on the journal. He grabbed blotting paper and once that was done with he closed the journal, putting it back in the drawer. At that moment, the door opened and Smith walked through the hall.

"Evening, sergeant," the boy said. He was leaning against the door frame with a funny grin on his face.

"That florist got home alright did she?" Cooke asked, trying not to show his amusement.

"What? Daisy? Yes, she's back safe and sound."

"Good, good. I'm glad you were there to see her safely home."

"It was a good suggestion of yours, sir." He hiccoughed. "Are you packing things now, sir? I can help," Smith said, coming to.

"That would be most useful, thank you. There's quite a bit to do still. All these old records."

The two of them set to work, sorting through the important files and the rubbish. Some things were placed in crates and others they left in filing drawers and cabinets.

"What's happening with all these things we're leaving in cabinets and drawers, sergeant?" Smith asked.

"Well, it will stay, fully organised by us, and then we will leave them here to be collected. They will be taken to the archive rooms at Bourton Constabulary. And will sit there until someone wants to see them."

"When do they go? Is it before we leave or after?"

"That I cannot tell you. It will be whenever they can spare someone to come down here, I suppose. Our little village isn't very important. Only one major crime has happened her in all the time there have been police here. Most of these files are lists of drunks and petty thieves and what they ate for dinner and breakfast before they were released back to their wives and mothers. No more. I wouldn't be surprised if it were all left here to rot."

"Really?"

"Sadly so. We shall see, I guess."

"Seems funny to think this place will be empty," Smith remarked, adding more papers to the rubbish pile.

"I imagine it won't be long. Someone will buy it."

"Really? An old police house? With cells?"

"I suspect they will get rid of them, Smith, don't you?"

"Well, yes, sir. I'd hope so. Got to have a fair bit of money though?"

"Probably. It's a nice house. I'm sure a family could turn it into something comfortable."

The men worked a few hours more, supping on cheese sandwiches and beer before saying goodnight. Smith was the first to head upstairs.

Cooke remained behind to tidy the last few things on his desk. He stared at it a moment, before a thought occurred to him: *my journal.* Opening the drawer he took it out and flipped through the pages. *If anyone else were to read this and I was wrong about what happened at Querney Manor... Or worse: I was right. I must keep this safe. Somewhere I can return for it if ever I have need of it.*

Walking across the hall to a brick room where the three large cells stood empty, Cooke looked around. *In a cell? No, these will be the first things to be removed.* He continued scanning the place until his eye stopped. *Yes, that'll do. Everyone needs a fireplace.* Kneeling in front of it, Cooke was careful to place the book just behind the chimney area, to stop it from getting burned. *There.* He stared at it for a moment, hoping the day would soon come where he could retrieve it and catch the real murderer of Mrs Eleanor Forrester.

CHAPTER 19

"Ooh, let's get the kettle on, shall we?" Deborah asked as she closed her sister's front door behind her.

"You're just like mum. I'd totally forgotten," Lissa removed her jacket, fanning herself with one hand. "Doesn't matter if it's boiling hot, the kettle goes on." Lissa laughed. "You don't fancy something stronger, do you?" she looked at her sister with a grin.

"Well, I suppose I am on holiday… Oh, go on then," Deborah agreed, grinning back as she took her walking boots off.

"Jonathan, make us some cocktails, will you darling? Go on, there's a good boy," Lissa implored her husband.

"Och, go on then," he replied, "come on Peter, we shall make our fair ladies and ourselves something to drink after our long walk."

"Huh, well," Peter followed his brother-in-law, mumbling something as he went.

"Hi kids! We're back!" Lissa yelled up the wooden staircase. Two muffled responses came from their bedrooms; Lissa shrugged and laughed.

"What a wonderful walk that was," Deborah said, sitting down in a large tartan wingback chair in Lissa's front room. She curled her feet under herself in the big seat, away from the cold, hard wood floors. "That little cottage just by Loganlea. What a place to live! The middle of nowhere."

"And you thought Bourtonshire life was quiet."

"I know. I'd go mad there," Deborah sighed, tucking her hair behind her ears, "Peter would love it, I'm sure."

"Hmmm," Lissa responded.

"What?"

"Oh nothing. Come on, let's go and get our cocktails. I need to make a start on dinner."

"I'll help," Deborah said, getting up.

"No you won't," Lissa looked sternly at her sister, "you are my guest. You shall sit and do nothing. Read that old book you've had your nose in for half the time you've been here."

"I will. I'll read it later. It would be nice to cook with you. Like we used to," Deborah put her arm around Lissa and the two of them walked down the wooden hallway to Lissa's kitchen. It was a riot of colour; Lissa had decorated it in greens and oranges and browns. There were little knick-knacks everywhere including a colourful pottery chicken for housing eggs, orange salt and pepper shakers, big, ornate wooden spoons and crockery on the walls. It was as comforting as their mother's kitchen had been.

"Ah, just in time," Jonathan said, handing his wife and Deborah a dry martini each.

"We're going to make dinner for later. Beef pie and neeps," Lissa told Jonathan, kissing his cheek.

"We are lucky men, aren't we, Peter?" Jonathan smiled.

"Yes, yes, we are," Peter replied, getting a cigar from his pocket. "Care to join me for one?"

"Uh, well," Jonathan looked sideways at Lissa.

"If you must, do it outside" she said, walking away from her husband's embrace. "The children are both home from school and I don't want them breathing in the smoke." She took flour and lard from the pantry.

"I'll leave it for now, eh, Peter? Might read the paper instead," Jonathan picked up *The Herald* from where it had been left on the kitchen table this morning and indicated for Peter to follow him to the living room.

"I'll join you after this," Peter said, waving his cigar and slicing off the bottom of it into the bin. He went through the kitchen doors and out into the garden, making his way to a set of garden chairs and a table toward the back, under a weeping willow. Deborah stared out at him, biting her bottom lip.

"Come on, tell me, what's going on?" Lissa asked her.

"What do you mean?" Deborah turned away from the window and looked at Lissa.

"What's going on with you two?" she asked, adding cold water to the flour and lard. "Since when does Peter smoke cigars? And read the bloody Telegraph?"

"Oh, ha. Yes. He started reading that a few weeks back."

"He doesn't chat as much either. Doesn't seem quite at ease and," Lissa lowered her voice, "neither do you. What's going on? I can tell something isn't right."

"Um, well," Deborah's voice choked, her eyes beginning to well.

"Oh, love, I didn't mean to upset you," Lissa left her pastry and put floury hands around her sister.

"It's nothing," Deborah wiped her face with her cardigan sleeve.

"Like heck it's nothing. Come on, Tell me. Drink your drink and talk while I get the pastry going."

Deborah did as she was told and sat, "It's just," she said, gulping before taking a sip of her martini, "since we moved I feel like so much has changed."

"Well that's normal, you don't have familiar faces and places around you."

"It's not just that. Peter has changed. Little things: The Telegraph, cigars, but more. Some things only a wife would notice. Things like the way he talks to me. He's gone most of the time. He stays at the chambers' flat more than he is at the house which *he* bought and got *me* to move out to. He wanted this country life, but it's me that has to live it. And being out there with all those country windbags..." she trailed off. "He just wants to talk to the men. Chat about golf -"

"Golf? I didn't think he played," Lissa said, dropping her pastry on the wooden surface.

"He doesn't. But he wants to. He wants to go to the club and have me cook him dinners and clean the house and get his slippers and pipe. Well, his cigars."

"He never used to be like that," Lissa tutted.

"I know. I think being in the city stopped all that. I don't know. That sounds wrong. The Quernerys isn't all backwards. There are some perfectly nice people there. But Peter hasn't got to know any of them. He only wants to talk to the landed sort. He and his mother like to talk about all the fancy people they've rubbed shoulders with. It's a side to him I didn't know was there." Deborah drank and let the tears fall down her cheeks.

"Now, now," Lissa offered her a handkerchief. "Your life together in London *was* more metropolitan, yes. But that's not everything. You're apart from each other a lot. No wonder you are both changing in different ways. And it can't be helped with his commute. I can't blame him for spending time in London for work, but honestly, Deb, it feels like he's chosen his cake, made you eat most of it and only has little bites if it suits him. Could he not take a job closer to your new place?"

"He never would. He's Head of Chambers now. It's too prestigious for him. He'd never abandon the role. Plus I can see how much he enjoys telling all the country knobs what he does. His eyes sparkle in the same way yours do when you see cake," Deborah smiled through her tears.

"Hey!" Lissa laughed, throwing flour at Deborah who ducked too slowly not to get it down her front.

"And we can't move back," Deborah put her head in her hands and drank deeply from her martini. "He'd never agree to it. I'm trapped."

"Oh my lovely sister," Lissa sat down next to Deborah and put her arms around her. "Come on now, sip your martini, there's a good girl. I'm going to get this pie made and we can chat about how to make things better."

Lissa went back to rolling her pastry out before swapping it with beef in the fridge. They talked for a while about their trips out in Edinburgh and The Pentlands. Deborah was amazed by the beauty of the botanic gardens.

"Going there reminded me how little of my own research I've done," she said, opening a bottle of Matteus rosé.

"I'm not surprised. You've been distracted by this whole murder thing."

"I have, I know. But this diary I found is fascinating. The sergeant, Cooke, is his name: I like him. I don't really know why... he seems to have... integrity. Has a good nose for things. He talks about the village and the people in it in detail and I feel like I know everyone there. Oh, and I live in his house! I mean, how queer! It's not just a book I picked up at the library. From what I've been told and worked out, our dining room used to be his study. And our living room had cells."

"That's spooky, Deb," Lissa said, shaking her head as she stirred onions in a large orange cast iron pot.

"Isn't it? I think our room was his. There have obviously been changes to the house - no sign of cells anymore!" she laughed, "but to know he walked through the same door, put his coat on a rack in the same hall that I put mine on. It's..."

"Creepy."

"Incredible. Oh, and he went to a summer garden party at The

Manor in June, just like I did. Though it seemed like a *very* different affair. In those days they invited the whole village along. There were games like hoopla and Punch and Judy shows. The thing I went to was a horrid mixture of toffs and skinny modelling friends of Diana all guffawing and showing off their pound of flesh."

"Prude."

"No. Not prude. I saw more hairy chests that day than I ever want to see again. You'd say the same."

"I quite like a hairy chest, you know," Lissa winked and added floured beef to her pot.

"Yuech. I need another drink now, you dirty old hag," Deborah laughed.

"Me!? Ha!"

At dinner, Deborah, Peter, Lissa, Jonathan and their two children ate together and talked of Deborah and Peter's journey to The Highlands the following day. As they spoke, Deborah's heart sank.

"It has been so wonderful to see you," she whispered to Lissa, squeezing her hand.

"You'll see us again soon, I'm sure," Lissa replied. "We need to visit this famous Coppers End for one thing," she stood up. "Right, you two," she pointed at her teenage children, "you can help clear up. Deb," she looked at Deborah, "you can go and sit down. I'll bring you a dram. It's your last night. You *have* to partake."

"Well," Deborah smiled, "if you insist."

"I didn't think you liked whisky," Peter said, standing up with plates.

"I don't. At least I don't think I do. But I'm in Scotland. If I don't try it here, when will I ever?"

Deborah made her way to the living room, back to her big cosy tartan chair near the fireplace. It had been a warm day, but the evening was cooler so she put kindling on the fire and got it going. Once it was roaring, and Jonathan had brought her a rather large dram of something very smokey, she opened Sergeant Cooke's journal where she had left it. She was nearly finished and was now into December of 1920. Peter sat down in the same room, and eventually Jonathan joined her. She took no notice of them as she began to read about the work Cooke and Smith were doing to close down their little police house. *He seems so melancholy, knowing that everything about his life was going to change.* Ignoring all passers-by of her little corner of the room, Deborah's attention was caught by an entry made just after Cooke had returned home from Querney Manor's Christmas get-together. As she read all noise around her was muffled and forgotten and she was only jolted from her thoughts as she heard her name being called.

"Deborah," it was Peter. "We need to leave early tomorrow. I think it's best you start heading to bed."

"Oh, Peter!" she said, louder than she had anticipated. "You know we don't need to leave at the crack of sparrow's fart. I don't know why you're rushing me. I'm reading something interesting. Let me finish."

Peter shrugged and made his way out of the room and went upstairs. Deborah kept on, leaning further and further forward in her chair. *The ring. The bloody ring,* she thought.

"Rupert had the ring," she said aloud, finishing up that entry. It was the last in the journal altogether. "Oh my god," she said. "Oh my god."

"What is it?" Lissa came in from the kitchen.

"It's this book. Oh shit."

"Come on, tell me. What's wrong?"

"Cooke doesn't think they caught the right person."

"What? The killer?"

"No."

"Really?"

"Yes! Really! He thinks it was the brother. He was sure it was the brother. He hadn't quite pieced together the how and the why of it all. But the brother had the missing wedding ring."

"The what?"

"Oh, I can't explain. Not now. Her killer is still alive. At that house. Oh my god."

"You don't know that."

"But I do. I've read so much of what this man has written. I told you: I like him. He's intelligent. He *knew* there was something wrong with the case all along. That things didn't add up. Also, he thinks Eleanor Forrester wasn't this party-mad girl that she was made out to be at the inquest. He was making plans to speak to the old steward, Mr Barnatt. He thought he could shed some light on a few things."

"Well did he?"

"I don't know. He had traced the steward and made a note of his address in London, and where he worked after leaving Querney Manor. But it finishes before it tells me whether he found him or not. Oh my goodness."

"Come on, there's no need to panic like this. It's fifty years old."

"But the killer is still there. Still alive. Like nothing happened."

"You don't know that. There may be another journal for all you know, explaining that he looked into it and found that his theory was incorrect."

"Hmmm, I suppose," Deborah scratched her chin. "But I searched the fireplace. There was nothing else there."

"Didn't you say there was all sorts in cabinets and boxes? And things stuffed into the walls?"

"Yes, but I've been through the cabinets. And the things in the walls were for insulation. This was hidden in the fireplace on purpose. There's no reason to put it there other than to keep it from someone. Oh my..." she trailed off, pacing the room. "I have to do something about this," she said, leaving the living room and pacing up the stairs.

"What? What do you mean? Why you?" Lissa called after her.

But Deborah was already at the top of the steps and down the hall to her bedroom. Peter was in his pyjamas and getting into bed.

"I'm going to London tomorrow," she said, grabbing her suitcase and handbag, making sure everything was packed properly for an early getaway in the morning.

"London? What? Why? What about our holiday?"

"Oh, hang the holiday, Peter. This is more important."

"What is? What's happened?"

"The killer is still alive. It's Rupert Bingham."

"What? You cannot be serious."

"I am. Deadly serious."

"No, no. You cannot change our plans. I don't want to go to London. I've made arrangements to meet with people on our walking tour."

"Oh, you can go, Peter. There are trains from here to Inverness. And buses. I'm sure you can figure it all out. But *I* am going to London."

"No, Deborah. I forbid it."

"You -" she paused, swallowing, "*you forbid it*?!"

"I do," Peter gulped.

"Forbid?" she whispered, taking a breath. "Who are you? I don't recognise you. Where is the affable, fun man I married? The one who didn't want to be a boring old fart like his father? The one who didn't want a little woman like his own mother for a wife? You are *forbidding* me? Bloody hell! Tomorrow morning I am driving to London to go to the Public Records Office, then I shall make my way back to The Querneys. You can come too if you like. But don't expect me to talk to the man who forbids me to make up my own mind to do something. If you don't want to come, have a lovely holiday, I'll see you when you get back.

Now off you go downstairs. Take a blanket, you can sleep on the sofa tonight."

It wasn't easy for Deborah to fall asleep, but she forced herself to. The journey to London would be long, and she was filled with adrenalin. *What happened at Querney Manor? Why didn't Sergeant Cooke get his man? What help can the steward give? Why would Rupert Bingham kill his sister and how on earth is he still living free, in that house, like he didn't?* Her mind raced, but when she woke early in the morning, coffee, nervous energy and desperation to find answers got her into the car after leaving a note for Lissa. *She'll understand, unlike Peter,* she thought, as she went towards the A1. *Oh Peter, what on earth am I doing?* Deborah nearly turned round, before remembering how he had forbidden her to go to London. She put her foot down harder on the accelerator.

After a couple of hours, Deborah stopped at a petrol station to use the loo and bought a bottle of lemonade and a cheese sandwich from the man behind the counter. She ate it in the car and was careful not to drink too much too quickly. She wanted as much road behind her as possible. *Where should I stay?* She pondered, all at once realising how little she had thought this whole thing through. As she continued her way south she made all the decisions she needed to: where to stay, who to make enquiries with, what to do after. *The first port of call will be to find Barnatt, if he is still alive. If not him, his children or someone who knew him.* Deborah bit her lip, the uncertainty of this mission coiling itself around her body, causing it to tense. Inhaling deeply, she made further plans in case there was no Barnatt anymore. *I will just have to take a chance,* she decided.

Eight hours after leaving Lissa's home in Morningside, two petrol stops, three toilet breaks and two horrible sandwiches later, Deborah arrived at a bed and breakfast she knew near Belsize Park. Pulling in round the side of it, she breathed a sigh of relief at the 'Vacancies' sign. It was too late in the day to do anything now. Her enquiries would have to start tomorrow.

At first light, Deborah was awake, planning her day. Once she had dined in the chintzy, old-fashioned breakfast room on fried bread, bacon and eggs, she left the bed and breakfast and walked to the tube station. To Chancery Lane she travelled, and located the Public Records Office quickly. At the reception she was asked her business by an old man with a stoop and a head so bald he looked like a wrinkled baby.

"I'm looking for the records of a man. Births, marriages, deaths. Hopefully not the last one of those," she added quietly.

"Do you require assistance with the records?"

"Um, I don't know?"

"You will, I'm sure. They are very extensive, miss," said the man. "If you make your way to Archive Services, on the first floor someone will make themselves available to you to start you off."

"Thank you," Deborah said, leaving him behind and clutching at the notes she had made earlier on and placed in Cooke's old diary.

A younger man in a grey suit with a brown woollen tie was sitting at Archive Services. The name badge on his shirt was Thomas.

"How can I help you?" he asked with a wide smile.

"I'm looking for records."

"You've come to the right place. I'll need a little more information than that though," he grinned.

"Oh, yes," Deborah spluttered. "Right. A man. Cyril Barnatt. Born 1894. Steward to Querney Manor House in Bourtonshire, but then moved to Whitehouse Mansions in Richmond in London in 1920. He worked for local government then, for a land surveying service. That's all I know."

"Actually that's a fair bit. We can look at Bourtonshire records and London records, *and* government records and find things that match up. You may be in luck."

Several hours later, she was.

"It's got to be him, hasn't it?" Deborah asked Thomas. "It all adds up."

"It looks that way."

"He is still alive. I can't believe it. Seventy-nine years old. It's a shame we don't have his address though."

"But there's the daughter's. Jane. And an address in Richmond."

"I hope she's still there."

"This seems very important to you," he asked casually, closing a book they had been using.

"It is," she replied. *It really is.*

Deborah and Thomas made their way back to the desk through the maze of records and information booklets. Deborah yawned but felt a shock of nervous energy pulse through her body as she realised the answers she was looking for might be in Richmond-upon-Thames. *I must keep going,* she said as she half-ran to the nearest station, hoping and hoping that Jane Barnatt still lived on Queens Road and that she may be able to tell Deborah the whereabouts of her father. The tube journey took an age as she slumped slowly west on the District Line. Twice she fell asleep on other people's shoulders, only realising when they had got up and her head had fallen to the side without anything to lean on. By five o'clock that evening she was there. Knocking on the door, Deborah felt a mixture of exhaustion, excitement, dread and hunger. It opened and behind it, a friendly-looking woman in her late forties stood in front of her.

"Can I help you?" the lady asked.

"It's possible," Deborah could barely speak for nervousness. "I'm hoping you are related to or maybe know a man I am looking for. Cyril Barnatt? He may be able to answer some very, very important questions about something I am investigating. My name is Deborah and I've come a very long way."

"Well," the woman said, "I'm Jane, his daughter, I suppose you had better come in."

CHAPTER 20

Cooke stirred his hot cocoa and went back to his desk. January was always misty in this part of England but this year it seemed particularly so. He had returned from a beat around his new patch - the inspector's orders so he could get to know the place better - and the cold was settling in his skin. There had been no stars to see in the sky and no familiar faces to say hello to like he used to. After rubbing his eyes, he looked at the other officers. The lights in this room were brighter than those he lit at this time of night at Coppers End. As he blew on his cocoa he thought back to the bed he had there, the one he could go to at any time because he knew The Querneys were asleep.

"Cold out there, was it?" asked his inspector, a man named Rivers.

"Yes, sir. Very much so, but nothing I'm not used to," he smiled at the man. He had spoken to Rivers a number of times on the phone before starting work at this constabulary and had met him at the inquest into Eleanor Forrester's murder. Other than that, the man was a stranger. A fair man for the most part, Cooke had decided on his first day with him, but gruff too.

"Anything to report?" Rivers asked him.

"Nothing. I shall say so in my report."

"It's good for you to understand the geography of the place more," Rivers explained to him. "You're no stranger to Bourton, Cooke, but policing it is a different matter. It's a bigger place than you're used to, you and I both know that. We have more crime, sadly, and more of it is sordid."

"Not just someone pinching the odd turnip!" shouted one of the other sergeants from across the room.

"Ha!" laughed the desk sergeant who had left his station to join them and was standing by some shelves opposite Cooke. "We should call him 'Turnip', shouldn't we?" he added. Officers of all ranks joined in the laughter.

"All right, all right," shouted Inspector Rivers. "Back to it. And you," he turned to the desk sergeant, "hurry up handing that paperwork over and get back to your post."

"Yes, sir," the desk sergeant said, placing some papers down on an empty workstation and scuttling back to the front desk.

"So, Turnip," the Inspector said with a rough and low laugh, "file your report from that beat you just took. Shouldn't take you too long to write 'nothing' should it? Then start looking into this theft," he placed a folder of paperwork on Cooke's desk. "Happened a short while ago. Look sharp about it. This may be your third night shift in a row, but this is a Friday evening and it's a race day too. Expect a fair amount to do."

"Yes, inspector."

"Right, on with it then."

Cooke drank his cocoa quickly and began looking at the theft he had been handed. *Old lady...* he read. *Hand bag taken from café... Three witnesses.* Cooke read through the statements taken and the descriptions of the perpetrator. He shook his head as he saw that one of the other customers had seen it happen and thought it was a young boy with dark hair, the waitress had thought it was a short, but older man with mousy-brown hair and a dark hat on, and the victim had thought it was a woman. *What am I to do with this? Is this just busy work for the bumpkin?* Cooke rubbed his chin leaving a red mark. His eyes scanned the room to see what his colleagues were doing. *Perhaps this is a joke on the new boy.* The contents of the bag were a comb, some boiled sweets and a small purse with a few pennies in. *A young constable could sort this out.* Cooke shifted in his chair and waited for the laughter to peel from the inspector or some of the other, more jocular policemen he worked with. He expected them to gather round and point at 'Turnip' being given a pointless case that the most junior of officers would simply file before making a cup of tea for the old woman and apologising for the fact she will, like as not, never see her handbag again.

Sighing, Cooke signed a few of the pages, took a note of the victim's address, went to the filing room to process his report from his own beat around Bourton this evening and a few others that had been gathering on his desk. In the filing room, Cooke placed each report in the correct place but something caught his eye before he closed the wooden drawer. He pulled out the paper he had seen and took a closer look at the signature of Constable Jacob Smith.

"Huh," Cooke said to himself. He and the boy had worked together once since they were transferred, but only their first day. Smith had done night shifts while Cooke worked the day, and vice versa. He had wondered if that had been done on purpose by the inspector, to force them both to work with others. It had definitely been good for Smith, whom Cooke had seen on a shift change two days ago, laughing with some of the younger constables before heading out for a beer. *It's good for him,* Cooke had thought at the time. *He should have boys his age to work and have fun with. Not middle-aged old me.* He put the papers back and left the room at once.

Back at his desk he looked at the clock. It was after ten now and the inspector had been right. The noise from the front desk was louder than before as people had been brought in for various reasons, most of them seemingly drink-related. One of them was a very well-dressed woman who also apparently earned her money in a less than moral way. Cooke could hear her shouting at the desk sergeant about how unfair it was to be treated as though she were some common madam.

The night ticked on and Cooke went out onto the streets again. He dealt with four situations, all of which he brought in: one case of brawling (two men, both the worse for drink), two cases of pickpocketing (both by the same young boy), and another was a man for being intoxicated (and urinating in a public place). In this last case, Cooke put the man in a cell to sober up. The stink of urine burned the back of his nose and he scrunched his face as he closed the cell door. He had been at Bourton Constabulary for ten days now. *I hope Friday nights aren't all like this,* he thought, picturing the old kitchen in Coppers End, with its warmth from the coal fire. Smith floated into his mind again, and he remembered the bacon sandwiches and strong cups of tea he and the boy had shared during cold, dark nights. In that police house they had only ever had three cells and there hadn't been one occurrence that Cooke could recall where they were all occupied at the same time. *I'm tired,* Cooke realised as he walked back to his desk and sat down; it was a little thing, not like the grand, dark wood one he had sat at looking out on the village of The Querneys. *I'm not sleepy, but I'm tired.*

"Turnip!" shouted the inspector from his office. Cooke sat up with a jerk and went to find out what he was being called for.

"Yes, inspector?" he said, standing to attention.

"At ease," Inspector Rivers said. "There's been reports of a break in and I think you are the perfect person to attend," he grinned.

"Thank you, sir?" Cooke wasn't sure if this was a joke either.

"Don't look so worried. It's at your old place: Coppers End. We received a call from the village by an old lady who lives near to the house. She says she heard breaking glass and that there might be something moving around inside. Most likely it's a cat, but needs must. I told her we'd send someone to take a look and if there's anything in it, someone will pop round in the morning at a more sociable hour to take a statement from her."

"Of course, sir. I'm sure you are right about it just being a cat. Nothing ever happens in The Querneys."

"I'm aware of that. Look lively, it'll take you about thirty minutes to drive there in case you had forgotten. Do you want to take a constable with you?"

"No need, inspector. If it is a break in, I will likely know who they are and deal with them effectively."

"Good. We're busy tonight. Come back quickly," Rivers waved a hand in dismissal and Cooke left him to his office.

His feet moved quickly across the room to his desk, Cooke was in a hurry. *This is perfect,* he thought to himself. He checked for his pocketbook and pencil and took a quick glance around at the other men at work. No one was paying him any mind so he opened his third drawer down and removed a brown paper file. No one watched as he walked out the door to a car, sat down in the front and opened it. There wasn't much inside, just a couple of papers and an envelope. He read back to himself what he had written down over the last few weeks since his transfer to the Bourton Police; since the incident at the Christmas party at Querney Manor. All the little mysteries and possibilities that were unanswered. He made the decision a few days after leaving The Querneys and moving to Bourton that he wouldn't give up on trying to prove his theory in the Eleanor Forrester case. Cooke cursed himself again for not making a note of the old steward's new contact details from his journal before he hid it. *Maybe that was rash,* he wondered, *I cannot remember now why it had seemed so important to hide that diary.* It was only a memory of a feeling now. He removed the letter from its envelope to double check its contents. Cooke had written it over a week ago, deciding it best to have the letter to Barnatt ready for when it became possible to get his address. Now that time had come. He could go and retrieve his journal and get the man's details. He read to himself in a whisper to make sure there was nothing he had left out:

34a Union Road,
Bourton
Bourtonshire
BO1 4NY

Dear Mr Barnatt,

I apologise to you for contacting you out of the blue in this way. You and I have met several times. My name is Sergeant John Cooke, and up until recently I was the sergeant at Coppers End, the police house in The Querneys, Bourtonshire. You were the steward to the late Mrs Forrester on the Querney Manor Estate. I investigated her murder. I was never able to contact you during the investigation and subsequent inquest: you were in London at the time of her murder on business for the estate and you were quickly made redundant by her brother, Rupert Bingham who had decided there was no longer a need to fill that post. I have felt for some time that there has been some sort of error in this case. One of those errors is that I never interviewed you. Call it instinct if you will, but now I believe I have evidence that the wrong man was found guilty of her murder. You may have seen in the papers that it was a vagrant who later died but was found guilty at the inquest. Whatever force this is that drives me to want to contact you and understand what it is you might know (but may not even realise it) pushes me still and I would speak with you as soon as it becomes possible for the both of us to meet or correspond. I ask this with the utmost urgency, so that *evidence may not be destroyed and that we catch the person I believe to be Mrs Forrester's murderer. I have not named him here for obvious reasons but all shall become clear when we are able to speak. I apologise for the dramatic nature of this letter. However things have changed and it is not easy for me to keep investigating this case without sounding some sort of alarm.*

Yours etc.
Sergeant John Cooke

PLACING the letter back into the envelope, Cooke put it all together in the file and started the engine. The drive was quiet and dark and the hour was late. Cooke's watch said it would be two o'clock very soon. He rubbed his eyes and thought about what he might find. Time moved slowly and Cooke felt like his arrival might never come. But come it did and he pulled his car into the space in front of the house, just as he had done many times past. Before the war he had driven a horse and cart, afterwards he had been given a car by the main constabulary making journeys through this part of the country from farm to farm and from Bourton to Coppers End so much easier.

The village was dark and quiet. The few lamps near the houses were still lit and the mist was worse out here than it had been in the town of Bourton, making the light from them pale and fuzzy. The cold air froze in his throat as he breathed in. Turning to the house he looked for a sign of broken glass or another disturbance. And there it was. The window of his old office had been smashed from the outside. Cooke peered in and saw shards on the floor where his desk once sat. He listened intently for any sign that whoever had done this was still inside but the air was still and soundless. Pacing his way to the front door, he held the handle, his fingers feeling the edges of its hexagonal shape. He had done this only weeks ago when he said his final goodbye to the place. He had never locked Coppers End when he was the sergeant here, but he knew this time it would be. Taking the large key from his pocket, he placed it inside the lock and turned, along with the handle of the door. It creaked as he pushed. It was a sound as familiar to him as his own name.

Inside, the furniture and filing cabinets he and Smith had struggled with and pushed into the hallway were still there under dust sheets. *No one has come to claim them yet. I wonder if they ever will. Or will the new owners simply shove them, forgotten, into the attic.* Cooke sniffed and noticed a musty smell lingering in the air. No scent of sausages frying or coal burning in the fires. He made straight for the room with the broken window. It was empty now, with just a pile of broken glass on the ground and dust settling on the window sills. He poked the glass with his pencil but there was nothing else of interest so Cooke made his way into the other rooms. First to the kitchens. Nothing there but empty cupboards and the signs of mice taking advantage of the lack of humans.

Onto the cells. The room had only one small window to the back so it was always a dark room, but this night it was even more so. A tiny sliver of misty light made its way though leaving the rest of the place in pitch black shadow. The meagre illumination cast itself on the diagonal as far as the fireplace and the wall above it. Cooke scanned around, wishing he had brought something to see better with. Something caught his eye. Something bright was on the ground in front of the fireplace and it glimmered in the tiny shaft of light from the window. He stepped towards it, knowing in his head that the house must be empty by now. Whoever had broken in seemed long gone. Even so, his heart percussed loudly as he walked through this black room where once he had housed petty thieves and drunkards. He peered at what had caught his attention, bending down to look closer. Crouched he could see it was nothing but an old spoon, probably found in the cells by whomever had let themselves in tonight; an old relic from when he and Smith had provided porridge to those who had sobered up by morning. He held it in his hand and smiled to himself, wondering if it would be wrong or strange to pocket the thing as a souvenir of his time at Coppers End.

His reverie ended quickly when he heard footsteps at the door to the room. He looked up into the face of a man he recognised, a face illuminated in the morsel of grey light that came from the window.

"So -" Cooke began. Rupert Bingham coughed and looked directly at something behind Cooke's right shoulder. Cooke began to turn but couldn't. A large strong hand pushed into the back of his neck, forcing his face down. He tried to move but whoever it was had the advantage of weight and height over Cooke who was crouched awkwardly. The last thing he saw was an eager look on Rupert Bingham's face fading into darkness and the last thing he felt was the thick rope fall round his neck and tighten on his throat.

CHAPTER 21

Driving back to The Querneys from London was frustrating. The going was slow because of an accident on the motorway; the car stood still but Deborah's mind was electrified. Meeting Barnatt had opened her eyes and she grimaced with exasperation at the motionless traffic. *Cooke wanted to speak to him and he never did. He never got the chance,* she repeated to herself. After arriving at Barnatt's house in Richmond the day before, when Jane had opened the door, Deborah had no idea what to expect. The woman was wary but kind and showed Deborah to the living room. Deborah had explained her visit in the best way she could, given the nervous energy powering her body without the aid of proper sleep or food.

"You see," Deborah had said to the woman, "I'm looking for Cyril. Your father, I believe. He was the steward at Querney Manor in 1920 when his mistress was murdered."

"That's right," Jane said, looking at Deborah in sympathy. "He's told me about it before. But I don't see how we can help you now."

Deborah explained further, adding that she was afraid the real killer was never arrested.

"And worse," Deborah finished off, "If it is who I think it is, he is still alive, and living a wonderful life in the splendour of a beautiful home, and has *never* faced justice. I know that the officer investigating it all, this Sergeant Cooke, he thought several times that your father may have some answers to a few things. And I agree. I don't really know why, but I do. Is he still alive? If so, would you be willing to tell me where he lives now? If I can get to the bottom of this, justice may finally be done."

"Goodness. You are on rather a mission. An exciting one as well. It doesn't seem quite real."

"I assure you it is."

Well, as a matter of fact my father is still alive. He has lived with me for a number of years now, after my mother died. He is old and frail but still has most of his wits about him. I can't promise you he will be able to tell you anything you want to know, but I can't see the harm in finding out."

Deborah's entire body heaved a sigh of relief. *Oh my god. I may get my answers,* she had thought at the time.

And I did get answers, she remembered, sitting in the car and impatiently tapping the steering wheel. It hadn't been that easy, Cyril Barnatt was hazy about a few things, but Deborah had found what she was looking for.

Jane had gone to his room on the ground floor. He walked slowly with two canes but he managed, with his daughter's help, to sit in a comfortable armchair.

"So, you live at old Coppers End, do you?" he asked smiling, after they had made introductions.

"I do. Thank you so much for speaking to me, Mr Barnatt. I understand this will have come out of the blue, and I appreciate your daughter's kindness to me and your time in speaking with me."

"Oh, please. I like to reminisce," he said. "And call me Cyril. Times have changed have they not? I always hated being called 'Barnatt' in my day. I had a first name after all." He looked away out of the large bay windows of his daughter's house. "So, what did you want to ask me about? I tell you, it's not that out of the blue really. You're not the first person to contact me about what happened in The Querneys."

"I'm not?"

"No. I had a couple of letters in the mid or late twenties. Was it? Yes, I think. From the old butler, uhhhh, what was his name? C-c-c-c..." he faded away looking into the distance.

"Carter?"

"Yes, that's the one! Takes me back, it all does. That house was so grand. So beautiful. Have you seen it?"

"I have, yes. It's still quite grand, even now."

"Do they look after it well? Mrs Forrester always did."

"Um, well, I think it has been harder to do all the necessary upkeep in recent years."

"Of course, of course. Even back then, you know, that was the beginning of the end for a lot of families like theirs. I was taken on by Mrs Forrester, well, she was Miss Bingham at that time, in uhhh, gosh... end of 1918, I think it was. So I only worked with her for the best part of two years or so. Lovely woman, she was. Devoted to the estate."

"Was she? What do you remember about her?"

"Oh, well, she was funny. Very funny. And *very* modern. Worked with me until she was about to pop with her child. It wasn't the done thing in those days. Especially for a woman of her class. Lots of people - and I'm sure I overheard the staff gossiping from time to time - thought she shouldn't have been running the estate anyway. That she should have given over the day-to-day things to her brother, or her brother *and* husband. She insisted on being in charge, however," he sipped a cup of tea that had been brought to him by Jane and Deborah smiled inwardly about Eleanor Forrester. *Good for her*. "Well, I didn't know what to think at first, but my golly, she had a good head on her."

"Oh yes?"

"Absolutely. Sharp as a sabre. Like I said, lots of houses going down after the war and that Spanish Flu. Inheritance tax and so on. People selling everything up. Eleanor Forrester had some ideas of what to do to keep things going in the best way, and I really do mean that. She knew what to sell, what to farm, what to hold on to. It was my job to know those things. And she was a natural. She really was. Her brother though," he paused.

"What about him?" Deborah moved closer to the edge of her seat.

"He... well, how can I put it? What was his name? Uhhh, Roger?"

"Rupert."

"That's it. Rupert. He wanted to be in charge. That much was obvious. He interrupted our meetings constantly. Followed his sister around all the time. Badgering her about this and that. I imagine he was putting in his ideas for what she should be doing. I heard what happened to the estate after she died and he took over proper. The whole place fell to shambles. In so much as he lost lots of land. Had to sell more and more to pay off taxes and debtors. After they lost their prize pigs he never reinvested. You know -" he shifted in his chair, "they were another idea of Eleanor's. She wanted to change up their farming to make more income. And she was doing it. But then they were stolen. And then she died. And her brother didn't invest in more. He only just about managed to hang on to the mill, which I heard saved him for a little while. In the second war, he managed to find a way to lease it to the government to make weapons. And for that they knighted him. Can you believe it? He made money from the war and they gave him an honour?"

"Goodness. He told me he was knighted for services to the country."

"Oh, still alive is he? Well, I'm sure he would say that."

"I get the impression you didn't like him," Deborah leaned forward.

"No. Well, not especially. There was just something..." he paused. "Can't put my finger on it. But I did like Mrs Forrester. She was a good employer. I was sad when she died and I was sad when the brother told me not to return. I wanted to pay my respects but I decided he was grieving so I left him to it."

"What did you think of the reports of Eleanor's character in the papers and at the inquest? It must have been hard for you to hear about her secret life."

"Ha. Oh, well, I'm not sure I totally believed that. I suppose Bingham knew her better than anyone, but it never made that much sense to me."

"It didn't seem to make much sense to Cooke either. The sergeant investigating it, I mean," she paused. "Didn't you say Carter, the butler, had written to you? What did he want?"

"Gosh. I must cast my mind back. It was so long ago. They were odd letters though, I remember that. His first letter I think implored me to speak with him. He didn't say why or anything. And the second one, uhhhh, well, oh," Barnatt looked off into the distance as he thought.

"Honestly, there's no pressure to remember, I don't want to tire you out," Deborah said.

"You won't. It's been interesting to go down memory lane, as they say. Now, let me think... the second letter. That's it! A damn shame it was. I remember it. He was on the verge of going into a poor house. I remember him saying that. He was angry. Raving. Didn't think he should be there and needed to talk to someone who knew the house. He made strange accusations. But, yes, I remember. It was so rambling that not much of it made sense."

"How odd. Can you remember any of the specifics?

"Oh. Now you're asking. Let's see..." he bit his lip and closed his eyes. Deborah edged forward on her seat. "Oh yes. I remember. He said that he had been let go from the manor house. Rambled a lot about treachery. That you couldn't rely on people. It was very sad. He was clearly in a bad way. Said things like he would get what was coming to him. I don't know if he was talking about himself or another person, mind. As I said, I remember reading it and wondering what on earth had happened to the man. He was always so… fastidious, staid, dependable. His face never moved. The ceiling could have collapsed while they were serving tea and he would have gone on as though nothing had happened."

"He sounds like a formidable man," Deborah said.

"Oh, he was. When I read that second letter it was clear that he had fallen in many ways. No longer running the house he loved. And he was proud too. I remember that. Couldn't let anything get in the way of making Querney Manor a shining beacon in the county. Or country, even. Obsessive. Even in that letter he wrote. Yes, he had lost his job there but still spent a few pages talking about the honour of the house. Said it had been besmirched. But, and I suppose this is interesting, not by the person we thought. I'm sure there was more about betrayal. And doing things he wasn't comfortable with. That came up a few times. He was obviously very distressed when he wrote it. He even talked of Mr Bingham."

"Did he?"

"Yes. Not much. Said he was the devil. And he'd always liked Rupert. I know that. Mr Carter had made it clear to me a number of times, in his own very discreet way, that he thought Rupert Bingham should have been in charge of the estate."

"Really?"

"Yes, but as I say, he was very subtle about it. And never let it affect his work. God forbid." Deborah smiled but her head was swimming. *What on earth does this all mean?* "I don't remember much else of the letter," Cyril Barnatt continued, "but I think I've given you the gist."

"You have, you really have. It doesn't sound like Mr Carter esteemed Rupert Bingham in the end."

"No. Most certainly not. I only wish that I'd been able to contact Mr Carter after I read that letter."

"What happened?"

"I tried to find him but he had moved on from the address he had supplied. I never heard from him again. I heard he died soon after…" Barnatt looked at his hands. "I feel ashamed I didn't make the effort to write back or find him sooner. I had known the man well at one time, but by then I was working a busy government job, with a wife and a young child. I didn't find the time soon enough."

"Please don't worry yourself about that, Mr Barn- Cyril, I mean. It was a long time ago. He may have wanted to reminisce about better times," Deborah said soothingly.

"Or get some money out of you, dad," Jane spoke up from the kitchen where she had been eavesdropping.

"Perhaps. Either way, I shan't know," Cyril stroked his chin. "Was there anything else you wanted to know?"

"Possibly. I'm still trying to take all this in. What you've told me is that Eleanor Forrester was excellent at her job, an intelligent, interesting woman, modern but you didn't think she had a habit of partying like a 'flapper' - that's what they called her in the papers."

"Absolutely. Stuff and nonsense. You never really know what goes on in anyone's life, but if that was true, I'm a monkey's uncle."

"Why did you never say anything?"

"Oh, well. I thought about it. I read the stories in the papers after the inquest. I was shocked. I wasn't sure what to do for a long time. It wasn't my business anymore, you see? At a party, oh gosh, when was it? Uhhh, oh yes, it was New Year's Eve going into 1921. I heard someone make an awful joke at her expense and I shot the man down, verbally, so to speak. I decided I should say something soon after that."

"And did you?"

"I wrote to the old sergeant who had first investigated the case. Late on in January of 1921. Or it might have been February. I don't know what I thought would come of it. The inquest was done and dusted and couldn't be changed. But he may have been able to do something, I suppose."

"Did he?" Deborah moved even further to the edge of her seat.

"Oh, well. I'll never know. After what happened."

"What happened?" Deborah tried not to sound shrill.

"He hanged himself. In that January. So I heard. I had a friend in government working with the police who knew I had worked out there. He told me about it."

"Oh." Deborah put her hand to her mouth.

"I'm so sorry you didn't know. It was hushed up because it would have been quite the scandal. I heard from an old friend Cooke wasn't enjoying life after they moved him out of Coppers End and into Bourton. Went back there one night to investigate a break-in. He left a note and hanged himself."

"Do you know what the note said?"

"I never saw it. Sorry."

"No, no need to apologise. You have been so helpful. I'm just sorry I didn't know about Cooke's death. It must have been very well hushed up. No one in the village has mentioned it."

"No. Those in charge decided there had been enough scandal in one village for a lifetime, so they did all they could to keep it quiet and do a quick burial. That's privilege for you. The word means 'private law'. Did you know that? Very apt, given the circumstances."

"Very." Deborah's heart ached. She took a tissue from her handbag and dabbed her eyes. "This will sound silly but I really feel like I've got to know him through his journal and his work. I've studied it all these past few months. I liked him. He was a good man."

"He was, I believe." Cyril Barnatt nodded.

Back in her car, Deborah shed another tear as she finally began to move through the traffic. Half an hour later she was coming off at the junction and she was only twenty minutes away from The Querneys. Her heart pounded hard in her chest. Breathing deeply, she tried to calm herself but it was useless. She was coming back to a home that seemed so different, so unwelcoming, so full of darkness. This was a house of suicide, a village of secrets and murder. *How had I not known about the suicide? Did Peter know? In my house! Where I live and sleep!* Anger rose inside her and she pressed her foot down harder on the pedal. Soon enough she was pulling into the drive in front of Coppers End. Deborah sat in the car staring at the house and the bricks and looking at the front door. *How can I call this home again?*

She knew she needed to go in. The next stage of this investigation was in front of her: gathering her thoughts and all the evidence before heading down to Querney Manor. *And calling the police. Maybe.* That part wasn't decided yet. Debrah had no desire to be laughed at for wasting their time.

"Okay, come on," she said to herself, and got out of the car. Her legs were stiff and she was bone tired, but Deborah pushed herself onward. Once through the front door she knew immediately that she wasn't alone. There were voices coming from the kitchen and she realised at once who they were.

"What are you doing here?" she asked, her voice raised.

"Where have you been?" Peter replied, walking through the kitchen door towards his wife, accompanied by Theresa Slate. "You drove away from Lissa and Jonathan's without a word, just a little note! I've been worried sick."

"I needed to go, I told you that. How did you get back?"

"The train, of course. I didn't know where you were going. I was worried for you. I got back here two days ago and there's been no sign of you. I've been going out of my mind with worry," Peter turned to their guest. "Luckily I bumped into Theresa here. She's been very helpful."

"Oh, I've jus' been makin' cups o' tea and bringin' over sandwiches and bits to eat. You don't have a thing in and Peter has been too busy worrying about you to look after himself."

Deborah looked at him and saw for the first time that he was rather unkempt. His normally clean-shaven face had thick stubble and he looked exhausted.

"Oh Peter, I'm so sorry," Deborah put her hand on his shoulder. "But I had to go. I have found out so much and I think I understand what happened."

"Deborah, you have no idea what I've been through. And your sister. I spoke to her last night and she's planning on catching a train down tomorrow morning to help look for you. We thought you had disappeared off the face of the planet!" he exhaled loudly in relief. "Well, you're home now. That's what matters. And you've found out whatever you had to. Can we move on now please?"

"Move on?" Deborah stepped back. "No! I have to go. Now! I need to go up to Querney Manor immediately. And I think, yes definitely, one of you should call the police!"

"Wait, what?" Theresa stared at the two of them.

"Peter, you explain, I'm gathering a few things together and then I'm marching up there to confront a killer."

Deborah left Peter and Theresa standing open-mouthed in the hallway as she stormed into the dining room where she had left all her folders on the Forrester case. She put them in her arms to join the journal she was already holding and walked to the front door.

"Wait!" Peter shouted after her.

"I can't! He did it!" she turned, holding the door knob, ready to pull it shut. "He killed his sister, I cannot just leave it now that I am so sure he did it. He wanted the house and the estate. He killed her for it and somehow probably diddled the daughter out of getting her inheritance. I'm less clear about the second part of that but all the evidence points to him being the killer! I'm going. So please just do what I ask and call the police!" Deborah pulled the door shut fast and decided against walking. She was exhausted and she didn't want either Theresa or Peter trying to follow her and make her stop.

Opening the car door she sat down and pulled away quickly, seeing Peter and Theresa watch her go in the rear view mirror. *No turning back,*

I have to follow this up. Rupert Bingham killed his sister so he could control the estate. He hated her ideas and thought he could do better. Deborah bit her lip as she pulled into the house. There was a feeling of unease deep inside. *What if I'm wrong? And why did he take her ring? No, Cooke said it was him, and Cyril Barnatt was sure the stuff about her being an immoral floozy was wrong. Rupert Bingham must have made it up to discredit her and provide a reason for her being murdered by a stranger in the middle of the night. A stranger he somehow framed. Another innocent. Bastard.*

Deborah stepped out of the car with renewed, violent energy as she advanced on the front door of Querney Manor. She raised her fist to knock but paused, pushing at the front door instead. If it was chance or just the usual way they did things, Deborah did not know, but she found it open. Pushing it slowly, Deborah peered around into the hall. It was empty. She looked at her watch. It was three thirty on a warm summer's Wednesday afternoon. *They may be in the garden, or at work, or shopping in Bourton.* Treading lightly Deborah made her way further inside.

There was no sound but the ticking of many grandfather clocks, each slightly out of sync with each other. The feeling of seasickness in her belly became worse as she realised she was technically breaking into someone's house. She shook her head, resolving to keep moving. This time Deborah knew where Rupert Bingham's annexe was so she went straight there, making sure to keep out of sight from anyone on the stairs or the upstairs landing. Once outside the door to his room, Deborah stopped herself and began to feel ill. *What am I doing?* She pursed her lips and realised that at no point on the journey up here had she decided what she would say. Deborah held her hand up to knock once more, then changed her mind. As before, she turned the handle and pushed it silently open. The room appeared as it had the last time she had been in it. The desk, the photographs, the neatly folded bed. This time Deborah took her time to listen out for anyone behind her or in the adjoining bathroom. *No one. I'm alone,* she decided.

She knew exactly what to look for. Even so she took a sharp intake of breath when she realised it was still there even after all this time. *The old cigar box.* Gingerly, Deborah opened it up and she stared inside.

"Yes!" she said, louder than she had intended. But inside was a wedding ring, one she had read about a number of times before in the files Cooke had written fifty years ago. Deborah picked it up, flipped through the manila folder she had created to keep everything in order and found the picture she had of it. It was grainy and ripped, but the description was still intact. The markings and beautiful ornamentation all matched. *Rupert Bingham had his sister's ring. I don't know why. Either way, it proves that he did it and not that tramp. He must have taken the ring from her dead body, along with other things he decided would be used to prove that someone else did it.*

Deborah pocketed it and wondered what to do next. She turned around only to see Rupert Bingham in his wheelchair, staring at her.

"What are you doing in here? Again?" he asked. "Robert! Nurse!" he called out. "That blasted nurse. It's her day off. Robert!" he called again.

"Stop!" Deborah put her hand out to make him calm down.

"You want me to stop? You have broken into my room. Again. And you are riding through my things again. Who are you and what do you want?"

"You know who I am. I'm your neighbour, Deborah. And I want," she hesitated, "I want justice."

"Justice? For what?"

"Yes. Justice. For your sister. I know you killed her."

"What are you talking about?" He turned his chair to the door of his room, "Robert!" Rupert Bingham shouted once more.

"Listen to me," Deborah could hear her voice cracking but she went on, "I know you killed her. I know you took her wedding ring. For some reason I'm sure only you understand. But that proves it. The tramp you blamed it on had everything *except* her wedding ring. Not because he lost it, but because *you* planted the rest on him when you killed him too, but kept this one thing back."

"Are you mad?" he scoffed, his face twisting into a smile. "What a load of rubbish. Robert!"

"Stop that at once. I have the ring now. And I'm going to show it to the police. Along with everything else I have found out. You pretended that your sister, Eleanor -"

"Don't you presume to say her name," he spat as he hissed.

Deborah stuttered, "Y - you pretended that she went to all these late night parties and things and had too much to drink and would return at all hours. I'm not sure how you convinced the police of that. Did you get her maid to lie about it? Is that what you did? So as to add credence to the make-believe? By doing that you sullied her reputation and gave a motive for robbing and killing her to someone who could happen upon her returning home. You did that, didn't you? And then you found some unfortunate soul to take the blame and you killed him too. That's right, isn't it?" Deborah stood taller as the words began to flow.

"You know nothing," he smirked.

"You hated your sister, didn't you? And so you killed her."

"You are wrong Very wrong. I never, ever hated her. And I didn't kill her."

"Then who did?" Deborah shouted.

He looked at her shrewdly, his eyes squinting as he thought about her question. Then he looked around the room as though checking for the presence of others.

"You really want to know, don't you?"

"Yes." Deborah stood still and tall.

"My sister Eleanor was killed by a man called William Carter. *He* killed her. Not me."

"But, but - but -" Deborah shook her head. All of a sudden she felt very tired.

"Oh stutter all you want. The butler did it," he laughed. "Nice way to put it, I suppose. But it was *not* me. So be on your way now. I didn't kill my sister."

"How do you know he did it? That's suspicious in itself!"

"What!?" Rupert Bingham shouted. For a man reportedly so weak he used considerable strength to move his wheelchair at speed across the room and directly into Deborah's shins.

"Ow!" she shouted, pain screeching up her bones.

"You go through my private things and question me? Me? Who are you? You are nothing. Leave my house at once with your disgusting accusations."

Deborah's legs throbbed and her head began to pound from tiredness. *Should I just give up?* Before she could answer her own question, Deborah's eye was caught by the photograph of Eleanor Forrester on her brother's desk. She grabbed it.

"You're lying," she said, breathing to calm herself and forget the pain. "William Carter was the butler here and he was a good sort of man. Sergeant Cooke thought so, and so do I."

"Cooke? Ha," Bingham laughed mirthlessly. "More concerned about the closure of his precious police house than digging further into what really happened."

"Wait, so you admit it? You did it?"

"Good grief, you are stupid."

"Tell me what happened. Why do you have her ring? How do you know Carter killed her?"

Rupert Bingham looked Deborah in the eye and smirked, "Because I made him do it, " he said, blankly.

Deborah stared at the old, wrinkled, and twisted man in front of her. The stabbing pain in her shins was getting worse and so was the exhausted throbbing in her head. She looked up, distracted by movement. Robert Bingham had just walked in and was staring at his grandfather and Deborah's drained face.

"What's going on? Are you alright, grandfather?" he asked.

"Took you long enough to get here," Bingham scolded his grandchild.

"I was on the telephone," Robert replied, still staring at Deborah and the things she was holding in her hands. "What's going on?" he repeated.

"Your grandfather was confessing," Deborah said, keeping her voice as steady as she could.

"Confessing?" Robert said. "What are you on about?" His smile was patronising.

"He's confessing to the murder of his sister. Or incitement to murder. One of those."

"Good lord," the boy looked at Deborah with sarcastic pity. "You really are odd. And obsessed. I found you looking things up about that stuff in the library ages ago. And then again at your house."

"I've found out more than that since then. And he's just told me that he made another man kill his own sister. Tell him. Tell him!" she shouted.

"I did say that," Rupert confessed. "I didn't think anyone would hear it, alas you did, Robert. But I am not worried. Robert is a good boy and knows that if he sticks by me I will take excellent care of him in my will. Don't you, boy?" Robert stared blankly. "He would never speak out. And I am sure to die soon, therefore he will be very, very rich."

"So then," Deborah's voice was calm at last. "If you have no fear of recriminations, just tell me. What can *I* do about any of it?" Deborah forced herself to look calm and innocent.

"Indeed. What can you do? A strange local woman with a mad theory about a dying old man," Rupert sneered.

"Tell me what happened. What do you mean you made Carter kill her?"

"It wasn't hard," Rupert began, "he hated her. I knew it. He had loved her like a child once, but he couldn't stand how she was changing the place after our father died and left it to her. I tested the ground with him, seeing whether he agreed that a woman shouldn't inherit over a man. Of course the old coot agreed."

"But that can't have been it? You don't murder someone, and in such a violent way, because you don't like a few things they do. And why did you make him do it? Because you hated her too?"

"I told you," Bingham's voice was a loud hiss, "I didn't hate her. I loved her." He stared at the ground and leaned forward in his chair. For the first time Deborah thought she heard pain in his voice. "I loved her," he repeated. "I wanted her. I wanted her to want me too. I made her lie with me a couple of times when we were younger. But did she love me back? Did she thank me for my care of her? No. She just pushed me away. Got me sent to boarding school far from home. Made excuses not to be alone with me. Even got a lock on her bedroom door."

Deborah stared at the old man, aghast. She turned to Robert who was looking at his grandfather, his face a shade of green-grey.

"But - that's disgusting. I can't -" Deborah stuttered once more. "Why did you -"

"Why did I have her killed? Because she married that American idiot. I wanted her, but she chose him."

"But you were brother and sister," Deborah whispered.

"I know that!" Bingham spat. "I know it couldn't happen! Not properly. It didn't stop me wishing and wanting," he was breathing deeply, a rattling sound emanating from his throat. "I hoped. I wondered. Perhaps she'd change her mind and never marry and we could be together. In secret, yes, I knew that. But we would have been together. Instead that vacuous toad weaselled his way in with his money and Eleanor ate it up."

Deborah's mind was blank with shock. She needed more answers though. She coughed, "How did you persuade Carter to do it?"

"I told you. It was easy. He already didn't like her. And he knew we had been together, in a way that brother and sister shouldn't."

"He did?"

"I said that," he sputtered. "But I made him think that she was tempting me. Taunting me. Chasing me. That I was a victim of her wicked lusts. He wanted to help me. So he did," Bingham paused. "It took a while to plan and a while for me to work on him. We didn't want to just kill her. It had to be done right. We undermined her for a while. First by planning the robbery of the pigs. It made her look stupid and it cost her money."

"That was you?"

"Are you deaf? Or stupid? Why do you keep asking ridiculous questions? You were right, Robert," he turned to his grandson who was sitting, statue-still, on the bed. "She's an idiot." Deborah looked at Robert again, his face was fixed on his grandfather's. "So yes, we planned that," Rupert continued. "I knew we had to drug my sister to be able to move her. So I practised on the maid. I seduced her. It wasn't difficult. But it was disgusting. Every time I was with her I pictured Eleanor instead."

Deborah gripped onto the bureau she was standing in front of. *I feel sick. He is foul.* Nausea developed in waves and grew till she tasted bile in her throat.

"Anyway, the girl, whatever her name was, she trusted me. She planted the soiled evening clothes for cleaning whenever I asked her to and I repaid her with kisses, compliments and promises. People are so *easy*," he snickered.

"What happened then?" Deborah asked, swallowing.

"An accident. I gave her too much of the barbiturate. She died. Couldn't be helped. I was glad that the old doctor didn't care enough about the little maid so he never investigated properly. But I knew how much to give Eleanor now, you see. Enough to make her sleep so we could move her more easily and make it seem like she'd been using them and it had caused her to be less sensible."

"So you drugged her and Carter stabbed her. Is that what happened?"

"More or less. We planned it together. Made sure witnesses could attest to our whereabouts. Made sure the finger could also be pointed at The American if I needed it to be. Turns out I didn't. I gave her a dose of barbiturate just after dinner and then I…" he paused, looking into the distance. "She was on her bed. So beautiful. I kissed her face. I wanted her so much. She had kept me away from her for so long. Years. I could smell her skin as I held her that night. It was too much. I had to have her. So I lay with her one last time."

"She… she didn't wake?"

"A little. Those 'defensive wounds' that came up in the inquest. She didn't mean to fight me off. I am sure of it. I know she loved me…" his voice trailed off.

"I feel sick," Robert spoke suddenly.

"Don't be stupid, boy!" his grandfather turned to look at him. His eyes were wide and angry. "These things can be natural. And what I did saved my family! It saved this house! It would have all gone to that stupid man, Forrester, and their child if I hadn't made sure she never signed off on her new will! The child I wanted. I loved her too. She was part of Eleanore. But him? To have control over the house that had been in my family for hundreds of years? We made this village. We put the first quern in that mill and gave people jobs and an income. We built this place. I couldn't let him have any say in the running of it! And Carter felt the same. He helped me. I moved her body out to the forest by that tree and met him there. I… faltered. I couldn't do it. I loved her, can't you see that? He took the knife from me and did it. He was so angry. Disgusted by her in the end I think. It was so sad. He once thought of her as a daughter but not anymore. Not the girl who was teasing and seducing her brother and running the house in this new way, selling the London house and getting rid of tenant farmers. He cried as he put the dagger in, but he did it all the same."

"But she didn't seduce you," Deborah grimaced at the thought of Rupert abusing his sister. "You raped her. As a child. And then again, after you drugged her."

"Rape? What are you -" he shook his head fast. "I loved her. She loved me. I know it."

"And then you had her killed."

"I had to do it. There was no other way."

"Wasn't there? And what about the tramp? What about him? Did Carter do that for you as well?"

"No. He was shaken and weak. Didn't want to go ahead with it all anymore. I got rid of him a year or two later. He died in a poorhouse, with nothing. That's what happens if you don't stick by me. You hear that, Robert?" Robert nodded slowly.

"So who did that? Who killed the man who was framed?"

"Me. Of course. I knew how to kill someone that no one cares about and get away with it. No one cared about that stupid maid and no one cared about a man living on the streets."

"So you drugged him too."

"The first intelligent connection you've made since you came snooping in here."

"Why did you keep the ring?"

"I had to," he sighed, breathing ever deeper. "I needed it. A connection to her. I wanted to be with her. This way I am. The ring binds us together."

"You're despicable. Foul." Deborah had had enough. "What made you think you could get away with it? You nearly didn't, you know. Keeping that ring nearly cost you. Cooke found it. You didn't know it, but he did. He knew there was a connection between you and her death. He had it. He just hadn't fully grasped it yet. Had he not killed himself I know he would have done."

Rupert Bingham started laughing. It was a low, rasping laugh at first and it grew louder. He nodded his head and his belly wobbled as he twisted his face into a grimacing smile.

"What?" Deborah asked, unsure of things again and swallowing bile back down once more.

"Killed himself? I suppose you've heard everything else. Why not this?"

"What do you mean?"

"I know he knew about the ring. Saw him snooping during a Christmas do here at the house. So we did it. Carter and I. We lured him to the house and managed to very convincingly fake his suicide. His new colleagues didn't like him and didn't think much of him. They bought it so easily that he had decided not to go on, now that everything in his life had changed and he had lost what he felt was home. We wrote it in his note and strung him up ourselves."

Deborah's eyes widened. She couldn't speak. She forced herself to.

"How could you?" she managed. "Four people are dead because of you. Five, if you count Carter, whom you manipulated into killing Mrs Forrester and then abandoned when he grew a conscience."

"I did what I did for my house and my family. I have always taught my children to be ruthless if they need to be. Bernard married that dolt for her money, and Robert is learning much as well."

"I didn't know..." Robert's voice faded as he stood up from the bed.

"I know you won't say anything, Robert. You want your money, I know you do. You won't have long to wait. And you," Bingham looked at Deborah, "no one will believe you and won't give them the chance. Help me, Robert."Robert stared at his grandfather. "Don't just stand there," the old man said. "I've got her trapped with my chair. Get a weapon."

"What? No." Robert started walking backwards, his hands held up in the air.

"Come on boy! We can't let her go from here. You have to help me." The old man rammed his chair harder into Deborah. He stared into her eyes. His were bloodshot, angry, hungry.

She screamed, "Help! Somebody! Please." She tried kicking and pushing Bingham away but it wasn't any use. "Robert," she turned to him, pleading. "Help me, please. Don't let him hurt me."

"I don't know what..." Robert's voice trailed off, "I can't."

"Robert! Please!" Deborah shouted, trying to push herself away from Rupert. A foot wriggled free, finally. And then another. She started to run, only to feel a dull pain on the backs of her legs as she was mowed down by Rupert once more. Her hands had been full. Cooke's diary, all the papers she had on Eleanor Forrester's murder flew into the air as she came crashing down, face first, onto the wooden floor. She tasted blood in her mouth and her arm ached from landing on it. Trying to get up, she saw Rupert grab an old walking stick. He raised it above his head and brought it down on her legs, the only part of her he could reach. The pain in her left thigh burned as he raised it again.

"Stop it! Please! Robert! Stop him!" she yelled, trying to push herself up. *I'm so tired. Someone make him stop.* She was exhausted, but pushed herself further along the floor, ignoring the searing agony in her legs. Again Rupert thwacked her with his stick, this time reaching the small of her back. Deborah began to cry. "Stop him, please, someone," her voice was weak.

"Come on, Robert," she heard Rupert yell, pausing momentarily in his crusade to stop her by any means. "It isn't as hard as you think. We'll make it look like an accident. Or that we thought she was an intruder."

Deborah looked imploringly at Robert, "Please, don't," she tried catching her breath. "Don't do what he wants. You're not a killer. You've made mistakes. But that's because you've listened to *him* all your life."

"How dare you!" Rupert brought up the wooden stick once more. Deborah closed her eyes, waiting for a new burst of pain. But it never came. She opened her eyes to see Robert standing over his grandfather and trying to pull the weapon out of his hands. There was a struggle as Rupert was much stronger than he had ever seemed, but Robert got hold of the stick and threw it on the floor, well away from the old man. Rupert Bingham readied himself to rush his chair at his grandson, but Robert was ready and he held out his arms to keep the man at bay.

"Stop, grandfather. Stop. Enough now." His voice was mollifying and Rupert stayed himself and breathed heavily.

"You're no grandson of mine. You're out. You'll get nothing," his voice was low and calm and without any feeling.

Deborah pushed herself up to a sitting position. Lifting her skirt gingerly she saw welts and bruises begin to form. Standing up, she began to pick up all the papers that had floated to the ground, disordered and spread across the room. She wasn't thinking, she just needed to do it.

"Leave here," Robert told Deborah. "Leave those," he added. "Just go. Get away."

"I can't," Deborah didn't even know if it was her own voice speaking. "I need to get these things to the police," she picked up the wedding ring and put it in her pocket. "It's important."

At once there was a loud noise coming from somewhere in the

house. Lots of people rushing. Deborah looked up at the door to Rupert Bingham's annexe and saw Peter's face staring at her, followed by three police officers. *He's here*. Deborah walked over to him, leaving the rest of the documents on the floor, and collapsed in his arms, shaking with tears.

"You called them," she managed after several minutes.

"Of course I did! You insisted! I was worried you might be in danger. You know, because you said you were confronting a killer and all that." Peter held her tight in his arms. Two officers stood by Rupert Bingham, another surveyed the scene.

"We're going to have to ask you a few questions, Sir Rupert. And you too, uh, Mrs Gordon."

Deborah shrugged as Robert wheeled his grandfather out, flanked by the officers.She and Peter made their way out and followed the police van all the way to Bourton Police Station.

Deborah gave a statement and handed over all her evidence. They had been impressed. All of it had been studied: the files, the notes, the diary, even the little pieced together slips of paper. The investigating officer looked at Deborah agape.

"You did this?" he said.

"Yes," said Deborah, a wary tone in her voice. "Should I have contacted you sooner about this? I hope I haven't broken any laws."

"Well, no. I don't think," he flicked through the pile in his hands, "I mean... it's not a new case."

"No. And I had no idea what it would lead to."

"Of course, of course..." his voice trailed away as he read something off a paper Deborah knew had been pulled from her own attic wall only months previously. "And you really found all this. Just round your house?"

"Not exactly. As I explained to the constable who took my statement, I found it in the walls. Some of it. It was a very common way for insulating houses against the cold."

"My grandmother used to do that with old newspapers."

"Well then. The diary though? That I found tucked behind the fireplace. I think Sergeant Cooke, the author of it, wanted to hide it because he suspected Rupert Bingham and had written down his thoughts. He didn't want anyone to find it until he had proved his suspicions. Which, it turns out, he never got to do."

"Hmmm," the sergeant put the papers on the table and shuffled them together. He stood up when Deborah coughed.

"Ahem, don't you think this should be put right? Sergeant Cooke was murdered. He didn't commit suicide. It was hushed up and that... that isn't proper," Deborah straightened herself up in her chair and looked the sergeant in the eye.

"I shall see what I can do, miss."

"Missus. That would be the best thing don't you think? Cooke was one of your own. His former constable, Jacob Smith might still be alive as well. He deserves to know the truth of the matter too. I should say."

"Well, I'm not sure we have the time or resources to track down -"

"One of your number? A former police officer who worked in this very station? That's a shame."

"Well, it seems like you're very good at this, miss. Perhaps you can? I'd even suggest you becoming a WPC but, you know, age limits and all that." Deborah sat still for a moment looking intently at the man.

"Is there any more you need from me?" she asked.

"No, miss. You're free to go."

"What will happen to Rupert Bingham?"

"He's confessed. And his grandson has corroborated what happened today. He'll appear before a judge before long, miss."

"Missus. But he is aged and infirm. Is he likely to receive a prison sentence?"

"I couldn't say, miss. I wouldn't worry yourself too much about that sort of thing. Best leave that to us policemen and the other professionals, eh?" He handed Deborah her jacket and opened the door of his office. She stood and took the jacket from him, thanking him as she left. Peter was waiting for her at the front desk. He took her coat and held her hand. It was warm and old and comfortable.

"Let's go," she said, smiling at Peter who looked at her with affection and concern.

"Of course," he opened the door and they stepped out into the late evening light.

Half an hour later they were back at Coppers End. Sat in the car outside, Deborah's legs were heavy and sore and would not take her any further.

"I'm so tired," was all she could say.

"Of course. Let's go in, shall we? Have some wine? A bit of bread and cheese? You need to eat and go to bed. In the morning you can explain everything to me and tell me all about how you saved the day."

"I don't know if I can, Peter."

"Explain it?"

"No, I mean, go to sleep in there. A man was murdered in our house. Did you know before we moved in?"

"No. I was in such a hurry to buy that I simply offered cash and took the place. I had no idea about any of it."

"But it still happened."

"I did," he paused. "How about we stay tonight and tomorrow we find a hotel?"

"But what do we do then?"

"I don't know. But we will think better after a good night's sleep."

"Probably. Plus I have more work to do on all this."

"You do?"

"Of course. I need to find Eleanor Forrester's daughter. If she's still out there somewhere. She ought to know what happened to her mother. And Jacob Smith, if he's still alive. He should know that Cooke didn't kill himself. I highly doubt those officers will make any effort to find him. At least a couple of good things should come out of all this. At the very least."

"I suppose you're right. Plus, it's good that justice will be done for more than one Forrester girl."

"We had better go in. I know we must. Just for tonight though?" Deborah double-checked.

"Yes, we can sit in bed and eat cheese and drink wine and fall asleep and not wake up till late."

"Sounds good," she replied. Neither of them moved though, and Deborah yawned before turning to look Peter in the eye. "It's the first time we've felt close in a long while, Peter."

"I know. All it took was solving a murder."

"*I'm* the one who solved it," Deborah laughed.

"Yes, aren't you fabulous," Peter looked back at her and kissed her on the forehead. "And I'll be better. I know I've been a windbag lately but I promise to do better."

"You promise?"

"I just said so. I meant it."

Deborah smiled at her husband as he stepped out of the car before going round to help her. Peter went inside the house first, turning on the lights as he did so. Deborah took a last look around the hills that surrounded her house. They were clear now, their silhouettes outlined by the glowing moonlight. For a split second she thought she saw a man by the front gate. He was tall and in a dark uniform. *I know him*. No rope in his hand or round his neck this time. She smiled and blinked. He was gone. She turned away from the warm summer night and went inside for one last evening at Coppers End.

THE END

ABOUT THE AUTHOR

Stef Lyons loves books and loves writing. She lives in the UK with her family and their cat. In her spare time she cooks. She spends a lot of her time dreaming about moving to warmer climes, but then remembers she has ginger hair and pale skin so that won't be possible. This is her debut novel. She really hopes you like it.

Milton Keynes UK
Ingram Content Group UK Ltd.
UKHW010928210224
438226UK00001B/22